BUFFALO

BUFFALO

SYDNEY BLAIR

VIKING
Published by the Penguin Group
Viking Penguin, a division of Penguin Books USA Inc.,
375 Hudson Street, New York, New York 10014, U.S.A.
Penguin Books Ltd, 27 Wrights Lane, London W8 5TZ, England
Penguin Books Australia Ltd, Ringwood, Victoria, Australia
Penguin Books Canada Ltd, 2801 John Street, Markham, Ontario, Canada L3R 1B4
Penguin Books (N.Z.) Ltd, 182–190 Wairau Road, Auckland 10, New Zealand

Penguin Books Ltd, Registered Offices:
Harmondsworth, Middlesex, England

First published in 1991 by Viking Penguin,
a division of Penguin Books USA Inc.

1 3 5 7 9 10 8 6 4 2

PUBLISHER'S NOTE
This is a work of fiction. Names, characters, places,
and incidents either are the product of the author's
imagination or are used fictitiously, and any resemblance
to actual persons, living or dead, events, or locales
is entirely coincidental.

A portion of this novel first appeared in *New Virginia Review*.
Grateful acknowledgment is made for permission to reprint excerpts
from the following copyrighted works:
"Exile's Return" from *Personae* by Ezra Pound.
Copyright 1926 by Ezra Pound.
Reprinted by permission of New Directions Publishing Corporation.
"Ball and Chain" words and music by Willie Mae Thornton.
© 1968 Cristeval Music and Baytone Music.
"Respect" lyrics and music by Otis Redding.
Copyright © 1965 by Irving Music, Inc. (BMI).
All rights reserved. International copyright secured.

LIBRARY OF CONGRESS CATALOGING IN PUBLICATION DATA
Blair, Sydney.
Buffalo / Sydney Blair.
p. cm.
ISBN 0–670–83554–4
I. Title.
PS3552.L3464B84   1991
813'.54–dc20   90–50403

Printed in the United States of America
Set in Granjon
Designed by Cheryl L. Cipriani

for Abbie & Tom

What is the use of talking, and there is no end of
      talking,
There is no end of things in the heart.
              —Rihaku, "Exile's Letter"

I

DELIVERY

R aymond McCreary sits in the belfry sipping Jose Cuervo by the capful. He is hoping that by downing the tequila in tiny doses he can prolong its medicinal qualities and waylay the useless torpor that always gets him in the end. But tonight with the bottle cap is no different from the other nights. In the beginning, when things are still mildly illuminating, he remembers he is glad he walked off the job: the foreman was a jackass and everybody knew it. The other men had patted him on the back and acted as if they wished they had done the quitting. Ray likes remembering that. Then later, after arguing with Vivian about the wisdom of going through life free but broke, he tries to put his fist through the belfry wall and she goes off to bed, angry and hurt, while he sucks on his bruised knuckles. All that, and only a hairline crack to show for it.

Feeling sick, he leans out the belfry window, moaning, heaving, then manages to maneuver the steep steps back downstairs, where he passes out on a couch. His dog sleeps under the couch, white legs and paws sticking out like the ends of a bear rug. Much later, he wakes up shivering—the fire has gone out—and trudges to his room, where he slides into bed next to the lump that is Vivian.

They had argued about work and they had argued about other things, silly things, like the cigars that he chain-smoked.

"Why don't you go back to Camels?" she had said. It was she who'd persuaded him to give up cigarettes, never dreaming it would come to this. "Go back to your Camels, and then go back to your job."

■ ≡ ■

Ray lives in an old two-story whitewashed schoolhouse outside Charlottesville, Virginia, which, up till twenty years earlier, was where the local children learned fractions and English composition. The brick school that replaced it is fifteen miles closer to town, with low ceilings and a cafeteria and central heat and young whippersnapper teachers instructing their charges in how to feel good about themselves and the world they live in. In the old schoolhouse, you couldn't help but be self- and environmentally aware, Ray pointed out once to Vivian: the place was heated with wood, and when your fingers were cold, you couldn't write and that felt bad.

The windows of the old place stretch from floor to ceiling, framing dark pinewoods and fields where deer graze and wild turkeys sometimes settle. There is a boys' room and a girls' room—miniature equipment that seems to hit Ray and his friends midshin, though actually it is larger than that, and serviceable, just less convenient. And of course there is the teachers' rest room. And the drinking fountain. A stage. A belfry.

There are times—infrequent and usually late at night—when Ray questions the sanity of spending so much of his adult life in a child's world, but that was before Vivian, and, as she points out, it all depended on how you looked at it. People spent lifetimes trying to regain their innocence, relive their youth, see the world through the eyes of a child. Take Picasso, for instance. Surrounded this way, she'd said, you couldn't miss. Ray admires her ability to see things so clearly. For him, in those dark nights, only the odd anxious moments of insufficiency and shame pushed their way through—scorned friendships, awkward crushes, botched spelling bees. Maybe his life would have been different if he hadn't been appointed to the Safety Patrol when he was ten. The Safety Patrol kept kids walking politely to the right in the halls, kept them from being mowed down when crossing the busy streets after school, heading home. It was supposed to be an honor to serve on the Safety Patrol, but it had bothered Ray that he had to ride herd on his fellow students, and after a month or so, he took to encouraging the kids to break rank and race down the halls on the left, fouling the flow, or backward, upstream, willy-nilly, wreaking havoc with the current. For this, his badge was removed and his duties revoked.

In the main classroom there are sofas, and Mexican hammocks strung like webs, and on the stage is all of the stereo equipment Ray got cheap in Nam, and at this moment, Country Joe is shaking the very soul of the schoolhouse with the Fish Cheer.

Gimme an F! yells Country Joe McDonald.

F! moans Ray, knee-jerk.

■ ≡ ■

"Rise and shine, McCreary." Bullet is shouting into the phone. "Got a boat delivery for you. Forty-eight-foot trimaran; gotta get her to the islands before winter. Be at the Annapolis city docks at 0600 Wednesday."

"Jesus Christ, Bullet, what the hell time is it?" Ray squints at the clock, leans back on the pillow, phone cradled at his neck. Next to him, a slight dent in the sheets is all that is left of Vivian. He hears metal sounds from the kitchen but is too fogged to detect whether she is tossing things around with more force than usual or simply getting the dishes done. Either way, his head feels as if someone were pinging on it gently from within, xylophone style, on just the precise nervy spots that evoked the greatest pain.

The morning light, weak as it is, hurts his eyes, so he closes them. He hears Bullet giving forth over the wires miles away, inches from his ear.

"You still there, McCreary? What's up? You got a woman running you ragged?"

Ray hears water rattling against the tin shower stall. He wonders briefly what Vivian will say this morning, if she'll drag it on out, the wary dog dance.

"Tell her you'll set her up in piña coladas for the rest of her ever-lovin' days, and get on up here. I need a navigator."

"She hates rum."

"What's that?" Then, "Hey. McCreary. Speak to me. You coming or not? I got to get this thing rolling."

"Whose boat is it?"

"Mine. Blew the wad good this time."

Fatigue interferes with Ray asking, What wad. "Who else you got?"

"Two other guys, weird as shit but good sailors. We're taking her down to Morehead, then we'll go outside. Should be a good little cruise." He pauses and Ray pictures him pacing his kitchen, hair spiky from fingers constantly raking it, telephone cord stretched to the limit, loops limp and defeated. "Gotta get out of Dodge before the snow hits."

"Two things," says Ray, eyes open to slits. "You're sure the boat's seaworthy, and have you got anything left from the wad to pay me."

Bullet sighs. "Trust me."

■ ≡ ■

Ray has not seen Bullet for a couple of years, but he always knows what he's up to. Their friendship stretched back to the Marine Corps, Vietnam, R and R. That they are alive today is based on that single year-long interdependence, and they both know it. Way back, they hadn't imagined they'd be friends fifteen years later, but no one else had seemed surprised.

Bullet hadn't wanted to come home. "I'm just your basic, clean-cut, upstanding jarhead from Podunk, U.S.A. You think I wanta go back there? I love my wife and kids, I fought the enemy, and I'll even reenlist if they'll have me."

They wouldn't.

There were rumors of Bullet's zealousness both on and off the field. He was fearless in combat but bordered on the lunatic off-hours. Though the brass caught wind of certain things, it was hard to prove anything. They didn't have the time, or the resources, or the inclination, to follow up on any of it. The most they did was deny him a second tour, an affront Bullet never quite forgave them for.

"They're saving your sorry ass. You should be pulling time, or dead," Ray had said. "Consider yourself charmed."

Ray hadn't considered himself charmed, just undetected, if such a thing was possible. He had remained calm, more or less, off the field, had learned to tolerate the unevenness of the days in the jungle, the fractured nights, but even a man as vaguely uncommitted as Ray didn't stand around asking to die. When cornered, he was as crazy as anyone, could run just as fast. Or he fired back, or hid. Detachment, his instincts and luck had saved him as it had saved so many others. He never seriously considered deserting, or putting a gun to his head. He had not been wounded, and was grateful. His belief in God was shaky.

He hears Vivian bang out of the house, rev up her Datsun, and roar out the driveway, gravel raking the scarred side of his old pickup. He liked her immensely and was very much afraid he was in love with her.

"See you Wednesday," he says to Bullet.

■ ≡ ■

The trimaran sits wide on the water like a large woman anchored to a park bench, secure in her excessive breadth, regal

in her solitude. She reminds Ray of the mother of a boyhood
friend, who more than once had comforted him when he'd scraped
his knee or fought with her bully of a son. The boy had eventually
shot Ray in the eye with a BB gun. Ray had more than once
rested his head on her huge set of breasts, an immense cushion
of soft flesh between him and any poking bones. She usually wore
bright flashy blouses with pictures of flamingos or bananas or
palm trees—as if she yearned for a different life—but she never
seemed to mind when he dampened them with his bloody nose.
The boat is rocking gently in the wake of a passing Chris-Craft,
and Ray can almost see again the shimmering pink birds in the
flat green of her blouse, their thin fragile legs. Sometimes he
thinks if he could just find that woman, or someone like her,
everything would be just fine.

Bullet is perched in the rigging at the top of the mast, securing
a pennant. In the cockpit below, Ray sees two blond men in
aviator glasses. They are looking up at their skipper with something like amusement and awe, and in their gold-rimmed shades
he is reflected back on himself and the sky. So are the yellow-
and-black bees and papery-looking hive sewn onto the pennant.
The Severn River laps at the edges of the boat, secretive and
oddly comforting. A light breeze works its way through the
network of lines and stays and halyards strung between the masts
and hulls. The air smells dank and salty.

"OK," Bullet is saying. "Lower me down nice and easy, nice
and easy." A line snakes smoothly around the winch, tailed by
one of the blonds. "Hold it," yells Bullet. "Take me up a foot."
The man pulls on the line. The winch clicks like cards snapping
on bicycle spokes. Like an angel, like a saved soul, Bullet rises.
He tightens a bolt on one of the stays. "OK," he says, "OK," and
he motions with his flattened palm that he is done.

The men ease him down, though still he prevails as if twenty
feet above them. As he descends, he makes the sign of the cross.
"Pax vobiscum," he says to the blonds. To Ray, "Bless you, my
child." He bumps onto the deck, takes a last look at the pennant.

"Perfect." Turning to Ray, who is still standing on the dock, he says, "You're late," puts out a hand. Grasping it, Ray jumps aboard. The trimaran lists slightly with this added weight.

"What's she called?" Ray asks.

Bullet gestures skyward. "The *Honeybee*." Both men narrow their eyes as they stare straight into a bright October sun, trying to make out the pictures on the pennant. "Did you know," Bullet says slowly, "that bees are mentioned over a thousand times in the Bible?"

"No."

"But you know I keep bees at my place in Frederick."

"I guess I didn't know that either."

"Five hives. They swarmed the day Peg left, every goddamn one of them. Stow your stuff aft."

■ ≡ ■

Two days later, after dodging barges and oilers and the U.S. Navy at the mouth of the Bay, the *Honeybee* enters the inland waterway, and three days after that, they are in Morehead City. They refuel, restock the galley, stretch their legs for a day. They get drunk at the marina. The next day, at 0630 under fair skies and before a stiff southwesterly breeze, they enter blue water.

Out past the jetties the ocean sits cloudy and foamy and still. Screaming seagulls dog them, as if the boat were some lost whale in whose wake and confusion they might find enough food for a lifetime. The men see porpoises, always far off, wheeling through the water. Rays and skates slide past, silent as ghosts. The men breathe deeply, expectant and exhilarated to be finally on their way; the wind ruffles their hair, sweeps it back nobly, defiantly.

By the middle of the second day, with the help of a northwesterly, they are in blue water proper, though the sea is not blue at all out there. Pale emerald, the color of Coke bottles or bright spring moss.

As the wind picks up, the *Honeybee* slashes through the water, no matron now, but sleek and determined—the perfect lover— driven as much by instinct, it seems, as by Ray's careful computations. By the fourth day the wind is dead aft and very strong. The trimaran slices through patches of water where schools of fish sashay and flash; she skims the water's top like a dancer, just touching. She seems in control, the men as incidental as her destination. Or at least that is how it seems to Ray as he and Bullet stretch out in the cockpit, slick with the Swedish tanning oil one of the blonds brought. The oil smells like almonds, and the world seems not to exist, or to exist only here. Bullet clocks their speed at fifteen knots.

They sail south, and the sun gets closer and hotter. Any fresh food, meat especially, must be eaten or thrown overboard, so for three days, the blond who cooks serves Stroganoff, shrimp in garlic butter, chicken croquettes. The men are always hungry. They celebrate the halfway mark with a meal of fresh dolphin caught on a yellow bucktail. They watch Ray reel in the fish, watch its rainbow spots go gray, then back to a faded rainbow, in a matter of minutes. Sitting on the deck afterward, drinking Wild Turkey, the wind pushing them down to the islands, they feel as tight and content as a sleeping hog. The air is warm, the rhythmic rise and fall of the boat lulling and lazy. The sunset transforms the sea into a brilliant rumpled sheet of fuchsia and gold.

Ray plucks at his old guitar; one of the blonds passes him a joint. Bullet eyes the joint but says nothing. Even in Nam, Bullet had not indulged.

"Nightcap," says Ray. Bullet shakes his head in mild disgust and goes back to sharpening his buckknife. He is too full to grouse about it.

Ray begins to sing about the cuisine, the progress of the *Honeybee,* about what they left behind, what awaits them on the islands. One of the blonds tells them he used to sing barbershop, and hums a few strains of "Clementine." He is particularly fond of Ethel Merman tunes, he tells them; the rest of the crew know this, as he has been singing them nonstop since Morehead City. First time Ray heard him, he'd given Bullet a look, but now all they do is groan good-naturedly. They let him get away with it because he is such a good sailor.

"I've sung in glee clubs, I've sung in nightclubs, I've even sung in Carnegie Hall, but singing on the water is like singing nowhere else on earth," he says.

The men drink and sing and tell bad jokes and talk about women until the next watch, which is the blonds'. Ray takes a shot with the sextant just before the horizon fades, charts a course, then lies on the foredeck watching phosphorus sparkle and explode at the edge of the boat, listening to the three hulls slip through the water. And for the first time since the trip began, he wonders what Vivian is up to, what she'd said when she found his note. She'd probably cursed him till the walls shook; he was a fool, a weakling, a cad—he knew it. He was past forty, and feeling it. These days, he is thinking, life seemed at times to slow down dismally (insomnia, hangovers that lasted for days, back trouble), while at other times it moved along way too fast (glorious sunsets, bone-shaking sex), leaving him breathless and full of respect and wondering what the hell hit him.

Right now, at this moment, he feels a deep tenderness toward Vivian, no residual rancor over her giving him a hard time over cigars and jobs. He knows he really does love her, as much as he has ever loved anyone. That was what made it even worse, she had said: knowing he cared but that it wasn't always enough.

Enough for what, he had asked, and she had just shaken her head and looked away.

Ray lies there thinking about that, and her, smoking his cigars, watching the stars—phosphorus of the sky—then he goes below to sleep.

■ ≡ ■

Above him it sounds as if a giant tree is crashing onto the deck, tipping the boat, splintered branches skittering everywhere. Ray lets it pass and goes back to sleep. He knows things sound louder below, disproportionately dangerous. Mild scrapings on deck might sound like death itself.

The next time he wakes up, Bullet is leaning over him, face close and red, pulsing with blood, nose bulbous, ludicrous. "All hands on deck," he roars. "We got a gale coming on."

"Can't be. Red sky at night." Ray remembers the sunset had been scarlet. Glorious.

Bullet's eyes glitter, and for a moment Ray thinks he might slug him. "Look around you, for Christ's sake."

Ray looks around him. The boat is pitching and rolling, cans and duffel bags shifting from side to side as if drugged. Up till then, with what little consciousness he had, Ray had attributed the discomfort of the bunk and his spotty sleep to bad dreams. Now there is a loud crunch directly overhead, bringing a certain sharpness and immediacy to the morning. It sounds like a backhoe lumbering from one end of the boat to the other. Bullet rolls his eyes and mutters Sweet Christ. His knees bend, his legs lean with the movement of the boat. He looks like someone trying to maneuver a surfboard through the curl so he can take her on in to the breakline, hanging ten, gilding the lily. Except that he is wrapped in orange foul-weather gear, and a surfer wouldn't be caught dead in swells like the ones Ray sees when he pokes his head through the forward hatch.

"Shut the goddamn hatch," someone shouts, and he does, drenched.

The *Honeybee* lurches, tossing Ray onto the starboard bunk. He sits there a moment feeling the boat, rolling with the swells, waking up. Fishnet hammocks bulging with oranges, books, and flasks bang against the hull. Water spraying up over the portholes gives him the same submerged feeling he used to have when, as a teenager, he would take his cherry '55 Chevy through the car wash.

He gets up and goes to the head—later, he thought how foolish and methodical a thing that had been to do just then—where he holds himself steady with palms flat on the lacquered hulls, as if trying to exhibit some brute strength by pushing them out. Through the porthole opposite he watches the angry ocean, gray-green, agitated, opaque, trying to sink his ship. He struggles into foul-weather gear and slips up through the hatch, where he falls against one of the blonds as a huge wave catches them broadside.

"Tie yourself in, then get a life preserver," the blond screams, shoving a line at Ray. Ray wraps the rope around his waist, finds a life preserver, puts it on. Rain, coming from all sides and from impossible angles, lashes at the rubber of his coat.

The *Honeybee* seems all alone out there on the Atlantic. Her outer hulls slap and shudder, out of sync. It is as if her brain has gone haywire, sending odd messages to various flailing body parts. And suddenly there is entirely too much of her. She has become an embarrassment to the men aboard, a houseboat flopping around in clipper territory, inconvenient and troublesome as a spurned lover.

Ray makes his way forward to help Bullet and the blond reef the mainsail. The storm jib is already up and fluttering to keep her nose into the wind, save her from being banged around so much. Things seem under control.

It is while he is furling the mainsail that Ray notices the open buckknife taped to Bullet's forearm. He almost laughs, but the little he can see of Bullet's face is grim enough to stop him. He knows that in the heat of battle, so to speak, Bullet wanted to make the move, however drastic, rather than be moved upon. Whereas Ray, over the years, had discovered that often, if you just waited the thing out, it had a way of taking care of itself, with no blood shed. It occurs to Ray that Bullet might as readily turn the knife on any of the crew as cut the main sheets, if it meant saving the ship. A frightening prospect, which happily he has no time to dwell on. Yet as he fights with the mainsail, Ray finds himself envying the madness that moves his friend to arm himself against twenty-foot waves with a thin shaft of sharpened steel and a foolhardy bravado.

And then he is afraid.

Waves the likes of which he hasn't seen since sitting out the surf at Maui rise around the trimaran, breaking over her as if she isn't there. Even if the sails weren't slapping around and the shrouds weren't rattling and shrieking this way, the noise of the storm alone, of the wind and the rain and the sea, would be enough to deafen a man for days. Potentially hazardous to your health, Ray joked to Bullet earlier in the cruise. Like chainsaw bucks. Red dye no. 2. Agent Orange.

At Maui that day they had pulled two bodies out of the foam, along with brightly colored bits of fractured surfboard.

In the next twenty-four hours, all the men have bouts of seasickness—even Ray, who has never before succumbed at sea—and though the air temperature is mild, the wind cools them and stiffens their joints, makes old men of them. Everything below is sodden and uncomfortable. Sleep at first seems impossible, but eventually they get snatches of rest, tying themselves into the bunks. They subsist on whiskey and crackers and routine. They know it cannot last forever.

By the end of the second day, Ray thinks almost constantly of Vivian. And while not wishing her there to share the misery, he muses over how pleasant it would be lying with her in his old oak bed—woodsmoke smells, dogs, snow outside—covered with quilts and comforters they would later kick off, not needing the warmth, not wanting to be hampered by that weighty collection of patchwork and down.

■ ≡ ■

Bullet is on his way forward, and he is not wearing a safety line. The wave that gets him crashes over the hulls of the *Honeybee,* making her tremble as if someone has taken a sledgehammer to her. After three days of suffering, each man has wished himself anywhere but there. Yet the moment he falls, the moment Bullet hits the water, he calls for help just as frantically as they would have, his cries thin and shrill.

Ray is on watch. Yelling below to the blonds, he works to free the life ring. He throws the ring where he last saw Bullet, then goes to work on the dinghy line, tangled and twisted as heavy-gauge fishline. He gives up on the line, pays out thirty feet of his lifeline, and jumps in. Nobody tries to stop him.

It is unlike any swimming he has ever done. Though he is a strong swimmer—in high school they'd been honing him for the Olympics, but in the end he dropped it, lacking the necessary hungry edge—now he has no more control than if he were caught in a weir. He chokes on mouthfuls of salt-water. The lifeline wraps around his legs and seems to pull him down. He screams and curses and goes under. He comes back up and, gulping for air, sinks again. He struggles to keep his legs still while he loosens the line, which takes tremendous will, because what he feels like doing is kicking and pushing and bouncing his way right out of the water and into the air, back to someplace safe.

The line seems cemented in knots; his fingers are sluggish, as if frostbitten. He sinks and comes up several times, and finally his legs are free. He looks for Bullet, and when he can't see him he almost panics, almost gives it all up, but then there it is, the orange life preserver with Bullet's head leaning against it—white face, black hair. Ray thrashes and fights to get to him. Sometimes he seems very close, an arm's length away; the next moment he is a speck of something tiny and dark and insignificant. This seems to go on for hours.

It is only when Ray is forced to stop, when, exhausted, he lets himself float, that he begins to feel the movement in the waves, feels their life, senses the patterns. After that he swims in the troughs and rides the crests. He lets the sea do the work and suddenly he is there, almost on top of Bullet, and he sees his face clearly, head resting on the inflated pillow of the preserver, eyes closed, mouth open. He looks lazy and disinterested.

Ray yells and the eyes open, and what he sees there in the strange lull that the ocean seems to offer up as a reward for his efforts is the same thing he has seen in his own eyes in the morning straight out of bed, in the middle of the night after raucous lovemaking, in the middle of the night alone, tripping or so drunk he thinks his own image is a lover's and he kisses the cold mirror before passing out on the floor. It is a look of wonder and knowing and fear, and it asks for nothing.

■ ≡ ■

Back on board, the men lie senseless and wet in their bunks. If the boat is still pitching and rolling, they hardly notice. Once Bullet reaches over to put a hand on Ray's arm. "Thanks," he says, in a voice so full of emotion that Ray, embarrassed, can only say, "No problem." Bullet's fingers press hard for an instant, then the hand drops off. Looking down, Ray notices the buckknife is gone.

■ ≡ ■

Next day no rain, no wind, no clatter. The *Honeybee* is be-calmed in the middle of the Atlantic. The sea is mirror flat, that bright and hard and still—no apologies. The sun, hot and high overhead, is equally bland and bright. Their complacency and perfect steadiness—their fickleness—annoys and humbles Ray. Sitting in the cockpit studying charts, trying to figure out how far off course they've been blown, Ray wonders how he could ever have viewed the ocean as playful and inviting. Perhaps, in fact, he never has. Right now, even in this dead calm, the sea looks about as inviting as a sleeping shark. He says this to Bullet, who is arranging wet clothes and sleeping bags and cushions on every available surface and line. Bullet snorts, says, "Just like a goddamn woman," which isn't what Ray had in mind at all, but he lets it go. To his way of thinking, women were just as tough and mysterious as the sea but slightly more predictable, and kinder in the long run. At least he hoped so, and he thinks uneasily of Vivian. The blonds, back behind dark glasses and a little wan from the ordeal, are nonetheless perky. The singing one has started back in on Ethel Merman ("I hear music and there's no one there, I smell blossoms . . . ," et cetera)—a good sign. Satisfied he can lash the tiller midships and sail or drift in the right direction, Ray strips off his clothes, hangs them out, and stretches out to sleep.

They sleep, and the *Honeybee* drifts. There is no hurry now. Eventually the wind picks up, and seven days later they hit land. Literally. Bullet, in his excitement at finally reaching Charlotte Amalie, rams the *Honeybee* into the dock of the first marina he sees. Except for a crack in the gunwale, no damage is done.

The first one ashore is the singing blond, who kisses the ground, Pope style. After the men calm down and secure the boat, they hit the bars. They drink together, they drink in pairs, they drink alone, they reconvene and do it all again. They take over the town, terrorizing the tourists with their sweaty irreverence, boring the locals, who have seen it all before. They wander everywhere and run into each other in bars, on the beach, along the crooked hillside paths that snake through the town.

Two women from San Diego who say they are doing conch research buy Ray rum all night. They tell him where the good diving spots are and then they take him to their pink stucco cottage overlooking the sea. They produce a bong and they sit on the floor on rice mats, smoking and giggling. Ray can't remember when he has heard so much giggling. There is little talk of conchs. It is hot and the women take off their clothes, inviting Ray to join them, but like everything else on the island, they seem too big, too tan, larger than life. If they were noise, they would be ten decibels too loud, they would be puncturing his eardrums. He excuses himself when the girls begin to dance, and takes a shower, lurching and tilting as if still in the throes of some tropical gale. And there, again underwater, it all comes back in dizzying flashes: the green Atlantic, the rainbow hues of the dolphin, steel drum rumblings, rum. The pink stucco, the giggling, sapphire lagoons, Bullet's dead face. He lets streams of water wash it all away, and he thinks he could stand there forever, and does, until one of the women raps on the door and calls to him, "Are you still alive in there?"

He spends the night on the beach under a huge kapok tree, and the next day dives for a conch to take to Vivian.

- ≡ -

Ray did not generally spend much time thinking about the future, and he tries hard to ignore the past. But on the flight back to D.C.—rosy conch for Vivian carefully packed in worn T-shirts in his duffel bag—he reviews the details of the trip and falls to swinging neatly, for a change, into imagining how things might be (given he made it to the next day, an inevitability he still did not take for granted). He tries not to dwell on how hurriedly he'd left things with Vivian a month or so earlier. If he had been able to reach her by phone from Annapolis, he probably would not have gone. But he had not had time to call.

He sent several postcards from Saint Thomas, though, paving the way for his return. The postcards had pictures of flowers and insects grown to an unearthly size and color, which seemed accurate enough to Ray. Also, no one on the islands seemed to work, which Ray knew wasn't true, but that was the point: nothing was obvious there. And no one moved fast—they ambled or strolled. Anything seemed possible.

"You got to get rid of that mainland mentality," Bullet said to Ray when he expressed doubts about life in the tropics. He poured Ray more tequila, which they were drinking that last night in Charlotte Amalie instead of rum. But Ray had found the limitlessness too heady and a little scary.

Out in heaven, the plane drones soothingly. Below him, Ray watches patient rivers and streams taking their sweet time to get to where they have to go, unperturbed by intervening mountains and lakes and rhinestone towns, and he savors the moment's easy peace, knowing it won't last.

■ ≡ ■

Ray orders a drink. He feels the need for fortification. He wonders again whether Vivian will be glad to see him, if she'll even be there. Hundreds of times since he's known her he's asked himself whether it was more courageous to struggle to work it out with her or go it alone—valiantly—and spare her (and him) the difficulties and disappointments of a life together.

"Courage got nothing whatsoever to do with it," Bullet had said. They were still at it with the tequila, could still, amazingly, form words. "Jesus H. Christ, McCreary. You either do it or you don't. Don't wallow around in purgatory. Cut everybody a break, you know what I mean?" He shook his head in disgust and downed the shot. "Jesus H. Christ," he said again.

Ray had thought about pointing out Bullet's failures with Peg, but hours of talking couldn't untangle that one. And he was glad he hadn't told Bullet that sometimes he considered Vivian too young for him, or too nice, though the truth of it was she was only a few years younger than he, and sometimes she wasn't nice at all. Not at all. Maybe he just considered himself too old, and without answers, therefore lost and unworthy. Vivian was far from helpless; she was tough and smart and jogged daily and would probably have money socked away when he was pitiful and penniless. She had a certain endurance he felt he lacked.

She liked him, she said, because he made her slow down.

He liked her because she was honest and funny and she listened to him. Also, she was very pretty. And wasn't it getting to be time, after all, to settle down? In middle age, didn't you settle down, not just because you wanted to but because you had to? He was in excellent shape for a man his age—had the body of a twenty-year-old—but he didn't quite have the stamina of yore, and sometimes when he thought about all the work he had still to do, he felt very very tired. Being fit helped; he saw it as part of day-to-day living: you split wood, loaded the stoves, built houses, pushed your truck out of endless mudholes and snowdrifts, swam in muddy ponds, threw sticks for the dogs, ate, slept, dreamed, screwed, dove for conchs. Settling down didn't mean giving it all up; there was no need for fat and boredom and indolence. It meant, he hoped, reaping the benefits. It meant reaching the peace.

Speeding along in the plane, already Ray feels as if he has drunk way too much. He lets himself slip into dreaminess; he is glad Bullet isn't there putting his two cents' worth in.

Ray has been with many women over the years, lately many of them young, and he had found those last few women before Vivian especially easy and uncomplicated, probably because they had so little in common with him. If he had bothered to mention Da Nang or hooches or the DMZ, for instance (which he never did), it would have floated past them like dead leaves. He understood that, because when they talked about nuclear war, he just couldn't seem to get into it.

He had liked the way they seemed to need him; he liked being in control. Who didn't? Vivian didn't seem to need him, and he liked that too.

Before the trip, when he thought about all this too long, Ray would come down with a splitting headache that he sought to ease with dope and too much alcohol. Now that he was rounding the bend, turning the corner, so to speak, leaving Bullet and the bright islands and the eternal sun behind, he would make lucid lists every night of things to be done the next day. And he would do those things, by God, he would consult those lists and scratch things off, and by the end of the day—the end of his life—he would be able to point to the spent and blackened pages and say that, at the very least, he had done his best.

Ray leaned back in his seat, his drink nearly gone. He felt

relaxed and resolved. Purposeful. Leaving Bullet always had this effect. Conversely, whenever they got together, it didn't take long before Ray felt as if he was halfway round the world, even if they were simply sitting on someone's sagging porch drinking a beer. Could be Australia, could be Tibet, could be the goddamn moon, centuries from anything real. It always happened.

As far back as he could remember, they'd ruined nights out for their girlfriends and wives with their private jokes and soldier talk. The one time they'd gone to Hawaii for R and R, they'd eaten dinner—all meals really—as if at any moment they might all be blown to kingdom come. They ate fast and sloppily; they loved every bite. On the dance floor, they had embarrassed the women by abandoning them and dancing with each other in a sort of frenzied tribal stomp, or, when slow-dancing, had slid their hands all over their partners, hiking up their skirts in back, slipping hands inside blouses—wandering fingers—so that the women, laughing at first, would eventually refuse to stay out there on the floor with them.

"We might as well be *doing* it right here in front of the whole platoon," one woman had complained, knowing what was coming next.

Which wouldn't have bothered Ray at all, let alone the rest of the platoon, considering where they'd been just forty-eight hours before. The women were fine in the bedroom but glum in groups. The men didn't understand them, and didn't much care. They figured everything would be fine when they got back home and their hair grew out.

The next time Ray and Bullet left Nam, it was for good.

Ray orders another drink. He leans down to check the conch under his seat. It is there; through layers of canvas and cotton he can feel its hard, pointed edge. Finding the conch was a good sign, he'd decided; it was whole and perfect and as beautiful as anything he'd seen. And he'd gotten this far without losing or chipping it, another good sign. He hopes Vivian will forgive him. He had practically burst his lungs diving for it, had been about to head back to shore when it presented itself. That was how it had seemed: everything underwater stagy and artificial, big and bright, almost more than the senses could bear—glittering black-and-yellow fish, wavy coral (every color), the occasional slinky barracuda, the thuds and thumps of far-off propellers and engines. Out of the water, its colors softening in the afternoon sun, the conch seemed more manageable, though still retaining its mystery and, for Ray, some sort of inexplicable power. Ray liked it better that way, preferred the subtlety, thought it more real.

Though he could have done with a little less reality when he caught sight of a sea turtle, huge, belly-up, dead, floating and bobbing about with a clumsiness Ray found almost embarrassing. Maybe because he had seen the creatures out in the middle of the Atlantic, where they shot through the water with surprising speed and grace, as if they alone, in all their bulk and antediluvian ugliness, had been made absolutely and only for the sea.

It was time to go home.

When he left Bullet behind in L.A. years ago, after the war, they hadn't been sure if they'd ever see each other again, but such speculation had seemed completely beside the point. They were going home, on their separate flights—and in one piece—back to what they assumed were strongly constructed homes and lives. Ray recalls vividly the moment he first saw Priscilla when she met him at National and drove him back to her apartment on F Street in her battered yellow VW. She was his girlfriend, or so he'd called her when the other men talked about wives and whores and onetime or lifelong loves, but in fact he had never quite known where they stood with each other. And he wasn't going to worry about it now. She wore a ragged fur coat and a blue workshirt and old jeans and fringed knee-high moccasins. Also no underwear, he discovered later, to his delight and mild alarm. The lack of this most basic layer of clothes made her seem overly available, and not just to him, was his uneasy thought.

She looked good, she looked good, he said to himself as she maneuvered the little car through early-morning traffic. Washington looked gray, as usual, and a little stern and forbidding. It had been fall then too, he realizes, the trees losing leaves, getting ready for a winter that could be heavy with snow, or without it altogether.

Was it twenty years back?—at least that long, more like twenty-five—that they had spent many high school weekends in his old De Soto, gulping down sloe gin in Coke, Romilar, vodka in just about anything, in the interests of getting high, feeling something, anything, whatever it took. He remembers fondly the purple lights on the De Soto's dash, the Spaniard's proud helmeted head sanctioning somehow their amorous adventures.

He breathes in: the musty upholstery of the De Soto smelled for an instant like the inside of this plane. He smells Priscilla's perfume—Intimate, was it? Percy Sledge moaning away about how when a man loves a woman, he can do no wrong, et cetera, James Brown proclaiming this is a man's world. He remembers watching her face—chin tipped up, mouth a little open—as he pushed aside stray strands of her brown hair to work at the buttons on her blouse. Everything had been fine. Unfinished, fumbling maybe, but just fine.

After he enlisted, which he'd done against his parents' wishes and for lack of anything better to do, he had written to her constantly—daily, once he got to Nam—and though some of the letters never got past his grimy rucksack, most made it back to the States. Still, based on the frequency of her replies, he sometimes wondered about that. Her replies to his letters were sometimes chatty, sometimes spare, usually noncommittal, and always always always late. He could not know then, realized it only years later, that even if he'd been at Harvard, or living right next door, or in NYC, or working graveyard at the local paper mill, her replies would have been just as terse and spare. He couldn't blame everything on Lejeune and the jungle and the lousy U.S. Postal Service.

The plane bounces gently, shimmies through a pocket of turbulence. Ray's drink slips over the edge of the glass, dampening his fingers. He blots his hand on his jeans and begins to fool with the complications of lighting a fine Cuban cigarillo, when the flight attendant walks by, reminding him he is in No Smoking. He puts the matches away and leans back to doze.

He had not been in love with this girl Priscilla; at least he'd told himself that over and over when he didn't hear from her. But in all likelihood he had been. They had not "gone together," had never talked of marriage.

After Lejeune and before Vietnam, he came back to visit her in D.C. She was busy growing her hair and protesting the war along with everyone else, and there seemed to be very little to talk about. He would find himself laughing too often, too loud, and at the wrong times, a habit that annoyed her and took him years to shake.

They went to a Marine Corps dinner-dance in Quantico, where he made sure to have their picture taken. In the picture, she is wearing a white dress with wide sleeves, and her hair is falling over one eye. She looks sullen and mildly drunk, which she was. He is facing the camera head-on—also drunk—eyes bright as the insignia on his chest. His arm is around her, but she seems to be leaning away. He remembers feeling very very happy.

In the many times he studied the picture after that, he tried to remember if he'd forced her to do it. Had she objected to having the picture taken, as some girls did, through vanity or insecurity? Or was her discontent broader than that? Anger at the world at large? Or maybe her annoyance was reserved simply for him.

The day he came home for good, they went straight to her apartment, where she proceeded to roll a gigantic joint as soon as they walked in the door. These days the perfect hostess, she said as she rolled, has Jameson in the cupboard and good Mexican weed in the drawer. He smiled back and was glad she stopped there, that they weren't listing the litany of drugs they'd done, boring themselves and each other beyond reach. He didn't bother telling her that the dope in Nam was so good and plentiful you could be high all the time, if you wanted, and that after a few hits, you felt as if the top of your head had been blown away, simply lifted off and removed, shunted off to heaven, and without the aid and assistance of M-16s or any of that artillery shit.

He met some of her friends that day, who didn't seem to trust him. He didn't much care for them either. He listened to them talk about Grateful Dead concerts and student strikes, but the few times Priscilla prodded him into telling what he knew, he couldn't seem to get it out, and they didn't seem to want to hear. She had one friend in particular who was in SDS and from Queens, who Ray suspected was a lover. He rode a big black Harley and wore octagonal black shades at all times. Ray could just see Priscilla riding behind him, hair flickering out in back, cheek against the nap of the cool black leather.

"Did you sink any ships over there?" was the first thing this man from Queens asked Ray, who thought it pointless to reply.

Instead he told about the guy that got malaria. Nobody he knew took the malaria pills issued with the rest of their gear, because what most of them wanted more than anything was to be stricken and shipped out. And this one guy did, in fact, get malaria. Feverish and half crazed, he had wandered off and disappeared one day. No one knew where he was, but no one reported him, in case, by some fluke, he was out there actually enjoying life.

Two months later, and there he is again, miles from the camp where they'd last seen him, and it was as if he'd just come back from an evening stroll on the Strand, say, or returned from an overly long movie or a pressing call of nature. He didn't know where he'd been, or who had taken care of him—he muttered something about an old woman, fire, and food—but he was cured, and they folded him in and simply carried on as usual.

"We did a lot of that," Ray said. "I'm doing that now."

"Far out," someone said.

The dude from Queens, who had been listening hard, then talked at length about the nightmares that fucking soldier would have to endure all his livelong days.

There was silence, and then, for some inexplicable reason,

Priscilla began to talk about her dog. She had been leaning on Ray's arm as he told the story, and now she was talking about this dog that some musician friend had found beside the road, wounded and dying, and this guy had given the dog to her. Laid it on her, is how she put it. Ray thought all this hip talk the most affected crap he'd heard in a long time, even though he and his Marine Corps pals had talked constantly in specially coded slang. But they'd needed to, having much to escape. He forgave the talk in Priscilla, though, and, in fact, wanted desperately to know what to say and do in these strange United States.

She loved this dog, Priscilla was saying, she *loved this dog,* though it had turned out to be a colossal pain in the neck, a sick lemon of a dog, that took every cent she had to keep alive.

So turn it loose, Ray was thinking, let it go.

The dog was deathly ill, full of worms and bad blood and some degenerative disease she couldn't remember the name of that was eating away at it like lye. God knows, she said as she patted the fitfully sleeping animal next to her, I could do with a little harder heart.

When he watched Priscilla looking up at him, surrounded by her stoned-out friends, Hendrix wailing away in the background, she seemed indistinguishable from the enemy, hiding with camouflage and grenades and smeared black faces. For an instant, she was someone he would just as happily have blown away, given the opportunity and appropriate weapons. The next instant he imagined her naked and felt weak-kneed and foolish.

Ray got up to leave. The talk stopped. They watched him. And then Priscilla stood too, put a hand on his arm, asked if he wanted to go for a walk. He said he did. Outside, they moved down the straight gray sidewalks in silence, apparently aimlessly, though within an hour they were back at her apartment, and everyone was gone.

She was slow in letting him touch her. She seemed nervous at first, anxious, but once they were in bed, and he asked her what she would like him to do, she said everything. They made slow, edgy love, and he felt as much as he had in a long time what it was to be alive. Sometimes as he watched her, he felt he'd never known her, which was probably true, and not so much unnerving as just a bit odd. His dog tags, when they brushed her neck, breasts, stomach, felt good, she said. His hair was too short, though; lucky thing he was born handsome.

Toward the end of the night, because they both knew he would leave in the morning, they were kinder to each other. But then the chain around his neck caught in her long, tangled hair, and she'd twisted away, half in anger, half in frustration, and had actually started to cry. To his alarm, then—and now, sitting on the plane speeding back to D.C. and Vivian—Ray felt the pressure behind his eyes that suggests the possibility of tears. He remembers the light from the streetlamp filtering through the venetian blinds, dusty and noisy somehow, striping them. Upstairs, someone seemed to be doing the "Mexican Hat Dance" but without the music. In the alley next to them, a garbage can lid clanked. Priscilla, her hair, the whole place, smelled of the jasmine incense she loved—dusty and foreign.

She had just been saying she felt safe, happy, and now she was in tears, and for the first time since he'd been issued them, Ray removed his tags. By now they were hopelessly stuck, and he had to cut them out with nail scissors, a job he performed with great gentleness and care. She sat with her back to him, leaning his way now and then when he inadvertently pulled. While he worked, he joked a little.

After that, he wanted to go but she wouldn't let him, and when he presented the tags to her, she accepted them so solemnly he doubted—for a moment—her sincerity.

In the morning, drinking coffee, they hadn't known what to say or how to act, so they moved into a light arrogance that hadn't worked either; they were young and ill-equipped to handle their own small confusions, let alone each other's. They lacked whole chunks of information on how the world worked.

In the next few weeks, Ray wandered the city. He stayed at the local Y, or with people he chanced to meet. He hung out in parks and bars. At the all-night bakery on Wisconsin Avenue

they got to know him so well that they actually offered him a
job, which he turned down. He had severance pay and didn't
need the money, but wasn't much inclined to work anyhow. Also,
the women working in the bakery were so heartbreakingly pretty,
he didn't trust himself with them in the middle of the night,
steeped in all that sugar and bright light.

A small blond with a head of wildly curly hair gave him so
many free doughnuts he was tempted to ask her to move in with
him—he would find a place, a job, she could continue working
at the bakery, sleep all day if she'd a mind to. They would lead
blissful lives, would die together, grandchildren ringing the bed,
singing lullabies, everyone chewing fresh doughnuts. As if this
were all to be true, Ray checked out of the Y, prepared for
anything. But that night, the blond introduced him to her small,
sharp-eyed, bearded old man, and Ray was thankful he'd kept
his dream of a life with her to himself. He said goodbye and
walked down to the Reflecting Pool, where a bunch of people
were hanging around partaking of all sorts of drugs under the
nose of Lincoln himself. Ray had always liked the statue of the
seated Lincoln—benign and huge, protective and powerful. Like
God, or the best of all fathers. Big Brother, but a benevolent one.
Sometime during that night, Ray is certain he climbed into Lincoln's lap, waiting for a pat on the head, or the lift and lull of
Abe's deep voice reading bedtime stories. Or he might have
dreamed that. Those days it was all the same.

It had turned unseasonably warm earlier that week, and the
group had stayed outside all night doing things Ray couldn't
remember and didn't much want to. He awoke the next morning
in a tiny dark apartment near Dupont Circle with eight or nine
of the bunch scattered around on old mattresses and cushions,
cats everywhere, men and women indistinguishable. All moving
slowly in the aftermath of the night, body parts—or what Ray
saw of them—interchangeable. Soft moans and breathing, light
snores. A mass of legs and arms and long-haired heads. It was
about as far as Ray wanted to go with the flower children, and
he emerged from that place and the nightmare of the past few

years, into the wan Washington morn, miraculously clearheaded and intact. Walking down Connecticut Avenue with his duffel bag and pack, he felt as if he had just recovered from a particularly bad whack to the head. Now, though, he was coming back, yes indeed, he was coming back, he felt it in every stumbling step— and he walked and walked and walked, till he realized how hungry he was, and then he stopped for some coffee.

He ordered a huge breakfast, just about everything on the menu. Vivian would have been disgusted, he thinks, that he'd bounced back so heartily. Once, she said he was like an animal that way: I mean that when you're hungry, you eat, she'd said, and when you're tired, you sleep, and when you're broke, you work, and when you're flush . . . Her voice had trailed off, flagged a little when she saw how he was looking at her. He was thinking she was being unnecessarily critical, but mostly he was agreeing with her. He said, Doesn't everybody? and she'd said, Of course, but it was just that he was satisfied with so little. That's just not true, he'd said, though he had to admit, silently, that he liked things simple. And while there was nothing much he could do about it short of becoming someone else (and Vivian assured him that wasn't what she meant, the fact was she almost envied him), he tried, after that, to appear more complicated than he actually was.

In an offhanded and optimistic moment, while digesting the meal, Ray closed his eyes and let his finger land where it would on the D.C. map embossed in blue and green and siren red on the place mat in front of him.

How much of our destiny is linked to hunger, menus, chance, he thought as he peered at what lay beneath his index finger: Capitol Hill, pinnacle of freedom and truth. I shall go there, he said to himself, I shall sally forth—he was feeling that good— and, paying his bill, he walked across town to the Hill and was hired right off the bat at the first of the many renovation jobs going on there.

Right away Ray felt at home with the crew in those spacious skeletons of houses. He felt as if he had arrived. This was what he was meant for. Nobody cared what he'd done or where he'd been. All they cared about was whether he could hammer a nail true, which he could thanks to all the time and sore thumbs he'd put in as a kid. One or two of the men were fresh from Nam. Best goddamn job I ever had, said one burly man from Colorado, blond hair down to his shoulders. A couple of others were fresh from the stir. Same goddamn thing, said the burly man from Colorado, which made Ray wonder what he'd meant by the first comment.

The foreman, owner of a string of dilapidated row houses, was named Sharkey; he said little and had a pretty set of purplish gashes down his left side. Sharkey let Ray stay in one of the houses they were working on, along with two guard dogs that snarled and paced endlessly on the other side of the Sheetrock.

The flight attendant brings Ray another drink. This is the last one, he says to himself. Though he'd not been able to reach her, he assumed Vivian would be there at the airport; if she really wanted to, knowing the date of his arrival, she could discover which flight was likely to be his. She wouldn't be pleased if he stumbled to meet her in National Airport, and she had not been amused, he was certain, at the way he'd left the schoolhouse that day. Why was he so concerned, all of a sudden, about what she thought of him? He gulps down the drink and realizes he is nervous. He wishes he were with her in the schoolhouse, so that he could look at her and touch her, all along explaining as best he could the nature of man. He feels finally he is making sense of it.

Back when he was working for Sharkey, he would have been unable to explain much of anything. Sharkey's girlfriend Nan, junkie turned real estate agent, made sandwiches and Campbell's soup for Ray and Sharkey every night on a hot plate. They dined on a piece of plywood propped on cinder block in what would one day be a bay-windowed, skylit, very expensive living room. Every night after dinner they had coffee with or without whiskey. Sharkey did not drink, Nan rarely. Once, when Sharkey was away, Nan brought the sandwiches as usual and made soup for

Ray. When they'd finished and were leaning against the framing, drinking coffee, dogs moving restlessly next door, Ray leaned over and kissed her, in gratitude and what might have been pure love. They kissed long, but just that once, because of Sharkey.

Once or twice that winter, Ray thought he saw Priscilla draped across the back of her SDS friend, Harley idling loudly at the corner of Seventeenth and Penn, or roaring up Massachusetts Avenue past the embassies, toward the cathedral, where Ray sometimes went to hear the music. But he couldn't be sure. Plenty of Harleys around then, with black leather jackets and clinging, long-haired girls.

Several years later she sent him a wedding announcement— a photograph of her in a floppy straw hat and a miniskirt with holes cut discreetly in it (looked to Ray like Swiss cheese) and the man he assumed was her husband, bearded, with very long hair and an embroidered Mexican wedding shirt. From then on, they'd kept track of each other. They had sometimes joked about how, after all the disastrous lovers and marriage, they were probably intended for each other and each other only. They could joke about that, and about how they were getting older though not necessarily wiser, but they could not joke about the cancer that she reported to him matter-of-factly in a letter a year or so earlier. When Ray read the letter, he felt as if someone had struck him square on the chest with tremendous force and malice, and he had spent that afternoon and much of the evening wandering in the woods near his house, gasping for breath as if he were the one doing the dying.

The pilot announces they are about to land. Ray drains his glass and checks the conch one last time. The plane taxis down the runway, wheels bouncing tentatively. Across the river, D.C. looks alive. After the sleepy brightness of the islands, Ray looks forward to the deprivation and chill of winter in Virginia. He braces himself for the landing. He feels himself flatten out against the back of the seat, feels nailed to the upholstery behind him, spread out over it, momentarily without bones.

He does not see her in the crowd as they disembark, but he

is unable to see clearly right off anyhow, for some reason, cannot discern faces or distinguishing features in the crowd. He certainly hopes she is there. Besides everything else, his truck is still up in Annapolis; he is without wheels. He is broke. He supposes he can hitch down to Charlottesville, but he is feeling a mite weary for that. Still, he could if he had to. She would be at the school-house when he arrived, probably working out. She'd be on the mat on the floor in front of the woodstove upstairs, legs strong and beautiful like the rest of her. All she would be wearing would be rose-colored underwear—if that—and the fine gold chain he'd blown three paychecks on. A chunk of her hair would be loose and lying across her cheek like a scar. Aretha Franklin would be cranked up, so she wouldn't hear the car or truck that delivered him, wouldn't hear him sneaking up the stairs, avoiding the creaky spots. The dogs would be dozing, subdued by the music.

He'd leave the conch out in the hall and would watch her a moment. Her face would be flushed with concentration. The dip of her hip would entice him. She'd suddenly see him and give a little scream. He'd walk in and promise not to frighten her next time, and she'd say, Next time? but would be close to forgiving him. And then, before she could move or say anything more, he'd say, Sssh, stay there, close your eyes, and she would, because she trusted him. And he'd unwrap the conch and hold it carefully against her ear. She'd open her eyes, surprised at the coolness, and would be about to speak. Sssh, he'd say again, still holding the shell. Hush. Just listen.

- ≡ -

Ray had fallen in love with Vivian instantly. Or so it had seemed.

It was late spring. He was sitting in The Virginian, local restaurant extraordinaire, wondering where his waitress was. Usually he brown-bagged it, but this day he had to get away. He'd spent hours haggling, first with the owners of the house he was building, then with the foreman, about some minute architectural details that looked good in the plans but would be impossible to implement in wood. He was scribbling on his napkin—yet again—about what it would take to go independent, when, to his right, the midsection of a body covered with a bright blue apron appeared. "Can I help you?" the torso asked. He looked up into a set of eyes that seemed to know far more than the day's menu, and he said yes, she certainly could. Her eyebrows were raised and her hair was braided, but coming out everywhere, and he said, as best he could, "Two enchiladas, extra sauce, and two Dos Equis."

"Will someone be joining you?" she asked.

And he said, in what sounded to him like a phrase fraught with significance, "Not just yet."

When she came back later to check his beer, she stretched out across the booth before him, and when she did, the tip of the pencil that hung from a red plastic lanyard round her neck touched the tabletop just barely, delicately, balancing precariously for one full minute on its leaden point. She happened to look down and see it, and then he had another thrill—she let it stay there a split second longer and smiled at him. "*Au pointe,*" she said.

"*Olé,*" he answered weakly.

It was the most intimate moment he'd spent with a woman in years, even taking into consideration his particular weakness for the waitresses at The Virginian. He was enchanted.

He wondered if he hadn't finally and completely just plain lost it, gone round the bend. He needed a vacation. He needed a new job. Perhaps he was in the wrong line of work, surrounded always by men and tools and noise and hazardous working conditions: everything from shaky scaffolding to fiberglass insulation. Maybe he needed no job at all. Maybe he needed therapy, no doubt a lobotomy. On the other hand, maybe what he needed was this woman and her pidgin French.

He thought he heard someone call her Vivian.

A few days later, Ray went to the optometrist to have a piece of sawdust removed from his eye, and he asked the doctor, while he was at it, to give his eyes a thorough check. He hadn't had them examined in years—not wanting, naturally, to hear the news—but lately his bad eye had been acting up. Actually, his vision was excellent—the result of putting in many long hours as a kid recovering from the BB gun wound inflicted on him by a boy he had once considered his best friend. His father bought a book called *Sight Without Glasses,* and even before he left the hospital, Ray and he talked about acuity of vision, exercised their good eyes and Ray's bad one, so Ray could continue his youthful dream of becoming a fighter pilot.

Ray had not made it to fighter planes, and he had spent more miserable days and nights than he cared to remember slogging around in the jungle. But he remembered fondly those days with his father—in his recollection, anyhow, few and far between.

The optometrist put drops in Ray's eyes to dilate them, and then, after doing the check and proclaiming him well, just getting older, turned him loose on the world, half-blind and disoriented, a little queasy. The doctor recommended that Ray wear goggles when working from here on out. His office was in a huge, glaring mall, and Ray wandered the place for a time, not trusting himself to drive. He ended up at Penney's, where he spent what seemed like hours mulling over work boots, size 10½. He never shopped at Penney's—never shopped anywhere, for that matter: bought most of his stuff mail order.

The optometrist had given him a pair of disposable paper sunglasses that reminded Ray of the innocent old days of 3-D; he replaced them with his own shades. He wandered the rows of shoes, trying unsuccessfully to focus on their finer points—the smoothness of the leather, the tightness of the joints. Now and then he'd pick up a boot, run his fingers over the stitching; he would knead the leather in an effort to detect quality. He felt adrift, disembodied, and didn't much like it. Which surprised him, given the countless times over the years he had willingly put himself into every frizzed-out state under the sun, thanks to a constant and substantial flow of drugs. It hadn't been sordid and grim like today's crack and coke; it had been flower power and free love and be here now, babe. Though in a way Ray had cashed in on all that without feeling the slightest bit political. Feeling political took too much work. He had made it through the war alive. Wasn't that enough?

"I'll try this one, size ten and a half." Ray said this to the saleslady. He sensed, rather than saw, her disapproval of the way he was lingering in her shoe section.

"Yes, sir," she said, and went fussing off while he sat to wait.

Then he heard Vivian. Or smelled her. Knew she was in the vicinity. She was standing in front of a rack of track shoes, slightly blurred and bluish, asking how much a particular shoe cost. Something about what he could see of the way she was standing intrigued him. Her left knee sloped gently back under faded jeans in a sort of inverted curve, weight all on that leg, hip out. He imagined her parents constantly upbraiding her for not standing straight, as his had done. He liked the leg. He liked what he could see of the rest of her. He wondered if her magenta pencil was safely hooked to the end of her lanyard, tucked between her sweater and blouse, nestled against her breasts. She unbuttoned her bulky cardigan and shoved up the sleeves as if it were ninety degrees in Penney's. Her hair was loose this time, flying every-where, out of control. In his visual haze, her head looked to Ray like an angel's—glowing halo of filigree. In that instant he de-cided there was nothing about her he did not like.

She stayed near the track shoes, while he pretended to be mesmerized by work boots. "What I should really get," he said aloud, for no particular reason, "are cowboy boots."

"Those we don't carry." The saleslady was back, armed with the boots, impatient to be done with him. She patted the boxes she'd set on the chair next to his. "Excuse me," she said, and brushed past him to help Vivian.

He hung around while the saleslady went to the back for track shoes. He strained for a glimpse—figurative—of Vivian. When he got up to test a pair of boots, he bumped into a rack of gaudy bedroom slippers, almost knocking the display over. He steadied the rack and went back to the safety of his seat, alarmed at the rate and volume of his heartbeat.

When he thought he felt Vivian looking directly at him, he chose the boots currently on his feet and made his way to the counter to pay. He forced himself not to look in her direction, though his vision was clearing just slightly now. The saleslady was wearing a locket with violets painted on it, and way too much makeup; he was relieved to notice the details, but he didn't feel the least equipped to carry on a conversation with anyone, especially with Vivian, whom he now desired passionately. As he reached for his wallet, he wondered wildly if Vivian's buying track shoes meant she was a mad jogger, and he prayed it didn't. He'd never be able to keep up.

The saleslady seemed relieved to be getting rid of him.

The wallet wasn't there. He patted the other hip pocket. Nothing. He cursed himself for not mending the torn pocket and checked again. He looked around the floor at his feet, checked the ground behind him, lifted the smooth soles of his new boots, did a sort of small, dancey shuffle to see if perhaps he'd stepped on the wallet, hiding it, squashing its contents, but knew all along this was impossible. His new tan Wolverines stared up at him, huge and stupid. His heart sank. He tried to reconstruct. "I know I had it when I walked in here," he said, but not in a heartfelt way. The saleslady was exasperated—that much he could see— and Ray wondered how long it would be before she called Security.

"You'd better take off the boots," she said unkindly, and he realized now, knew absolutely, that she had mistrusted him from the start, that she half expected him to bolt for the exit, new boots clomping on the hard bright tile. And maybe that was exactly what he should do to escape this awkwardness and slander. He felt himself grow hot: he wanted to throttle this woman with her violet necklace and aqua eyes.

"I'll pay, I'll pay," he muttered.

And then there was Vivian, holding out his sad-looking, stained billfold. "Is this yours?" she asked. "It was over there."

Ray followed her pointing finger to the row of chairs where he'd been sitting.

"I think it is," he said. He patted the torn pocket, then reached up to remove his shades. It might be safe now to expose his eyes, let her see him. "Got a hole in my pocket," he couldn't keep himself from adding, yanking the glasses off with such a flourish that the loose right lens fell out, disappearing under a rack of Weejuns.

"You're having a hard time today," Vivian said, laughing, and it was true, but he was able to look right at her now and see that her eyes were bluer than he remembered, and guardedly kind. She popped the lens back into its frame, held the glasses out to him. She felt warm. The wire frames of the glasses felt cold, both in his hands and back on the bridge of his nose. He thought he smelled lavender mixed in with leather. He squinted to see her more clearly, thought perhaps he should remove the glasses for good. She was looking at him curiously.

"Do people even wear Weejuns anymore?" he said in his confusion.

She shrugged and laughed again. "Is everything OK?"

Did she remember him? "I've just had my eyes checked," he said. "They put in those drops."

"Huh," she said, easing back to the track shoes. "I was wondering." The saleslady rustled the bag with his old shoes. "Fifty-nine sixty," she said.

"Way too much," said Ray, but he paid in cash.

Vivian was still appraising the track shoes. He had to pass her in order to leave. "You work at The Virginian," he said, stopping next to her. "You write down the orders." It all sounded far more serious than he intended, much too much like bald statements of fact that she might or might not wish to refute, rather than light chitchat meant simply to get her attention. When he saw she wasn't inclined to answer, he said lamely, "Great enchiladas. Really good sauce."

Vivian pushed back her hair, looked at him quickly, went back to the Reeboks. She seemed to be waiting for him to go, but it was too late to retreat. Too much at stake, so he blundered on. "Would you like to have a drink later?" he asked.

And for the first time that he could see, she looked at him, really looked at him, at the new boots and torn jeans and black shades and general disorientation, and she said, "Only if you keep the glasses off."

■ ≡ ■

Over drinks he learned she taught art to elementary and high school kids and that sometimes she waitressed.

"I think it's great that you write the orders down," Ray said. Of course, she wasn't wearing the pencil around her neck, as he knew, in his heart of hearts, she would not be.

She answered, a little huffily, "I studied painting, not waitressing. Besides, everyone writes it down eventually so they can ring up the bill."

"I love it, I love it," Ray said quickly, not wanting her sudden seriousness to ruin what little leeway they'd made. "It just seems, well, antiquated." She looked at him oddly.

She taught art and she'd also, back in Tucson, where she'd lived last, taught aerobics to middle-aged women. "I understood them," she told Ray, "being one myself."

He decided not to gallantly protest her age, instead, half fascinated, half horrified, said, "You don't lift weights, do you?" and she said, "I have."

After the drink, Vivian went with Ray out to the schoolhouse. He supposed she couldn't imagine that someone so inept at keeping track of his wallet, or keeping his glasses in repair, could be perilous company. She trailed him out in her Datsun pickup, the practicality of which both pleased and slightly annoyed him.

She seemed not to fear him, and had certainly pitched right in there on the couch, had seemed to enjoy herself. No one took off clothes—serious business in that cool night. They would have had to go to bed immediately to avoid the discomfort of being naked without central heat. They kissed, Ray tentatively unbuttoning her blouse in order to work his way down her winter-white skin, but she said it was getting late and moved away a little. She said right off the bat to sleep with him was not her wish. He said it wasn't his either, though secretly he ached for her.

She liked his dogs.

"What's your name?" she asked the one that had been snoring next to the couch ever since their arrival. The woodstove was cranked up now, baking them. The kettle of water on top of it hissed and sputtered where drops of water seeped out through imperfect but fine-looking seams. The night had turned sharply colder, Ray noticed when he went to get more wood from the porch.

"Frenchie," said Ray.

"Frenchie." Vivian rubbed Frenchie's ears. Frenchie twisted her head this way and that, taking full advantage of the sudden kindness of a stranger. "I'll have to sketch you someday, Frenchie," she said. Then she said, her back to Ray, still addressing the dog, "Is he always this amorous?"

"Are you asking *me*? Am *I* always this amorous?" Ray asked.

"I was asking Frenchie," she said, "but yes, I meant you."

"Not at all." It was the truth. "And you?"

"What?"

"Are you always this amorous?"

"No," she said. She looked at him over her shoulder, and he admired the way the weak lamplight cut vague shadows across her cheeks. "No." She was still patting Frenchie. The white dog, Geronimo, wandered over to Ray's side of the couch, wanting similar treatment.

"Then?" Why was he asking all these questions? He should just keep quiet and lure her back to him. He stretched his arm out across the back of the couch, tentatively touching her shoulder.

"Then what?"

Jesus Christ, he thought, but he said, "Why are you here?"

She thought a moment. "Maybe I felt sorry for you, losing

your wallet, your sensitive eyes." She laughed and, before he could feel offended, squinted her eyes, lowered her voice, said, "Wolverines, size ten and a half," mimicking him.

Had he looked so lost? "I needed the boots," he said.

She said, Oh.

And stop patting the goddamn dog.

She kept on with the dog, looked at Frenchie attentively, as if the brilliance of their communication necessarily excluded all others. A few silver strands of Vivian's hair caught what little light there was. Then she said faintly, as if not fully engaged in the thought, "You looked a little forlorn. You're certainly nothing like what I expected."

"What did you expect?" Ray was edging his way across the couch to her. He was ready to hold her against him, have every inch of her touching every inch of him. He was weary of looking into her blue eyes.

"I guess," she said, her voice low now—he was very close to her—"I expected you to be quieter."

"Don't let the glasses fool you." He was instantly offended and stood up to get a drink in the kitchen. It was cold there; he found a bottle of whiskey and poured himself some. Behind him, he heard the door creak open and her footsteps coming closer. He wished they would just stop talking so they could go to bed, or she would go home. In spite of what everyone said, words left plenty of room for misunderstanding; sometimes talk complicated the simplest of acts. It was exhausting, and always enough was left unsaid so that by the end of a conversation there were still murky, untapped waters. By and large, Ray stuck to a general but friendly silence, with intentions vague and mysterious, things only remotely implied.

But he knew Vivian wouldn't go for that. He could see she was one of them, one of the people requiring answers. She poured herself a drink and touched her glass to his. "Don't be so thin-skinned," she said.

"I'm just a little tired."

She looked around the kitchen, touched bunches of herbs

hanging along one wall. "I love this place," she said. "And I like you."

"You do?" Never had he felt sillier. She put her glass down, put his down for him, and stood as close as she could to kiss him. "I wouldn't have driven all the way out here if I didn't."

Frenchie came clicking into the kitchen, brushing against the back of Ray's legs on her way to her spot between the counter and the fridge. Holding Vivian, Ray watched his dog watching him with baleful eyes. I like her, he mouthed to Frenchie. He stood back, let Vivian's hair fall from his hands back around her face.

"You're very beautiful," he said, and for once she said nothing, simply smiled.

Then she said she had to go, and they were outside, standing next to her pickup, shivering from the cold and the general excitement of each other, and he said, "Do you realize you're the only other person I know that's my age? What happened to everyone? Where'd we all go?"

She got into her truck, turned on the ignition, then rolled down the window while the engine warmed up. A song crackling on the radio was an old one they both knew.

"We listened to all that music and smoked all that dope and now we know everything, don't we?" Ray said. Vivian was humming along, smiling. "Maybe we just don't recognize one another," he said.

Vivian eased her truck into reverse. "I know in a heartbeat," she said. Meaning me? he was thinking. He put a hand on her door to stall her.

"Why don't you come out for dinner tomorrow? I'll make some pasta. We can throw it at the wall. Pasta al dente: if it sticks, it's done."

She said she would. He walked along as she continued backing, his hand on the door like the Secret Service. "By the way," he said, "did you find the shoes you were looking for?"

Vivian patted some boxes next to her. "Kangaroos. Size eleven and a half."

"Won't they be a little big?"

"They're for my daughter." She was moving forward now, picking up speed. The dogs eased away respectfully from the truck.

"You have a daughter?"

"And a son. They live with their father."

"What are their names?" he called out after her, but she didn't hear, at any rate didn't answer, and in the next instant she was out the driveway and well on her way home.

■ ≡ ■

"Don't you miss them?" he asked her at dinner the next night.

"Of course I do." They were sitting at the cable spool in the kitchen, eating his slightly underdone pasta. She had praised the food, the spicy pesto, which he thought was very nice of her. Now, suddenly, she looked tired. She looked past him, out the darkened kitchen window. "I wanted some time alone. For a while, anyhow." She finished her wine, continued staring past him.

"I understand that," said Ray, but he didn't really. His desire to be alone was necessitated originally by having to be, by not being able to charm a woman into diving into life with him. Over the years, he'd come to depend on it.

They ate in silence, then she said, "I consider all this temporary."

"All what?"

"All this." She waved her hand through the air, at him, the table, their cooling food. Then she sighed. "All I really want to do right now is paint."

"Are you going back?"

"To Tucson?" Vivian twirled pasta round her fork. Outside in the fields the bobwhites were giving forth. "Maybe. It's beautiful there this time of year."

"Beautiful here too," said Ray.

She nodded, was quiet awhile, then said, "Yeah, it is," but still it took her a little too long to meet his eyes, and whatever questions he had for her would just have to wait.

When it got to be summer, good and hot, she spent more and more time at the schoolhouse, swimming in his pond and the nearby river, helping him plant a garden. She brought a few boxes of painting supplies out; he got to loving the smell of oil and turpentine, loved the names of the paints: cadmium red, cerulean blue, vermilion. He built her an easel—couldn't build it fast enough—found himself wanting to give her all sorts of things. She'd set up the easel in the fields and woods around the schoolhouse. He liked watching her paint, thought, in his limited experience, that she was very good. Didn't always understand exactly what she was up to, but loved that too—the mystery, her privacy. But for all her seeming candor, he couldn't get much out of her about her husband in Tucson and the children. It was tender territory, he understood that, and they hadn't known each other long enough for him to push it. Still, he was curious, and a little jealous. For her part, she became exasperated when old friends, including women, turned up, either over the phone or in the flesh. He and Vivian kept things loose to the point of irresponsibility sometimes, but that, he told himself over and over, was the deal. That was the deal, and that was the beauty of their friendship, or whatever it was. Neither was held accountable to the other, they lived their own lives, had their own muddled pasts, and it was nobody's business but their own.

■ ≡ ■

Later that summer, Ray, for no particular reason, had a party. It was mid-July and very hot. They were several hours and kegs and lost conversations into the party when Ray, who was in the kitchen, heard someone pop a cork and shout *Happy New Year!* Someone else, not Vivian, was pushing her barely covered tanned bosom against him and was whispering into his ear. He assumed she was suggesting something erotic, otherwise why so close? but it was noisy in the schoolhouse and he could not make out the words. He heard the *s*'s in her words, felt their tiny bursts of breath. She smelled like limes and was waving around a glass half full of strong-looking, greenish stuff. Mint julep? Ray wondered, and pulled back.

"Are you alone?" he shouted above the screaming stereo. Glasses seemed to hop in place on the shelves with the vibrations; rattling plates nestled closer, settled like shifting earth during a quake.

She raised her eyebrows as if she were asking the question. He wondered what Vivian would think if she walked in right then. He wondered if he cared what Vivian would think. Perhaps he had been seeing too much of her. Of course not—he was crazy about Vivian. Perhaps he had been drinking too much Mount Gay.

"I came with Jack, but I'm always alone," said the blond. "You know?"

"That Jack?" Ray twitched his head toward a man in cutoffs and no shirt, who was taking a stab at being Jimi Hendrix but without the manic flaming guitar and the lighter fluid, certainly without the afro. People had given Jack plenty of room to do his thing. At first they had stood around, egging him on, clapping and saying *All right!* but now, bored, they left him to do it alone, which is all he really wanted in the first place. Jack was big, with a big beard, and had, at that moment (though Ray had no trouble imagining it otherwise), a shining, beatific monkish look to him. His scalp, protected by a few hairs resembling scars, was ancient and red. Ray had never seen him before. The blond either.

"That's Jack." The blond paused to lick the salt from the rim of her glass, the salt on her lips. "Jack's mean, but you look meaner."

"So do you," he said, and drank to her health. She smiled at him.

"Whose place is this, anyhow?" she asked, taking a piece of ice from her glass and crunching on it thoughtfully. "That Jack can really belt 'em out," she said with what sounded to Ray like deep admiration.

"That he can," said Ray. Then, past the fluff of the blond's hair, he saw Vivian watching him. He waved and said to the blond, "Catch you later."

"Not if Jack can help it." She smiled. "It's now or never." He gave her a friendly little hug and moved off through the people to Vivian. Her shoulders were tan and square under a purple tank top, and she was smiling at him, but he was not entirely sure of the look in her eyes.

He leaned down. "Having fun?"

Her curly hair was all over the place. Some of it brushed his cheek. She looked up, nodded. "You?"

"I am having the time of my *life!*" he called out to her, as if making it final from the top of Mount Fuji.

Later in the party, the goats got out and were hanging around the porch, curious, waiting for someone to do something—feed them, pat them, throw something at them. One of the kids clattered up the steps and began nibbling at a string dangling from a hammock. The moon was bright, and the weathered wood of the porch floor appeared wavy and white, barely there. Even the kid paused before stepping up.

"Isn't he cute," said the blond, who had followed Ray out onto the front porch. Inside, someone was trying to be Elvis, throwing his hair around wildly. Ray could see his shadow on the wall just inside the window, bouncing and jerking as if apoplectic.

"They eat everything," Ray said. "Where's Jack?" He was thinking how nice it would be to suddenly have instant quiet, instant calm. He was having a fine time and so was everyone else, which meant it would be some time before peace, in the form of sleep, anyhow, came his way.

The blond shrugged, put out a long arm bound in silver bracelets. "Come here," she said. She clucked to the kid the way she probably clucked to Jack, Ray was thinking. Then he thought, Where is Vivian? The kid nuzzled the blond's hand, nibbled at the closest silver bracelet, nuzzled her fingers again. She said, watching the goat, "If only they would put on the B-52s or the Pretenders or Sting, Jack wouldn't know what to do and then he'd pass out and we could go home."

"Jack's got good taste," Ray said, "tried and true," meaning the music but letting her think whatever she wanted. The kid looked at him, its rectangular pupils spooky in the moonlight; it seemed to agree for a moment on something Ray hadn't quite thought through yet. "They put goats in with racehorses to keep them from getting skittish," he said, "keep them from getting spooked." The blond patted the kid's head one last time and straightened up. "Too bad they turn into smelly old billy goats," she said, just as the kid bent its satyr head chin-to-chest and rammed sharp two-inch horns into her thigh right where the shorts stopped.

"Ouch!" she said, silver bangles clinking. "Stop it!" She tried to hold the kid off, twisted her body around as if she were inside a hula hoop. The kid poked at the backs of her legs, behind her knees. "Ouch!" she said again, louder this time, and then, "Help!"

It was Vivian, who had just come out onto the porch, that pulled the kid away from the blond and hauled it down the steps to the barn. On her way out, she glared at Ray.

"I'm sorry," he said to both of them, "I couldn't move," and he felt like laughing, wasn't sure why, knew it was rotten—the instinct to just turn around and walk off, leaving the blond to her fate with the goat. "I'm sorry," he said again. "He didn't hurt you, did he?" He thought he saw tears on her cheeks and was ashamed.

"I'm sure I'll be black-and-blue in the morning," she said, sniffing.

He gave her a bandanna to dry her eyes and helped her inside to look for Jack. And later, when Jack tried to ride one of the goats and Ray was getting him off before he was thrown or kicked clear to the next county, the bruised blond sat there on the porch steps still rubbing her legs, as sober as if Jack were a stranger and she hadn't been at the party at all, whispering into Ray's ear,

telling him secrets, wanting something from him. It was the last
he saw of her, or his bandanna. It was the beginning of something
with Vivian.

■ ≡ ■

Midmorning the next day, they are walking to the river.
Ahead of Ray, Vivian is moving fast, pushing aside low-lying
branches as they head for the Rockfish. She is wearing another
tank top, faded pink, and her hair is braided in some semblance
of order. It is very hot and humid, and Ray doesn't know why
they are going to the river after such a party, to say nothing of
rocky quasi sleep, full of lousy dreams and leering mouths.

He feels as if he's spent the night with a cattle prod. He is
getting to be too old to muster up the energy needed to bounce
back the morning after. Too many brain cells shot, too much
general murkiness, no payoff anymore. Or less of it, anyhow.
Vivian, on the other hand, seems to be full of zip and, now that
he thinks of it, has barely spoken all morning.

"What we should be doing," he calls to her, "is sitting on the
porch drinking Bloody Marys." She doesn't answer, pushes on
ahead.

He is thinking that by the time they get to the water it will
be pouring with rain, and he doesn't feel the slightest urge to
taunt fate and splash around in a river during an electrical storm.
He simply doesn't feel that lucky these days.

Vivian would swim in any river at any time. He knew that
and loved her for it.

"I have this great idea," he says to her back. She doesn't stop.
He wonders if the incident with the blond is bothering her. He
is sorry if it is, and says so. "Just stop and listen for a minute,
would you?" He catches up with her, holds her by the elbow.
She looks at him, and for a moment he falters. He can't quite
identify what he sees in her eyes, but it isn't friendly, whatever
it is, nowhere near the love he seems to be feeling with increasing

passion the more he watches her push through the woods before him.

"You know how my throat has been hurting lately?" he says, feeling stupid. Even his voice sounds stupid, low and ragged.

"Too much smoking," says Vivian. The dogs are panting next to her legs. She scratches one between the ears impatiently. "Well?" she says.

"I'll be talking," Ray says, "and suddenly I'll lose my voice, or it'll come out in some adolescent squeak?"

"I hadn't noticed." She waits, focuses on the precise center of his throat. She looks as if she is filled with the most unbearable, unremitting boredom.

"Well," he says, knowing it's too late to turn back, wishing he'd never begun. He feels he is tiptoeing with tremendous clumsiness along the most delicate of high wires. "I just have this feeling it's fatal, and my plan is you can nurse me along while I'm working on my final, definitive statement carpentrywise—house full of skylights and clerestories and cathedral ceilings, which I will bequeath to you, of course—and then I'll croak, but before I do, I'll have to face"—and here he pauses dramatically and yells out, "The Truth!" His hand is on his brow, his eyes closed. He feigns faintness, though in actuality he does feel a little off. He waits for her to ask, What truth? She says nothing. He wants to fall to his knees, confess his love, then keel over stone dead so he can avoid the unavoidable consequences of such a statement, but his legs stiffen and the words stick in his ailing throat and he says, "You could be a gorgeous widow, go around in black tank tops and too-tight skirts, try to keep that hair of yours squashed into a tasteful bun."

He waits for her to smile. She says, "I can't be your widow because we're not married—thank God—and by then my hair will be exactly one inch long all over, because I'm going to cut it, and as for your throat, you've probably got strep, so call the doctor and get some medicine and then just relax."

"It's gone on too long for strep."

Vivian pokes a stray hair back into the braid. "Stop smoking, then."

"Marry me so you can be my widow," Ray says. It just rolls off his tongue and out into the universe. He is appalled; he is in love. Inside his head, someone screams, *Retreat! Retreat!* He reaches out to touch her. She steps back.

"That's a terrible plan," she says. "Morbid." But he thinks he detects the slightest change in her voice, which makes him bold.

"It's a terrific plan."

"It's terrible," she says again, and now he realizes that he had it all wrong, she is more upset than he realized, she is on the verge of tears. "I don't want to nurse you back to or from anything. And I don't want to save you from anything, or wean you from anybody. And I *certainly* do *not* want to *marry* you. All I want," she says, "is to be happy, with you or without you. And I want to paint. And I want to see my children." He puts his hands on her shoulders, but she shakes them off. "So just please leave me alone."

Oh Lord, he thinks, oh Lord oh Lord. He puts his hands on her waist. Her tank top is drenched. "Just go on and do what you have to do," she says. "Don't worry about me." She turns around and goes crashing through the woods, dogs at her heels, a little off the path now. He follows, can hear her but can't always see her. He knows as long as they keep moving in this direction, they'll meet at the river eventually.

Once, he catches up with her and is behind her again, watching her move through the trees, muted sunlight flickering spasmodically over and—it seems—through her. Later, it seems impossible that he could have seen the spiderweb so clearly from so far off, or that it is even there at all. The web is gigantic, stretched between two oaks; it glints in the heavy air like baby hair, filaments lacy and fine, perfect symmetry. He watches Vivian head straight for it, and he wants to yell at her to duck, to watch out, leave it alone, but his throat hurts, or seems to, and the words never get said. She breaks through it as if it had no link to life whatsoever, as if it were invisible or, worse, as if she intended to destroy it.

For a moment Ray hates her for not seeing, or caring. He would have slithered under it like a copperhead, would have slunk along dragging his belly like a wolf. Would have skittered past like some small gray vermin. He would even have been the goddamn sacrificial fly. Anything to spare the web, keep the precarious balance.

Vivian stops and turns around. She is brushing sticky bits of web from her cheeks, holds her hands away from her sides, flicks her fingers to get rid of the stuff. She walks back to him. "What's wrong?" she asks.

He points to what's left of the web.

At first he sees she doesn't understand, and, in that instant, he wishes he had never spoken, that he did not have to hear what she would say. He sees himself standing in front of the web, foolish and ugly and alone, like someone who has just had a haircut gone awry—far too much taken off in back, too little in front—and everyone is smirking at the botched job, saying, That's OK, it'll grow back. He can almost feel the shears dangerously cold at his ear. He wants Vivian to hold him, run her fingers through his still-thick hair, love him as if he is complete.

Instead she says, "You know something, Ray? You're a little bit like a racehorse yourself."

So she had heard him on the porch with the blond.

"I mean in that you seem to need to have somebody around to keep you on track, keep you from being spooked, keep you in love with someone, anyone, all the goddamn time." She is speaking very deliberately and slow, and it is scary. Ray is thinking he has never seen her so angry.

"I'm sorry," he says.

She is very close to him now and to his alarm begins, gently at first, then with increasing speed and force, pummeling his chest with both fists—it hurts—and finally he has to grab her wrists to make her stop. Then it's her turn to apologize, and they walk uneasily to the river, where he still cannot bring himself to tell her he loves her, but he does what he can to convince her of his devotion. They lie on springy green ferns next to the river, tasting the sweet rainwater and each other's salty bodies, lightning flashing on the water like sparks, not mentioning what they've said, but not, of course, forgetting.

■ ≡ ■

She is not at the airport, nor at the schoolhouse when he finally arrives after several harrowing rides with drivers who seem far crazier in every way than he. Fatigued by the journey, disappointed at missing her, unprepared for the cold—a light layer of snow covers more and more of Virginia the farther inland he goes—he fears she might have left him, but she was only at the Safeway, buying groceries. She said she was expecting him the next day, for some reason, she figured he was the handsome stranger mentioned in her horoscope, but today would do. Still, there exists now the mildest reverse between them, which Ray is unable to bridge, so he chooses, for the time being, to ignore it. He makes a tentative peace with the foreman, whose judgment he mistrusts, and he spends the winter months doing finish work in the condos that are springing up in nearby farmers' fields and gentlemen's woods. At Christmas Vivian flies to Tucson to see the children, and Ray holes up in his shop every night she's away. When she returns New Year's Day, he presents her with a walnut drawing table, which makes her cry. When she is unable to stop, he realizes the tears stand for more than heartfelt thanks, and that is when she tells him she is miserable without the children.

"It's as if someone has cut out a part of me." She gestures at her stomach. "There's this empty place where I can just about feel the wind blowing through, it's so cold," and Ray knows he should have known this earlier, or done something about it, that it should not have come to this.

"We'll get them to come, of course we'll get them here," he says, smoothing her hair. He looks past her sobbing head to one of the cracks in the ceiling; it looks like the San Andreas fault. He wonders if the ceiling will cave in, bury them alive, Pompeii. After he'd picked her up at the airport, they had gone into town to eat dinner, and now they were lying in bed watching new snow fall. She has been back exactly three hours and has been crying the whole time. She has cut her hair short, which he says he likes, though he prefers it long; she says she knows he likes it better long, all men like long hair on women except people like Vidal Sassoon, and what the hell does Vidal Sassoon know about women? She is wearing some sort of Navajo dress that Ray thinks is lovely, and says so, but it makes her seem more an exotic stranger than the woman he loves. He likes the idea of her being an exotic stranger, but most of all he wants her to take off the dress, he wants to touch her without its interference. She says she is too upset. He wants to say, Do it for me, then, but it sounds way too selfish, so he says, "We'll get them here for the summer. They can stay here. This place could use a couple of real kids."

"But I'm not sure that would work," she wails. "They'll probably drive you crazy. They're lively. I mean," she says, calming down a little, "they're kids, you know?"

He knew. He felt at times mired in near adolescence himself, but he was willing to give it a shot. "No problem," he says. "It'll be interesting. I've done all right with Darryl all these years." Darryl is his sister's teenage mess of a son, who admires Ray in a way that is largely misguided—Ray and his sister agree on this—and a little embarrassing. "Claude could probably use a break," he adds, and wonders when he will meet the great Claude, father of these children. No doubt they would like each other— get juiced, talk about what a wonderful woman their Vivian is.

"At first he was adamant. No! he says." She is practically shrieking. He wishes she hadn't cut her hair. She is sitting up, wiping her cheeks on her beautifully woven sleeve. "But he'll come around, I think. He acknowledged it was a lot of work."

"He'll come around," says Ray.

He wants desperately to have her naked under the sheets with him. The snow is sticking to the windowpanes in identical, feathery swirls. He holds her against him, feels her softness.

While she was gone, he missed her profoundly. Never in his life had he sat so long as when he stared out his shop window while he waited for the glue on the walnut to dry. He was glad no one was there to witness it. That listlessness had lasted just a day, but it was enough to scare him, as was his feeling of longing when she called to say she was extending her stay a few days and would not be back till early January. He had expected to spend New Year's Eve with her, though he usually avoided celebrating holidays, thinking them fat with sentimentality. This December 31 felt different. He got tremendously drunk all alone (nothing unusual), pulled out his old guitar, and sat on the porch to sing to the moon and stars and goats and chickens and, luckily, not to any neighbors, as they were miles off. He sang the nonstop can't-stop don't-wanta-stop down-home down-and-out desolation dehydration demarcation deep relation no stagnation full gyration deprivation titillation happy-new-year-old-acquaintance be here now blues.

He sang it loud and clear, and at the hour he decided was midnight, or close enough, he yelled out at the top of his lungs, *Happy New Year, Darlin',* so loud he was sure Vivian felt the tremors clear across this great land, clean into her heart.

Next morning, early, she calls. "Where were you?" she says. "I called at midnight," and that is when he realizes he was two hours early with his greeting and that at the proper time he was long since passed out, dead to the world, which was OK, but he had not wanted, above all, to be dead to her.

Now, tearful but hopeful, she leans against him, then presses against him, touches him, and soon they've maneuvered her new Navajo dress to the point where her legs are free and then finally she pulls it off and they make up for the night before. More than once she makes him stop, makes him slow down; she pulls away, pulls back, separates herself from him. She simply looks at him all over. Then she touches him again, but never quite in the same way, and after a time, he is practically out of his head with wanting her but not quite having her. In the end he is conscious of very little except he might die of heart failure if she keeps on much longer.

"I am completely out of control," he says once.

"Isn't that good?" she says, but he can't answer, and then she tells him she loves him, and he is so moved it almost breaks his heart.

■ ≡ ■

"Long time no see." It is two months later, February, very cold, and Bullet is standing at the front door of the schoolhouse, swinging a duffel bag off his shoulder. "I see you retrieved your pick-'em-up," he says. "I'd planned on driving it down for you, hoss. Had to hitch instead. Got stuck with a Witness for four hours, which damn near killed me. What a ride! Tried to convert me, and he almost made it too."

Bullet squints down the dim hallway. Ray squints at Bullet. It is early, and he is having trouble believing what he is seeing. In the distance, diesel rigs whine on highways connecting Charlottesville to the rest of the world. Ronnie the rooster is raising a racket, alarmed yet again at the rising sun, and Bullet's mouth is moving, his whole body is in motion. He reminds Ray of Kerouac's description of Neal Cassady. He told Vivian that once, and she said, All you guys fancy yourselves such free spirits, but she'd been laughing.

Bullet is shifting around the front hall, looking mechanically this way and that. "Said his wife running off with his best friend put him over the edge. Said the smallest thing could bring you to the light. I said, Just bring me to Charlottesville, man." He puts down the bag, locks Ray in a bear hug. "So how're you doing, hoss?"

"Doing pretty good." Ray shivers. He pulled on a pair of jeans

when he heard the commotion—dogs barking, someone pounding on the door to be let in. "What time is it?"

"Time to get started on the day," Bullet says.

Behind him, Ray hears floorboards creak. He pulls himself
out of the hug. "Vivian," he says, turning, "this is Bullet," but
he knows she knows exactly who it is. They have had it out about
Bullet and boat deliveries and cryptic notes. And don't ever leave
your dogs and the rest of us like that again, she'd said, or we'll
be out of here, we'll be long gone when you get back.

They have had it out and they have reached an understanding,
and now, without meaning to—and against all odds (Ray has
always thought, unreasonably, that he was sterile; you just had
smart girlfriends, Vivian said)—they are having a child. Off-
spring! progeny! descendants! responsibility! Sometimes Ray's
heart almost stops at the prospect, but more often it soars.

Vivian is wearing the old plaid bathrobe that had been Ray's
father's. She holds out a flannel shirt to him. The thin winter
light moves unevenly on her rumpled hair, but she is wide awake.
Geronimo sniffs the visitor suspiciously; Frenchie, bored, has gone
back to sleep in the corner. Bullet puts one hand on the white
dog's huge head, extends the other to Vivian. They shake hands,
and he says to Ray, "You didn't tell me she was such a knockout,
McCreary."

Ray smiles helplessly, first at Vivian, then at Bullet, and,
picking up the duffel bag, formally invites him in.

■ ≡ ■

"What're you doing back so soon?" They are sitting around
the kitchen table, waiting for the coffee to perk. Though it is
later now, the day is not much brighter than when Bullet first
arrived. Snow is forecast; the air has that steely smell to it.

Ray pours three cups of coffee. He has cranked up the fire
in the kitchen stove, but the mugs are so cold the coffee cools

almost immediately. Vivian pushes hers away a fraction of an inch, which confuses Ray. He knows she loves coffee. Then he remembers she is cutting back (in the interests of motherhood) on caffeine, aspirin and drugs of all sorts, alcohol—the real sacrifice, she'd said—so he takes back the cup and says, "I'll make you some tea," which he does.

"I thought the plan was to stay down in the islands for the winter," Ray says when they are settled.

"That was the plan, but it got a little dull down there. After a while, the only thing left to do is sit around and drink yourself to oblivion and eat squid all day. Gets a little redundant, you know?" Bullet pronounces the *d*'s in "redundant" as if he is beating on a drum with his tongue.

"Doesn't sound so bad," says Ray, and he begins to wonder how long Bullet is planning to stay.

"It got a little old." Bullet walks around the kitchen with his coffee, examining woodwork around the windows, testing the fit of the doors. "This is some place you got here."

"Keeps us young," says Ray.

Bullet knocks on the wall as if checking for rot. A small piece of plaster, the size of a quarter, loosens and slips daintily to the floor.

"Don't tear the place apart," says Ray. "Last thing I want to do when I get home is pound nails."

He feels Vivian watching him, watching them, as if they were some two-headed beast. Life in the amusement park. He can hear her thinking, So this is the great Bullet. He wants to include her in their nonsense, but then he wants her out of the room, miles away, wants her nowhere near the two of them. Next thing, he wants her back and Bullet banished to Siberia, or some godforsaken place, safely distant.

Bullet wanders the kitchen restlessly, nursing the coffee.

"Where's the *Honeybee?*" Ray asks. "You didn't get rid of her, after all that?"

"Got a good deal and decided to bail out. It took about six weeks for me to sell her, but it was time. Peg says she'll come back if I pay her way, the little darlin'." He rolls his eyes, groans, "Women!" His mouth splits into an exaggerated smile, and they watch his gold caps glitter. "She loves me more than she'll ever know."

He walks back to the table, puts his boot on the seat of the chair. Outside, snow falls lightly. Vivian is quiet; maybe she's sleepy, Ray thinks.

"Next stop Australia, land of opportunity, the last frontier. Not many places left." Bullet cocks his head and looks at Ray. "Nah," he says. "Just give me good old Maryland, or—where are we? Charlottesville? Give me good old Charlottesville." Then he says, "You know, McCreary, you and me could have had one hell of a time in the gold rush," at which point Ray thinks he detects a quiet snort emanating from Vivian's side of the table.

- ≡ -

"He's not a bad person," Ray is whispering to Vivian that night as they get into bed. They can hear Janis Joplin wailing away with Bullet: "*And I say whoa-whoa-whoa-whoa baby it ain't fair what you do.*" "Just a little crazy is all."

They had spent the morning in town, getting beer in case the snow stuck. Ray gave Bullet a tour of the local bars but was careful not to stay away too long. When they got back, they tinkered with the old truck's engine, patched a few sagging boards on the north side of the schoolhouse. They had bought an immense supply of groceries, more than Vivian and Ray consumed in a week, and spent hours concocting dinner, most of which was eaten by the men in a fraction of the time it had taken to prepare it.

Vivian left them to each other; it was Saturday, and she retired to one of the upstairs rooms to work on a series of paintings she was doing of the schoolhouse. Ray knew she was pleased to see him happy, fooling with his friend, but there was a limit, and he prayed he would know it when he reached it. She wasn't the sort of person to give him much warning.

"Doesn't he ever sleep?" she asks.

"Honey it ain't fair what you do."

"He can get by on pretty little."

"I'd say he's mildly deranged."

"He just misses Peg and the kids," Ray says, but even to him it sounds limp, beside the point. Like saying you wanted to move to Antarctica because you heard the skiing was good.

"We all miss our children," says Vivian.

■ ≡ ■

Next morning they are awakened by bells ringing.

"What on earth?" Vivian props herself up on one elbow. The house shakes.

"I feel like I've died and gone to heaven," says Ray, then he says, "Bullet. Routed old Ronnie."

He leaps out of bed, goes quickly to the window, peers out, as if he expects to see the jubilation of the bells rippling red-chartreuse-aqua through the crisp air, over the winter-cracked fields. He had spent hours on the bells when he first moved in. There were two of them, and whether through disuse or rust or neglect or age, they were silent. After a while, he'd forgotten they were there, that they'd ever rung.

"Kandinsky painted music," Vivian says, as if she's there with him.

"Kandinsky?" He looks over his shoulder at her. Her eyes are bright and dreamy, all at once.

"Come back here," she says.

He goes back. She reaches for him. They are wrapped in each other, in the clanging, which, like sirens or thunder, seems to eliminate all other sound. Their ears pound with the ringing, their bodies move to the beating of their hearts. The bells clang joyfully, as if proclaiming some grand event, and though Ray can't imagine what that event might be for Bullet, for him it is feeling good with Vivian, feeling wonderful with Vivian, and looking forward, for once, to the future, to the child. For Bullet, maybe just getting the bells cranked up again is enough.

When the ringing stops, it seems unnatural, overly quiet, and they lie there for a time but then are restless in the silence and talk about getting up. They hear the dogs scratch to come in at the back door. Ray wonders what they'd done—cowered under the porch, paws over their all-knowing ears? Had Ronnie the rooster died of shame? Had the goats taken off for points unknown? Or had they, too, been enchanted?

And then suddenly Bullet is there, bringing them coffee, sitting on the edge of the bed, talking talking talking. They congratulate him on the miracle.

"I felt like a priest," he says, winking. Then he says, "Listen. McCreary." Ray's heart sinks for an instant. "I was thinking we could check out the area for a vehicle, maybe a pickup or Jeep. Something that will get me where I want to go. Wherever the hell that is." He laughs and they marvel. "The West Coast. Tahiti." He winks again. "Maybe you could help me with the driving. Yet another cross-country trek. Do you good. You, too, of course," He nods to Vivian.

She pushes her hair off her forehead and looks at Ray. "You weren't planning on going out to California anytime soon, were you?" she asks.

"Hadn't planned on it," Ray says, and is surprised when he feels the smallest pang at denying himself the adventure. How swiftly our desires shift, he thinks.

"As a matter of fact," Vivian is saying, and Ray can tell she won't keep quiet much longer, "today we were going to visit your sister up in D.C." She says this to Bullet. "Lest you forget." This to Ray.

"I hadn't forgotten." Then he says to Bullet, "You can stay here, if you like. There's a lot of food, lots of wood."

Bullet picks up Vivian's mug and holds it out to her. "Didn't those bells sound sweet," he says.

No one speaks for a few minutes. Ronnie is crowing inanely and regularly, as usual, oblivious now to the bells and the angle of the sun. There is little sun; rather a gray sky again.

" 'The tintinnabulation of the bells bells bells,' " chants Bullet.

They listen to the goats clamber around on the front porch. Goats, thinks Ray: the smartest? certainly the most stubborn, the most directed of all the creatures on God's green earth, with the possible exception of women. He glances at Vivian, who says slowly, looking at him, "We should probably be leaving before too long. It takes a couple of hours, and I told Christine we'd be there around lunchtime." Her eyes say more. Ray waits for Bullet to leave so they can get up, get dressed, get started on the day, but Bullet sits a little longer, looks out the window.

"Beautiful place you got here," he says, "really nice." Then he says, quietly, as if still hearing the bells, "All of a sudden I'm thinking how maybe D.C. would be the place to find a vehicle. All those civil servants take such good care of their cars. . . ."

Ray waits for Vivian to kick him under the covers, or sigh in such a way that only he can hear, but she doesn't. She is watching Bullet, whose face—prehistoric is the way Ray had described it once—seems to be growing younger and smoother by the minute.

"That would be fine," she says. "We'd like the company."

Ray doesn't have time to be surprised; it's out of his hands. At the door, Bullet stops to say, "You know what else they got in D.C., don't you, besides politicians and crooks and statuary and all those smart women?" He sounds very far off, because this schoolhouse, this master bedroom, is so large.

"What's that?" Ray asks.

"They got the goddamn Nam Memorial is what they got." And suddenly Ray hears the bells again, deafening this time, ringing between his ears, in the thick of his skull, unrelenting, a flash of blinding color.

On the ride up, Vivian jokes with Bullet and listens to the men talk about things and people she does not know. Ray has promised that Bullet will not accompany them to Christine's tidy rancher. "We'll point him to some used-car lots," he tells her.

"This is Sunday."

"He'll never know the difference. He's not going to buy anything, anyhow. He's just checking it out."

He keeps a hand on her knee as he drives, and when Bullet insists on taking the wheel, Ray puts his arm around her, keeps her close against him, so that there is nothing between them but their coats, and almost enough room between Vivian and Bullet for one more person in that front seat, a very small person, perhaps a child.

Bullet drives the last leg of the trip, and before they realize it, he is taking them over Memorial Bridge and into the snarl of weekend traffic.

"Wrong way," says Ray, "I should have told you. Christine lives in Suitland, and the truck place is on the way. It's easy enough to get back," he says, meaning Virginia.

"I thought we'd make a little detour," Bullet says, "check out the Wall." And though she had promised his sister they'd be there for lunch, and Ray has not talked of going to the Wall, wanting to do it alone—if ever—neither says a word to stop him.

■ ≡ ■

They see it from a long way off, low and long and black. What little snow there is does nothing to diminish its sheen, cannot hide it. They see the people, not milling around like tired tourists, not browsing as if at a shopping mall or the National Gallery, not rubbernecking as if at the scene of an accident, or at a circus, but standing still, in pairs, or threes, or, most often, alone. Farther down the Mall, they see the Monument poking white and hopeful into the winter sky.

They drive slowly, and all three feel suddenly and unbearably hot. They tug at their collars, unbutton and unzip their coats, peel off gloves. Ray's grip on Vivian loosens; she feels him floating off, puts a hand on his knee, pats it. He looks at her hand, at her face, but distantly, seems not to make the connection.

They park illegally. A bus lumbers past, spewing black smoke. They work their way out of the cab of the truck, feet thudding clumsily on the iron ground. They don't bother locking the truck. They walk over.

"Some young kid designed it," Bullet says. "She's probably a goddamn pacifist."

The closer they get, the farther from sound and light and the world in general Ray feels, so that when they are almost there, it is as if they are standing in total emptiness—complete quiet— though there are horns and sirens and planes landing at National and an occasional person coughing. A shrill sort of hum runs through Ray's head and down around the avenues of his body, like an alarm system being activated that is supposed to alert him to everything but prepares him for nothing at all. Vivian seems to feel the hum where her arm touches his, and she looks at him, but he is looking at the Wall.

When they get close, she drops his arm and Bullet falls in beside him, and the men move out in front. They seem to have forgotten all about her. It is as if they are heading for the beach, or a bar, eyes on their destination, and nothing between it and them but a patch of sand or some narrow, dark doorway. It is the same unseeing way they are able to leave their wives, or lovers, without really meaning to, but never ever their children.

Ray hears, oddly, a seagull. He stops, loses Bullet, closes his eyes, hears waves crashing—impossible!—smells smoke, the dank greeny-black jungle. He looks around him at Washington— solid gray, immovable structures, wise Abe presiding. It is going to be all right. And when he runs his fingers over the names of his dead friends, he loves the pain he feels and he hates it. He cannot bear to look at Bullet, who stands farther down the Wall. He does not want to relive it all. And there is a terrible moment when, leaning against the Memorial, his eyes closed, Ray rests his fingers where the granite is smooth and clean, and imagines he feels, in that blank space, Bullet's name deeply inscribed, and below that, slightly less deep, his own.

■ ≡ ■

One night in late March, with the sharp smell of spring urging them on, Vivian and Ray sit at the kitchen table after dinner, planning the garden they will plant soon. In the middle of a heated discussion on how best to grow cucumbers, Vivian excuses herself, and when he hears the girls' room pipes clanking and whooshing insistently through the halls, Ray makes a mental note to go easy on the five-alarm chili next time. Vivian's famous steely stomach is not what it once was, though her iron will seems to be pumping along at its usual brisk pace. In five minutes she's back, looking a little pale. But I will stand firm on the cucumber debate, he is thinking.

And so he says, "Hills are the only way to go. We'll plant them on the south side so they won't take up so much room." He has always planted cukes in hills; she could do what she liked with the lettuce and spinach, but the cukes were his.

"I think," Vivian says, without sitting down—she is leaning on the back of her chair—"that I might be losing the baby."

Ray feels a sharp jab in his solar plexus, gives out a gasp as if she's thrown that punch. "What?"

"I said I think I might be losing—might have lost—the baby."

Geronimo, sensing danger, moves from under the table to a clearer spot near the door. Frenchie is already there, is always, wisely, near a door. The fire in the kitchen stove—they had just been saying they thought they had enough wood to last till warm weather—settles softly, charred logs giving way to untouched oak. Vivian looks past Ray to the noisy stove. "I've been feeling awful all week," she says.

"But that's par for the course, right?" He hadn't noticed

anything out of the ordinary this week, but then he'd been unusually busy starting up an addition the size of a small house for
yet another couple ten years younger than he and at least ten
times richer, and that always threw him off. She should have told
him she was feeling bad. He should have noticed.

"I just assumed it was the same old thing," Vivian says, sliding
into her chair. "But this is different. Something's going on."

Ray looks at her. He cannot believe his ears. Or the state of
his heart.

He breathes in. He breathes out. He says, "Let's call the
doctor."

She says, "I already have. He said to come in in the morning."

"Let's go now."

"He says to wait till morning. Unless something else happens,
he says we should just wait."

"Christ." Ray scrapes his chair back from the table. He needs
to pull himself together, assemble his thoughts, form sentences,
work them into shapely paragraphs, beautiful sense. He needs to
plant cukes in hills. He needs to make more money. She is waiting,
she is waiting. He needs to say the right thing. He goes to the
fridge for a beer.

"I've never had trouble like this before," Vivian says. She
watches him push past milk cartons and fruit juice to get to the
long-necked Buds. He closes the fridge door, opens the beer, sits
back down, gulps at the beer, grasps her hand in his.

"Tell me exactly what happened," he says.

She tells him what happened, that she felt her body dispelling
this *matter,* is how she put it—bloody tissue. Ray feels his stomach
turn slightly. "Not a whole lot," she says, "but it's not right."

He squeezes her hand so hard she winces, and he lets go.
"And what did the doctor say, again?"

He watches her rub her sore fingers. "He said it sounded
serious but that we wouldn't know what was going on till he
checked me." She is running her fingers through her hair now,
which looks darker for some reason and is growing out from the
mad Tucson cut. Ray can't help it; he definitely prefers it long.

"But I still feel pregnant," she says. "I still feel sick as a dog." And, amazing to Ray, a smile flickers on her mouth, but he sees, too, that her eyes are bright with tears, and he is thinking how surprisingly inarticulate she's being about all this, imprecise and short, as if she can't bring herself to say the words, mouth the strict medical terminology. "In fact," she says, clamping a hand to her mouth, her face now as pale as the moon, "I think . . . ," and she stumbles from her chair and down the stairs, and again the pipes clang their cooperation.

When she comes back, he pulls her onto his lap, and her eyes are again too bright, and she leans her head on his shoulder.

"You OK?" he asks, and he feels her nod. "I'll come with you tomorrow." He is making mental notes on how to keep the men going, how to make sure they get started early on the foundation. For once, maybe they'll get the thing dug right without his constant supervision. He could make it back there midday, meet with the owners and the architect, maybe knock off early, get back to the schoolhouse early afternoon.

A log bangs against the inside of the stove. One of the dogs moves from the door to the far side of the kitchen. Ray stares out the window past Vivian's head, sees a doe mincing daintily across the end of the field and takes this to be a good sign. Still, he wishes this woman curled against him would say more, maybe burst into tears, do something to force him to react.

"You don't have to come," she says. "I'll be fine."

"I want to come," he says, though there was a time when Ray would have relished being ordered to stay away, go about his business—no need to bother stopping what you're doing to do this thing for me, et cetera, et cetera. He insists. She resists only a little.

By the next morning, they are both ready for the facts. A restless but uneventful night has left them both drawn and tired and unremittingly anxious.

Trailing Vivian into town, Ray wishes he were in the cab of her Datsun, riding shotgun, passing coffee back and forth, or maybe a beer, listening to her scratchy AM radio, or simply watching the familiar landscape slip by, anticipating the bright possibilities of the day. He studies the familiar set of her head and shoulders from his vantage point several car lengths behind— they are traveling too fast—and feels infinitely remote, separated for those twenty miles or so into town by far more than yards of highway and worn molded steel.

■ ≡ ■

At the doctor's office, he waits for her in the parking lot. He strolls to a nearby drugstore, buys a *Daily Progress,* reads it cover to cover, which doesn't take long. Gets out of the truck again to stretch his legs. Morning traffic drifts by, pale-faced commuters headed for auto-drip coffee and tiresome bosses. Or wonderful bosses. He, Ray, has a hard time bearing bosses. Probably a short-coming on his part, he has begun to realize in his old age, but a fact, plain and simple. Likewise, he has a hard time being a good company man, no matter how small the company, or how brief the stint. Not that he doesn't work hard; he has put up siding in Januarys so severe that the owners have begged him to stop for fear they'll have a corpse on their hands by day's end. He has crimped seams on tin roofs in summers so hot he suffered third-degree burns on all parts of his body not adequately shielded from the maniacal eye of the sun. Blistered fingers and knees where he touched tin too long. Disgruntled men on the crew refusing to go up there with him, saying he could fry himself if he wanted to, but they sure as shit had stuff to live for.

And they were right, Vivian said when he mentioned it once to her. It doesn't make sense to push yourself that way.

Had to get the job done, said Ray, but these days he isn't driven to push his body to the limit so much as he wants to produce finished, substantial, time-resistant living structures. The satisfaction of the end is supplanting an earlier borderline manic interest in the means.

And certainly, these days, he has stuff to live for.

Someone in a vaguely familiar green Nova drives by, honks a merry greeting.

Belatedly, Ray waves. Automatically.

He feels removed from all normal activity, encapsulated by the urgency of the situation and his love for Vivian, and though this concern is unsettling, he finds it not unpleasant. He has not taken the time, or maybe has not allowed himself to take the time, to imagine what would happen if they lost the baby. He is, in his own odd way, a creature of routine: when the routine required his being a boat bum and reprobate, he did that. When the routine required his being a lover of women, he did that without too much trouble. He'd been loyal to crazy friends, a mediocre musician. Lately the routine has been to imagine the role and responsibility of father—husband!—and he has been, in his own sedate fashion, assimilating all that, taking it on. And he finds, to his surprise as he waits for Vivian this crisp morning, that he is unwilling to let fatherhood go just yet.

■ ≡ ■

An hour passes before Vivian emerges. Ray is dozing in the truck, warmed by a patch of sun pouring through the driver's window. He doesn't see her till she opens the door and he feels the shot of cold air she lets in on her side. She tells him the doctor thinks everything's all right—threatened miscarriage, he called it—and they'll know for sure when the lab results are in. In the meantime, she should take it easy. In the meantime, they should make very sure they—she and Ray—know what they're doing. And before he can push her to clarify just what exactly it is she means by that, she goes back to the office to use the phone; she calls the school, tells them she won't be coming in that day. When she finally comes back out, they leave the Datsun in the lot and drive to The Virginian to get some coffee, herbal tea for her.

"Let's just get it to go," Vivian says when they pull into the Loading Only space in front of the restaurant.

Ray gets one of the waitresses he once had a crush on to put a slug of whiskey into his coffee, and he and Vivian sit in Loading Only, warming themselves with their hot drinks. Ray stretches his legs out past the gearshift, touches her boots with his. "Cheers," he says, tapping her Styrofoam cup.

She smiles, but her eyes are overly bright again. "This could mean," she says, sipping at her tea, "that there's something wrong with the baby. Could be Mother Nature in her infinite wisdom setting us straight."

"Let's just wait for the lab results, why don't we?" Ray says. No need to leap to preposterous conclusions, to burden ourselves with what might be, he's thinking. Time enough to suffer over the real thing, if and when it comes to that. Holding off saved enormously in the heartache department; he, for one, could attest to that.

"If it turns out I am still pregnant," Vivian says, and now she's looking past him in that maddening way of hers, is staring at the passing traffic as if it's alive and speaking, just inches from where she'd be looking if she were looking at him, "then we should probably think about whether or not to go through with all this."

"With all what?"

"With having the baby. I'm not young"—and here she stops him, puts a finger to his lips because she knows he is, in his confusion, about to protest—"when it comes to having babies. And all I'm saying is we have a choice." She pauses. "I have had babies, and I have not had babies, and there's a twenty percent chance I'll miscarry eventually anyhow, and in a way it's as if we've been given a chance to bow out gracefully. After all," she says, making a sweeping gesture with her arm, an arc floating from her still-flat belly to the close air on his side of the cab, "we didn't really plan any of this, did we?"

She almost knocks his coffee out of his hand. If she would just stop talking, he's thinking. If he could just get a word in.

She says, "I have two great kids—soon to arrive: did I tell you I talked to Claude yesterday?—and I don't recall ever hearing you say you were aching to be a father. For that matter, we hadn't really figured out what was going on with the two of us, had we? The last thing I want is for you to feel you have to make an honest woman of me."

She lets out a small snort of disdain and sips her tea, giving him, for the time being, full benefit of her classic profile. Ray sets his coffee cup on the dash beyond the steering wheel. He sets it there gently while he gropes for words; if he chooses words unwisely, the air between them might, in a fit of inexplicable spontaneous combustion, spark and explode and ruin them for life.

He opens his mouth to speak, but she is quicker. She says, looking straight ahead, "And I don't know if I could handle it on my own. I mean, I know I could, but I don't know if I want to. There's no real reward in going it alone, you know? I've done that; I'm strong as a fucking *ox*." She practically yells out "*ox*," and now, truly, tears are rolling down her cheeks. "I know what I am, I know what I want. . . . " She stops a minute, sighs. "I just want to relax and live a little. I've had enough of life's lessons." She attempts a weak smile, brushes the tears off. Out in the street, brakes screech. Someone curses. A panel truck rattles its way up the hill. Ray puts his hand over to her chin, turns her face to his, makes her look at him.

"Don't cut me out, Vivian," he says. "I am not the enemy."

She tries to turn away from him; tea spatters onto her jeans leg.

"Maybe I'm losing the faith," she says, rubbing at the spots, and he thinks he sees just the tiniest flicker of fear in her face, but it's gone so fast he thinks he was probably wrong. "I don't mean to sound so cynical. I'm just tired." And she closes her eyes, leaves her face squared to his, but closes her eyes.

"Look," Ray says. "Vivian. Look at me." Her eyes flicker open. "I love you dearly. I love you deeply. You are my soul mate. I want to do this. I want to do this with you. I am ready." He takes her hand, places it over his heart, right on top of his camouflage down-filled vest. He places his hand over hers. "Here," he says. "Feel that. My heart beats only for you." He feels the silliness coming on, can't stop it. He is bursting with love. And resolve. He removes her hand from his heart, holds it out in midair between them. An old lady passing by on the sidewalk smiles at them. She is remembering how her sweetheart held her hand some fifty years earlier in the stern of a boat while punting on the lake. But the sweetheart is dead and gone—she does not need to tell Ray that; he knows—died in one of the world wars, or, mutely, in a very clean nursing home, and he, Ray, is here and alive, and this woman, this beautiful woman next to him, is also here and most certainly alive, loving him but not quite trusting him. He lifts her capable brown hand to his mouth, brushes it lightly with his lips, says, "Let's just fucking *do* it, Vivian," and he kisses her hand again. "I adore you," he says, and this time, when she smiles and says, Good, I'm glad, he knows he's got her.

■ ≡ ■

The lab tests are positive. They celebrate being back on track with a bottle of champagne, Vivian worrying a little over possible harm to the fetus, Ray convincing her a sip or two won't hurt. He ends up polishing off most of the bottle himself, but it really does feel like just cause for celebration. It feels as though they are united for once in every sense of the word. This feels good! he thinks.

They plant the garden, Vivian leaving most of it to Ray while she tackles painting the rooms for the children. Not only do they have to prepare some sort of corner for the baby, but they need to get rooms together for Vivian's children, Delia and Claude junior (real name Ramsey Claude, but Ramsey never stuck). Ray helps with the painting when he can, but it is clear she likes working on it herself, so he leaves her to it. She is getting bigger now, is unable to zip up her jeans without a five-minute struggle—the real test, she tells him.

"Once the jeans go, it's all over," she tells him. She ties the jeans shut with twine and wears his flannel shirts, soft and loose. The shirts hit her midthigh and make her look young, Ray thinks, teenybopperish. It is all very quaint and nice, most of the time, this blithe dive into domesticity. But there are times when Ray wonders just how well he knows his beloved.

Vivian has left the ceilings in the children's rooms for Ray, and he is balanced near the top of a teetering stepladder, working on Claude junior's ceiling one evening, when she tells him to be sure to leave a patch of the old paint untouched. "You can leave it someplace where it doesn't show too much," she says. "Maybe around the overhead light." She is standing in the middle of the room, squinting up at him. His arm aches from spending the past hour defying gravity, spreading the paint above him at this unnatural angle.

"You look like Michelangelo," she says, moving so deftly from the old-paint-patch business to high art that he wonders if he heard her right the first time.

"You want me to leave some of the old paint showing," he repeats.

She looks up at him, hands on hips. From his perspective she looks shorter than usual, stumpy and round. But downright cherubic. She wouldn't like that. She nods in answer to his question. "A painter friend told me to always leave space for the spirit of the old room to slip out, return to the air, so to speak. Makes sense to me," she says, and moves from this room to the one next door—Delia's—where he hears her humming away as she cleans up empty paint cans, stiffening brushes.

"Sounds Indian to me," he says. "This friend of yours Indian?" He has paused in his ceiling work; he is giving his arm the break it deserves.

"Irish," she yells back.

"Same thing," says Ray, but he leaves a halo of old white around the light, a magic circle surrounded by pale moss green stretching across the rest of the ceiling like a meadow.

And does the same thing in Delia's room, this time leaving

room for restless spirits to escape through a band of old yellow around the light switch by the door. It is while he is putting in shelves a few weeks before the children are due to arrive that Vivian mentions, with a casualness Ray finds mildly alarming, that Claude had tied off Delia's umbilical cord with a chalk line.

"We were renovating the kitchen, as I recall," she says, "and there was a foot or so of snow on the ground, and it was all pretty much a mess." She doesn't sound angry about it, Ray is thinking as he fools with the level; just bemused. And entertained by her youthful follies. He knows it wasn't all a lark; he knows, for example, that she was the one who left.

"You had the baby at home?"

"By mistake. She was early. We had expected to have the kitchen finished. No snow. Beethoven in the delivery room. You know."

"Sounds a little dicey," says Ray. They are standing back, admiring his work. She is looking at the shelves critically, head tilted to the side, but she is thinking of that day years before, he can tell. And he sure as hell did *not* know. There was plenty he did not know, he was beginning, more and more, to realize.

"It turned out fine, but I wouldn't recommend it."

"But a *chalk line,*" says Ray.

"Beautiful colors," says Vivian. "Chalky blue, her purple pulse."

"Ugh," says Ray, but Vivian is lost to him for the moment, out there with the torn-up kitchen and chalk line and quick-thinking husband.

"Claude was good in a crisis," she says. "A man of action."

Maybe so, but he couldn't hang on to you. Wasn't strong enough for that, was he? Not too quick on the draw in that department.

She looks at Ray, but he knows she's seeing Claude. "There are times you remind me of him," she says, and Ray almost chokes. "In that neither of you gets overly concerned about things. Or at least don't seem to. You just get the job done. I liked that about Claude."

"Survival tactics," says Ray. "No ulcers for Claude and me."

He keeps fooling with the level, placing it this way and that on the shelves, studying the fickle bubble, but what she has just said is one of the most ominous-sounding and altogether alarming things he has ever heard. He would like to say something profound to her, separate himself forever from Claude, but before he can think what that statement might be, she is talking again, she is back to being dreamy. Paint fumes, maybe. Unhealthy. Addled the brain. He should get her out into the fresh air, could do with a good deep whiff himself, clear his head, distinguish himself by word or act from all other men.

"Delia will like this room," she is saying. Then she says, "After the children were born, I got back into painting. I gave it all up when I met Claude—it seemed, at the time, completely irrelevant, and in some ways, I still believe that. I mean, painting is wonderful, and soulful, but it's no substitute for flesh and blood."

"Doesn't have to be, does it?" asks Ray.

"That's what I've come to learn," she says. "Anyhow, I started sketching the babies all the time, couldn't resist, and eventually I got back to painting." She runs her hand over the shelves. "These are perfect," she says. "Thank you. Lots of room for books." There are paint flecks in her hair that Ray now tries to brush out with slow-moving fingers. Lord, this body of his aches these days. The damp days of spring. She puts her hand to his, stops his clumsy movements. "I could never understand," she says, "how people said their lives ground to a halt when they had kids." She smooths his hand with hers. "Mine brought me to life. Claude never stood a chance. It was no one's fault," and with that, Ray's heart stops. He almost dies from hearing too much. He takes a step back. As if she suddenly knows what he's thinking, as if she's just noticed who he is—or that he exists at all—Vivian says, "But things are different now. Or rather I'm different." And she pulls him to her and kisses him long and very tenderly. And through sheer willpower and minutes later carnal desire (much easier to scare up), he pushes from his head the nagging notion that perhaps this was the way she'd kissed Claude, too, before things went wrong.

■ ≡ ■

In late May the lettuce and spinach are up, and in June the children come and the schoolhouse is filled with clamor and confusion. "Just as it should be," Ray says when Vivian rolls her eyes and remarks on how peaceful things used to be. Though shy at first, Delia, eleven, soon warms up to Ray, to the point where she chides him relentlessly: about his taste in music (gross), his taste in cars, specifically the battered pickup (trade it in), his worn, patched jeans (truly tacky). "Patched by me," he says, showing her his knees.

"I can tell," says Delia.

She says "chill out" to her brother whenever he bugs her, and she reminds Ray uncomfortably of more than one accusing girl-friend. "She's going to be a heartbreaker," he says to Vivian, who groans and implores God or whoever is up there to help her. But he can see that she is very very happy having them there, and he, implicated as he is in the whole affair, is equally happy for her.

He plays a lot of catch with Claude junior, especially after an assault—verbal type—from Delia. He remembers, from when he was a boy, how good the whonk of a ball felt in his glove, the satisfaction of catching a high fly. Sometimes Delia joins them, and to Ray's surprise, she catches most passes. "Good arm," he yells when she throws, at which point she crooks her elbow, bulges a bicep, says, "Feel this!" Playing catch, she invariably grows bored long before Ray and Claude junior do, announces her decision to stop, and moves on to something else. She spends a lot of time reading. But Ray and Claude junior enjoy throwing the ball for what seems like hours; they are in hog heaven is how Ray puts it to Vivian. And he can see that pleases her.

He sets up a small workbench for Claude junior in the shop,

provides him with his own set of tools; the boy spends hours pounding away, nailing wood scraps together, tongue poked out in firm concentration. He makes boxes, bird feeders, weapons of all sorts. Now when Delia tells him to chill out, he simply shoots her dead with his wooden gun.

Ray is careful not to advise Vivian on how to raise the children. She objects halfheartedly to the gun, but when she overhears Ray telling Claude junior that if some kid hauls off and hits him, he should hit back, she lectures him for what seems like hours after the children are in bed about how she has never—and she is not about to start now—raised her kids to be combative. She cannot condone violence as a way of getting through life.

"Protecting yourself isn't perpetrating violence," Ray says, surprised at her vehemence and a little annoyed. "It's a question of survival."

"I will not allow it," she says, and, since they're in bed, closes the conversation by turning her back to him and feigning deep sleep. He doesn't pursue it—after all, they aren't his kids—but the longer they stay, the more he realizes how hard it will be to keep from becoming entangled in their complicated little lives, and that gives him pause. Gives him plenty of time to contemplate the future and to be frightened thoroughly.

Because the kids seem to like him; they talk to him, ask him things, listen to his answers. They think he's funny; they laugh a lot. Once Delia slipped and called him Dad. It was enough to embarrass them both for days. And one night, he and Claude junior—without telling Vivian—climb up onto the old tin roof of the schoolhouse and try to spot shooting stars. While they are waiting, Ray points out the showy constellations and then a few of his personal favorites—the Pleiades, Cassiopeia; last time he saw those was out in the middle of the Atlantic, he says. They sit quietly, in wonder, Claude junior resting his hand on Ray's arm. At first Ray thinks he wants something, wants to show Ray a new star, maybe tell him a secret. So he turns to the boy, but Claude junior is looking up at the sky, waiting for shooting stars, and the only reason he is resting his hand on Ray's arm is that

Ray is there for the resting, as solid and comfortable and dependable as an old chair. And the boy trusts he'll always be there, that he can rest his hand lightly on the large arm of this large man anytime at all—whenever he is tired, or has something to say, or is simply sitting on a tin roof waiting for a star to flash through the sky.

Later that night, Ray tries to explain to Vivian how, now that he's said yes to her, it is as if the floodgates are wide open, the sluices are working just fine, thank you, and everything is flowing right along, but it's moving fast, maybe too fast, it is almost overwhelming at times, and he just needs to get away, slip off one last time like a spirit slipping through that bright strip of paint. Go see a few old farts of friends, touch base with them one last time.

She seems not to understand.

"Did it ever occur to you," he says, "that I might find all of this a little scary?"

"All what?"

"You. The children. Everything."

"Are we really so awful?" she says, and she is laughing, but he can see he's hurt her. "We are not the enemy, you know." Now she's talking to the dogs about him in that way she has. "Best tactic," she whispers into Frenchie's ear, "is to befriend the enemy. You find out they're just like you." She hugs Frenchie, looks up from the dog's fluffy neck to say, "Watch out, Ray. You just might end up happy." He doesn't admit to her that she just might be right, and he doesn't tell her how moved he was, on the roof, at having so small a person so close.

II

BUFFALO

Ray is sitting at Papa Stumpy's, waiting for Charlene to make his barbecue. He knows it is Papa Stumpy's because the neon sign outside says so; he knows it is Charlene because of her black-and-white name tag. It is mid-July and very hot. Charlene's smooth round face shines with heat, and he loves her for it. He also loves her for the barbecue, whose reputation extends far beyond the boundaries of this small town halfway between Charlottesville and Washington.

Ray is on his way north to visit every friend he ever had—they all seemed to live in New England, the old ones. And though he is making the trip with Vivian's blessing, more or less, he feels the need for a good and decent launching. The barbecue should do the trick. Vivian's children have taken over the schoolhouse, which is fine with Ray, though mildly alarming at first. They could use some time together, he reasoned. He also felt, as he had tried to explain to Vivian, like taking a final whack at tying up loose ends before settling in.

"That could take a lifetime," Vivian had said. "Try to figure it out before you get back." One thing Ray loved about Vivian: her ability to state things so clearly.

What Ray takes to be Charlene's baby is careening around the linoleum behind the counter in a yellow plastic walker. He is soft and plump as his mother, his eyes the same bright green. Though most of the Stumpy family, Ray soon learns, is still in Jersey, Charlene and Papa and grandson Joey are here, and so is cousin Rosie, who is leaning on the end of the counter near the cash register.

"So what's happening?" Charlene says to Rosie.

"What? You need to ask? I've been working my little heinie off for two days straight, that's what's happening. Jeez. Gimme a Coke, will ya?"

Charlene gets the Coke. Rosie turns to Ray. "Pardon my French," she says, and he nods forgiveness.

Charlene checks the barbecue. Joey bangs gently against her leg with the walker. "Careful, son," she says. "It's the only set of legs I got."

And what a set they are, Ray thinks.

He is a sucker for waitresses. Like most men, Vivian said; disgusting. And embarrassing. Waitresses don't want to be bothered with fielding your questions and comments and looks. It's one thing to be pleasant, but Lord.

Ray, who had always felt otherwise, wisely demurred to this voice of experience. She was probably right; most men couldn't resist flirting with waitresses.

They—she had added—*we* are not there to serve you in all ways. We're there to take your order and bring the food hot. Or cold, as the case may be.

But the tip matters, Ray said.

Of course, she'd said; it's a job.

Secretly Ray thought she probably was not speaking for all waitresses, but he kept quiet.

"Almost ready," Charlene says, giving the barbecue a stir. She puts grounds into the coffeemaker, pours water through the top. She straightens silver, sponges off the counter next to the grill. From the kitchen, someone busts into a lusty "O Sole Mio!" Ray feels almost deliriously happy: things are wonderful here, they're wonderful with Vivian, he's on the road.

Charlene spoons barbecue onto a bun and puts it in front of Ray. She puts a small bowl of coleslaw next to it. "Sorry to keep you waiting," she says. "The coffee will be ready in a minute."

"No hurry."

It was a good time to be taking a break. Not only with Vivian, but workwise. His work was at a standstill, with a new project to begin in September. All sorts of new projects starting up in the fall... Lordy, he was going to be a father. Vivian was six months pregnant but didn't look it. I feel it, though, sometimes, she said. She had sublet her apartment for the summer. When Ray tried to persuade her to give it up altogether, she had lost her temper, unusual for her, and said how could she do that when things with him were still uncertain.

Still uncertain! Was it marriage she was thinking of? He was willing.

"We'll see at the end of summer," she'd said.

He was shocked at how easily she seemed able to envision a future without him, though admittedly sometimes the idea of being a father, let alone a husband, made him weak in the knees. He wonders if his own father had felt such twinges. He wonders what his father had felt about most things.

He had said to her, "You didn't expect to be on your own forever, did you?"

She'd said, "I was fully prepared. I was fine."

"And now?"

"Still fine," but when she saw his face, she said, "No, better, much much better," and had kissed him. Then she told him that these days, she wanted everything she loved close at hand. Including you, she said, poking a finger at his chest, though she said she understood about the trip. It was then Ray realized he felt exactly opposite: didn't want to lose what he loved, but didn't feel he had to touch it or hold it tight up against him, either, to keep it real.

"Your coffee," says Charlene. "At long last." She smiles at him. Her charm bracelet dances on the flecked countertop. Her sweet perfume makes his head swim.

"Thanks," he says.

He thinks he is in love with Charlene, with all women. Maybe he will stay here with her—maybe she is the woman of his dreams, the woman with the flamingo blouse. They could spend the rest of their lives making pasta; he would toss it onto her smooth white flesh to test it. Pasta al dente: if it sticks, it's done. He is amazed at how easily he slips into the old on-the-road mentality that allows him to imagine a different life for himself—endless possibilities!—wherever he stops. Pick a life, any life. He knows it is ridiculous, total fantasy, to forget everything except what is right there in front of him. But it is irresistible. Back home he is always working, always doing something, always on. Historically, he has been unable to separate himself from what is under his nose (he is thinking this to himself, addressing himself silently as if he is someone else), has been unable to make the break, without artificial stimulation of some kind or another. Psychedelics, drugs of all sorts, alcohol, did the trick, at least momentarily, for many years; when they didn't work, physical distance was what was called for. Gradually he had eased out of all the bad habits, alcohol lingering relatively benignly (though the number of his alcoholic friends astounded him). But this business of hitting the road was the last thing to go and one he was loath to give up.

No need to go cold turkey, Vivian had said; moderation will do.

For some folks, says Ray.

Moderation will not do, has never done, for Charlene, he is thinking. She is at the other end of the counter, talking to Rosie. He watches them in the mirror on the back wall, Charlene's image broad and comfortable.

"Mario the martyr," Rosie intones.

"So what's the story with the new wife?" Charlene wipes off

the counter. "She young or what? Mario told me she was thirty-nine."

"Yeah, she's thirty-nine and I'm twelve." It is Papa Stumpy yelling suddenly from the back. Everyone laughs. They look over at Ray when they hear him; their smiles include him. He thinks he might ask Papa S. for a job, for the hand of his daughter, guardianship of the love child Joey.

"He told me she was thirty-nine—why shouldn't I believe him?" Charlene says when everyone has calmed down.

"Thirty-nine going on fifty," says Rosie. "She's no spring chicken."

"So neither is Mario," says Charlene. "He's at least sixty," she tells Ray. "And this is not his first time at the altar."

"Huh," says Ray.

"Mario has some major hang-ups," she says.

"The understatement of the year," says Rosie.

Ray watches Charlene break down a huge bag of chips into sandwich-bag portions. The barbecue is delicious, just as he knew it would be. He tells Charlene that, and she smiles her thanks.

She is large, way past plump, but her excess weight doesn't shift around noncommittally the way it does on some people. It seems absolutely necessary to her health; she is confident, lovely in her largeness. She has a beautiful oval face, a cameo face, Ray thinks; she occasionally resembles the portraits of the young Queen Victoria, but with a little more pizzazz, he decides; Queen Victoria could have used a shot of Italian blood. Her thick dark hair is arranged in a complicated network of knots, braids, twists, barrettes and clips and ribbons holding it all in place. Her head is a work of art, her body the apparatus holding it all up, displaying it. The functional column—Doric? Corinthian? The terms are vaguely familiar; Vivian would know. She would approve. She probably would want to paint Charlene, accentuate the perfect heart-shaped lips that chew at this moment, with vigor, green gum.

"Did I tell you Mario and his new wife had their first fight last week?" Rosie straightens up, walks toward the front door. "Over what?"

"This photo album of his. She gives him holy hell for some pictures she found of him and his old girlfriends slash wives. Cut her finger trying to rip the pages out."

"That's ridiculous," says Charlene. "I mean, a man's gotta live, right?"

I am in *love* with you, Ray thinks. Yes! a man's gotta live.

"I mean, the man is nothing short of sixty. What does she think, he hung out in a monastery all these years? That's the most ridiculous thing." She shakes her head, steps sideways to avoid being creamed by Joey. "Where's *her* photo album is what I want to know."

"Maybe she burned hers," says Rosie. "Shred the evidence." She pushes her back against the swinging door, lets it close again behind her. She stays in the diner. She opens the door over and over, her feet moving backward and forward to what Ray recognizes from the old days—from the very old days of his youth— as a slightly irregular box-step waltz. He and Vivian had unearthed some Ethel Merman 45s that belonged to her parents and had attempted the waltz—and fox-trot—several times on the stage at the schoolhouse. Ray had been clumsy but enthusiastic; Vivian had been, predictably, knowledgeable and unerringly graceful.

"I'd better be going," she says, not breaking time. "Charlene." It sounds like an order. Charlene stops clearing, stands at attention, gives her cousin a mock salute. "I'm thinking of going back to Jersey for a while. Jocko found me a job up there making seven-fifty an hour."

Charlene drops her hand. "Doing what?" She begins wrapping pickles in pieces of waxed paper.

"Putting little screws into light bulbs or something."

"Yeah? You'd go nutso in about two hours," says Charlene. Ray loves her for saying "nutso."

"At seven-fifty an hour, who cares? Besides, it would only be for a year, and I wouldn't have to pay rent."

"Why not?"

"I'd be living with Terry and them."

"So?"

You live someplace, you pay rent, thinks Ray.

"So Terry's father owns the entire building."

"Oh. You really think you'll do it?"

"I might. I'd come back loaded."

"Well, I hope you'll still speak to us peasants when you do." Charlene refills Ray's coffee cup; he was on his last swallow. He thinks she gives him a wink. "By the way," Charlene says as she pours, "whatever happened to Terry's brother Vito? Haven't seen him around lately. He split or something?"

"Vito is hiding out in New York. Vito owes Mario twelve hundred dollars. Vito owes Georgie five hundred dollars. Vito owes Jackie seven hundred and fifty dollars. Vito's on the lam, and guess what, nobody can find him. Vito is afraid to go back to Italy because they know where he lives there."

"So they're going to catch a plane clear over to Italy to collect a few hundred dollars?" She says to Ray, "Vito's not a criminal, he's just dumb."

"Ah," says Ray.

Rosie shrugs and keeps dancing with the door. "All I know is he's hiding out in New York and that's why you haven't seen him lately. I got to get going. Mario will work himself into a screaming fit if I don't get over there."

"He should have taken a longer honeymoon," Charlene says.

Simple, thinks Ray.

"Shouldn't everybody." Rosie holds the door open. "Look, I gotta go. Call me." She doesn't move. "What time you getting off today?"

"Six, but I'm going straight out." Charlene smiles as she wraps knives and forks in paper napkins. Joey the babe is quiet; he plays with a string of beads too large to choke on, Charlene assures Ray.

"Johnny?" says Rosie.

"Yeah."

Ray is crushed, momentarily peeved. It is as if Charlene has misled him, hoodwinked him into believing he was her only suitor. How could anyone else appreciate her as he did? If Johnny were to walk in just then, Ray would challenge him to a duel—*en garde!* Defend yourself and the honor of this lady!

Don't make me choose, Charlene would wail.

En garde! "He's a very lucky man," says Ray.

"Yeah, he's a lucky man," Rosie says to Ray, "but all of us cousins gotta suffer for it. I never see her anymore, and I have never even met this wonderful boyfriend that I know every single detail of his life and that she's been going with for two months now."

"Six weeks," says Charlene. "Six weeks and three days, to be exact."

"Six weeks," says Rosie. "Disowned by my own cousin."

"You'll meet him. We're still getting acquainted."

"She doesn't call, she doesn't even introduce me to her boyfriend." Rosie lets the door go. "Call me," she says as it closes.

"OK," Charlene says. "Ciao." They watch Rosie get into her Duster and drive off. "She's a talker," says Charlene.

Ray smiles and pays his tab. He walks out to the truck and leans against the back. Only been on the road a few hours and suddenly he aches for Vivian. Through the plate-glass window of the diner he sees Charlene cleaning up after him, Papa Stumpy's neon name flowing across her aqua uniform. It is so hot next to the highway he feels as if he might explode if he stands there much longer, but the barbecue was wonderful, and so was Charlene. He pokes his head back in the door. She looks up, eyebrows raised.

"Everything OK?" she asks.

"That barbecue was just wonderful," Ray says. Joey, sitting on his mother's ample hip, stares unblinking at this man. "Best I've ever eaten. And I have eaten some barbecue in my life."

"Thanks." The baby squirms; she moves him to the other hip.

"You could make millions, patent the recipe."

"Trade secret," says Charlene, "family secret." She smiles.

"Well, thanks," Ray says, instantly humble.

"You're welcome. Come back again."

"Ciao," says Ray. The glass door swings shut. He climbs into the cab of the pickup and starts the engine. In the rearview he can see Charlene watching him, her hand holding the smaller, plumper one of the baby as they wave goodbye. Next phone booth he sees, he stops and calls Vivian, who is surprised but pleased to hear from him so soon, and who tells him his sister Christine called just after he left because Darryl had run off again.

■ ≡ ■

Ray had planned to bypass Washington, with only an obligatory phone call—if that—to his sister. Now, out on the highway, skirting D.C., road signs flashing past like flags, Ray is thinking what discouraging names Maryland had given her suburbs: Beltsville, Waldorf, College Park, Greenbelt, La Plata, Suitland. Hard, punishing names, offering little hope. Virginia seemed to do better: Charlottesville—the name sounded fine, lyrical almost. He would stop in Suitland, but then on to New England: Connecticut! Vermont! Maine! where the names were sound and the people true.

He lights another cigarette—he is back to Camels—and, coughing a little, reminds himself it is time to start thinking about quitting again. Hot streams of air pushing through the truck's vents smell like dryer exhaust, though he knows once he is clear of these hot-rod Porsches and lumbering semis, the air will turn sweeter, the odor of tulip poplars, for instance, cutting through the heavy heat. Anyone with any sense, Ray tells himself as he mops his brow, was immersed at this moment in an ice-cold river or pond, lowering his body temperature by about a hundred degrees. Or he (or she) was entwined with a lover somewhere— and here he thinks of Vivian—giving himself over entirely to the heat. Passion, Ray had always figured, was worth any amount of discomfort, physical or otherwise. He fiddles with the radio, looking for some Dwight Yoakam, and then takes signs to Suitland.

Christine fills him in. No one had realized at breakfast two days earlier what was afoot. Christine and her husband, Jerry, had not thought Darryl meant it literally when he talked about wanting to get back to nature. He told them, between mouthfuls of French toast, that he wanted nothing more than to live with the earth, talk to her—the trees and the sky—eat hickory nuts, sleep in a grove of pines. Because, in his parents' view, Darryl was always lost in a haze of extravagant thought, often saying things they did not understand (or particularly like), and because he was always dabbling in poetry and painting, Christine and Jerry paid no particular attention that morning to his rambling cant. Nothing had seemed awry, though in retrospect Christine said she should have known their son was fueling up for the long haul—five helpings of French toast, and she and Jerry had simply thought the boy was hungry.

What they did say: we all want to live in harmony with nature, we weren't born yesterday, we were young once too. But we have to put food on the table, pay the rent, earn money to fuel the VCR, our motor home, pay for your college education. And incidentally, you'd better hurry up and get to your job at the garage, or they'll fire you. They had spoken kindly but firmly; this was not the first time. Of course it would be groovy to live off the land, they had murmured, but that's pretty much impossible here in Suitland, and you might consider how long you'd last without food and shelter and the other little amenities that make life just a tad more bearable. It might also get a little lonely out there.

I like to be alone, Christine says Darryl said, and I travel light.

Might have a hard time finding shot engines out there in the pines to tinker with, Jerry had said.

Darryl was a fine mechanic, a magician with carburetors and worn brake shoes. His parents encouraged him in this enterprise, having long since given up on law school or medicine or—Jerry's work—real estate. Poetry and painting were OK, though of course they had no idea what he meant by it all and were not convinced that he did either. All they really wanted, when it came right down to it, was for Darryl to make it through the difficult teenage years alive and in one piece.

When Christine found marijuana floating around the bowl of the upstairs toilet midmorning, along with various pills and powders and capsules she couldn't begin to identify—floating belly-up like so many dead goldfish—she panicked and called the schoolhouse, but no one was home. Then she called the police, but they said to give it twenty-four hours. That time was up last night, and she'd called Ray again but had gotten Vivian. Jerry had left on a business trip after the French toast breakfast and was headed home now, but it would be a while. What could they do?

"First thing off, we have to be calm," Ray says. "Second thing, he'll be back." But he doesn't believe it, remembering the many times he'd run off himself as a youngster, only to be found eventually. He never had returned voluntarily. "Sometimes, as adults, we run off," he adds, surprised at himself. "Marred and scarred."

"Is that what you're doing now?" Christine, his sister, asks. They had never been particularly close, had not seen much of each other over the years. It was only lately, in the past few years, they'd been able to accept each other's frailties. Darryl and Ray had always hit it off. Darryl was enchanted with this uncle who was in his forties—over the hill—but who was, despite this handicap, handsome and strong and savvy. In Darryl's eyes, Ray was as close as they came to human perfection: no flab, no mortgage, no children, no hassles. And Ray would add mentally, because he recognized the adoration: yeah, and no job, no (real) woman, no dough. Sometimes he hinted at his sorry imperfections, but Darryl would have none of it. Just look at all the women! Actually, Ray tried to explain once, there hadn't been that many, but because he'd never gotten around to marrying anyone, just one of his girlfriends seemed to carry the luster and sensuality and significance of at least ten of anyone else's. Plus all his affairs had ended amiably, which endeared him further to his nephew. Except for a svelte, smart TWA stewardess—they weren't called flight attendants then, Ray said—whom Ray had loved deeply but simply hadn't felt up to. Now, of course, there was Vivian, and he was happy to report to Christine that there was no end in sight with that one.

Most of all, Darryl could talk to Ray.

They find him that evening in the state park that abuts the Suitland subdivision where Christine and Jerry live. No one dreamed he might have stayed so close, or that after all this time, he would surrender peacefully. Ray is the one who spots him first; it is around dinnertime, and everyone is hot and tired, and suddenly, with no fanfare or warning, Darryl waves at Ray and the others, steps out from behind a huge white pine, swings a red bandanna overhead like a lariat—Ray's bandanna, actually, a birthday present straight from his head to his nephew's. He must have been watching them circle for hours, Ray realizes, the searchers sniffing and panting and following vapid scents like lost bird dogs. How he must have enjoyed the hunt, Ray thinks; how he must have chuckled at their earnestness, their ineptness, their coming up short, and all along so close! Darryl: the all-seeing center, the epicenter, for once, the swinger of the bucket. And all his friends and family, the whole goddamn police force, circling and tripping and toppling just out of reach like so many skewed satellites. What power and pleasure he must have felt in those hours!

But is he crazed, or just unhappy? Christine wants to know. Or both. Or neither, Ray suggests. He tries to talk to Darryl when the police have gone and they are safely back in the Suitland house, but they don't get far. "It was a little scary the first night," Darryl says to Ray, "but the stars were nice. The Big Dipper was right there." He is flopped out on his bed and jabs a finger up at the ceiling. He seems to have grown about ten inches since Ray saw him last; his feet are huge. "It was really nice. Peaceful."

"What about all the dope you clogged the toilet with? They're going to have to call Roto-Rooter, at the rate you're going."

Darryl give a short laugh. "I'm cleaning myself up; it's the cleansing purge. I'm starting over." He puts his hands behind his head, looks over at Ray. "You should know what I mean."

"I know what you mean," Ray says, "but next time, just use the trash can. And do me a favor: let your parents know. At least leave a note. They were sick about all this."

"They worry too much."

"They're your parents; it's in the job description." Ray isn't even there yet, in the parent department, but already he feels it, how it all comes back on you. Lord, Lord, he thinks, how does anyone take it on? Is what your children mete out to you directly proportional to how much you tormented your own folks? "I'll tell you one thing," Ray adds. "Your old uncle's goose is cooked."

Darryl raises his eyebrows.

"Vivian is pregnant."

"No shit!" Darryl sits up.

"No shit."

"God," says Darryl. "Was it an accident?"

"Nothing is an accident," says Ray, then he says, "It was planned." And then he says, "It should be one of the more interesting adventures of my life."

"I guess so," says Darryl, but he sounds doubtful. "God." He shakes his head. "So much for doing exactly what you want."

"We all gotta grow up sometime," Ray says. "I've done exactly what I wanted for a long time now." Which wasn't entirely true, but no need to split hairs now.

The look Darryl gives his uncle is that of a seventeen-year-old, and what more can he expect, Ray thinks. At seventeen, he wasn't near as wise as this boy.

Out in his truck, ready to pull out of Suitland, head north, Ray proposes to Christine that Darryl come to Virginia for a time. He offers to loop by to pick him up on his way back down.

"I'm not sure your living arrangement would be suitable for him." She says it kindly, but she means it.

"It'll be good for him; he can work on our vehicles, he can be a gofer at the site. He and Vivian get along well. Things are different now." He tells her they are expecting a baby and she congratulates him, with tears in her eyes, says she is happy that he is happy, are they married yet? that after the baby, nothing will be the same.

"That's what I'm hoping," says Ray.

Christine sighs in the white streetlight, and Ray wants to smooth her hair, cradle her, relieve her of some of the worry of her life. "Things will look better in the morning," he says, and offers her a cigarette, though he knows she is trying halfheartedly to quit. She shakes her head no and suddenly he sees her as a knee-socked teen, cardigan draped over her shoulders, bouffant hair, bopping around in her flouncy pink room to Elvis, the Shirelles, Little Eva. The Beatles and the Haight did not find a friend in Christine; she had stuck with the familiar, with things American.

Life didn't seem particularly fair, but what was new about that? Even Ann Landers never claimed life was fair. Their parents should have warned them; surely they had known. Someone should have told them not just about life's travails and blind corners, should have told Christine, anyhow, that even when you did everything right, more or less, you didn't automatically get a tangible payoff. You don't always get what you deserve. Nothing to cry about, but it was the truth. Then again, maybe it was just that you aren't rewarded (was he thinking of God here? he wasn't sure) when you are good, but when you are bad, shit happens. Maybe it was more that. Imagine if Christine had been bad.

She must be asking him a question, because she has stopped talking and is looking at him. "Well?" It is very hot, and the sound of Suitland traffic whining off in the distance makes Ray realize just how tired he is and what a long way off home is. And New England. There isn't much of a moon, and the smell of hot clipped grass is everywhere.

Not knowing how to answer, not having heard the question, he reaches out to smooth the gray glinting in her hair. Some of it catches in the creases of his hand, rough from the building he's been doing all these years. She is surprised at his gesture, but she leans against his hand, leaves her head there so long he finally has to gently retrieve it, as he might his shoulder from the cheek of a sleeping child, his wrist weak from the weight. By now they are both mildly embarrassed, but it is done, and no one died from the effort.

"You OK?" he asks.

She nods. "Jerry will be home soon." Ray pats her head awkwardly, and this time she looks at him curiously, as if he might possibly be running a fever or drinking heavily from some secret whiskey stash.

"Darryl'll be all right," Ray says. "He's young is all. But he's smart, and he knows you love him." It sounds lame, but Christine thanks him anyhow.

"You can stay another night here, you know," she says, gesturing toward the house.

"I'd better push on." Ray starts up the old truck. Christine's hand is still on the door. The diamonds Jerry has given her over the years glitter and shake. "One good thing," she says. "At least he came back—or let us see him—on his own." She looks at him with a faint smile.

Ray squeezes her hand, feels the diamonds poke at his palm. He watches his sister move up the sidewalk toward her house. She looks sturdy but very small, framed first by neatly shaped American box on either side, then by the monstrously tall columns that hold up the front porch. Just before the door, she turns to wave. "I'll call," he says, "and I'll swing back by on my way home," and in the rearview he watches as she lets herself in.

■ ≡ ■

He is in Connecticut six hours later and sleeps in his truck until midday. For two or three weeks, he wanders the countryside and the adjoining states, visiting old friends. They are all glad to see him; they stop their work long enough to catch up, they show off their pretty children, new and old wives and companions. But no one stops working for more than a couple of days, and no one seems to have a trouble-free life, though several claim they are happy. The plights of some of his friends leave Ray grateful for his own mild confusions: one man, for instance, was working hard at cultivating three love affairs (openly and honestly, he'd said hotly). Usually he managed well enough and all seemed satisfied, but there were times when he said he felt like pushing the lot of them (himself included) into some deep, dark pit. Another friend's teenage daughter had run off with the son of the high school janitor, and while the parents heartily approved of working with your hands (he is a psychologist, but she is a potter), they are distressed at the poignant, dog-eared postcards they receive daily from Portales (no return address), telling how penniless and lonely (and pregnant) their daughter is. Another friend had sunk what little money and faith he had into a farm he'd inherited from his father, only to suffer through the driest year in recent memory. Some friends drink too much, others love coke. Some are (still) in jail, some are dead. And one woman Ray has known for years, whose cooking and sense and good humor he has always admired, comes out to his truck one night—husband long since happily passed out and snoring on the worn couch—wanting to sleep with him. And when Ray refuses, citing long-standing loyalty to her husband, she tells him in low angry whispers just how arrogant she has always found him.

Maybe behaving honestly made you feel good in the long run, Ray thinks as he watches moonlight seep through the sprung seams of his camper, but it certainly wasn't much fun.

In the morning he calls Vivian collect from the already sun-baked phone booth outside the general store down the road. It is Saturday, he has been gone almost a month now, he is nearing the end of his journey—he can feel it, just has Priscilla left to see—and he wants to hear Vivian's low, easy voice right now, wants a little more fuel for the road. And he wants to check on her, make sure she's managing all right, but he knows she can take care of business for herself and her family, with no assistance from him. Spare me the needy, she had said to him once, and he can hear her saying it again, at this very moment, between the plaintive rings of the unanswered telephone.

■ ≡ ■

Vivian hears the phone just as she is putting her hand down to pull some weeds next to the spent Swiss chard. In that instant, a snake slithers past. At first she simply stares, the snake a highway of shifting gold and pink, rumbling along in silence beneath the ragged zinnias, tall as redwoods. One minute the highway, the next just blank earth and her own sharp breathing. Then she jumps back as if electrically charged and beats a retreat to the yard, fifteen feet off, where she stares so hard at the chard it seems to twitch involuntarily, mysteriously rifled by life, or some light breeze. The day is hot and steamy and dead calm. When her knees stop shaking and her eyes stop doing tricks with the chard, she goes into the schoolhouse to consult the snake book and drink a beer. It is only ten A.M., and she has not drunk a beer all summer.

This is the second time in three days Vivian has seen the snake. She knows it must be the same one, too close to the house and way too familiar. She knows from Ray's military-issue *Poisonous Snakes of the World* (color plates, exhaustively thorough descriptions of the reptiles, coded information concerning what antidote to administer when, and under what circumstances) that copperhead bites were rarely if ever fatal. For adults, anyhow. The snake book leaves little to the imagination. But she knows, too, that the bites are tremendously painful, having watched Frenchie suffer through one earlier that month. And she knows, or senses, the long-lasting, debilitating effects of such trauma on the poor old human body. Certainly Frenchie had looked for all of one night and most of the next day as if she preferred no life at all to the one she was currently having to endure.

The copperhead that got Frenchie was stretched out across the driveway in front of them like a stick of deadwood. Vivian had seen it and caught herself midstep, but the dog had bounced merrily on and, even after being struck, had not been able to comprehend the source of the pain. The snake had vanished and they went back to the schoolhouse, where Frenchie lay on her side on the front porch, panting in glaze-eyed despair, her paw swelling to softball size. Geronimo stayed close, nose resting on his paws, his brow furrowed, if such a thing was possible in a dog—Vivian was convinced absolutely that it was. The children had tried to soothe Frenchie, had made pillows for her out of old towels, and she had been dutifully grateful for the consideration.

Vivian hesitated only a moment before calling Dr. Tucker. Usually he chastised her, and the world in general, for its overindulgence of pets. She had cats, which were now commingling warily with Ray's dogs, and she hardly thought she visited the vet unnecessarily. People think their animals will live forever, Dr. T. had said the last time she was there, and he shook his head in mild disdain. He talked about prescribing low-cal dog food to overweight and discouraged beagles, tranquilizers for high-strung cats, the peace of the needle to the hopelessly sick and dying. Vivian had simply wanted distemper boosters for her cats.

This time Dr. T. said to bring Frenchie in immediately, which she did, and he had spoken in low, gentle tones to both of them while applying salve to the paw and shooting Frenchie full of antibodies. And Vivian wished, in her moment of relief, that he might tend to her in the same way, shoot her full of something to ensure that everything would be just fine—the coming baby, her two growing children, Ray: he, Dr. T., would insist on bed rest and round-the-clock care, prescribe something strong to ensure a carefree head, healthy heart, fine life, remind her she should think and ruminate over nothing, nothing at all, doctor's orders. Rarely did Vivian allow herself such moments, fearing the resulting possible lack of vitality it took to make it from one day to the next. But Dr. T. had instead patted her on the back as she left, telling her to call in three days if Frenchie didn't improve.

If she had caught the phone when Ray called that Saturday, she would have told him how she and the children had stood next to that small garden patch near the house, the one marked off by railroad ties, tipping back and forth, poking at the chard with their toes, searching for the intruder. They had watched the place where the snake had been, as if hoping for some kind of miracle—the chard would part, make a path like the Red Sea, someone would play Moses, and they would walk into it, through it, and onto firm, snakeless ground.

You never see them in the same place twice, she reminds herself while she drinks the beer. And that is the blessing and frustration of having seen one in the first place—that you know they are around so you are warned, but then you have to wait for them to show themselves again, you have to be patient, you have to set yourself up to be acted upon in order to take action yourself. She also knows, from the blessed snake book, that copperheads mate in the spring, and give birth—live—late summer, early fall. Those are their busy times, she explains to the children, as if describing the tourist trade.

Late that afternoon, Vivian's friend Jane comes. She is just there overnight, checking on her goddaughter and her pregnant friend. It is as hot and still as it gets in central Virginia in August, and while the women sit on the porch having a drink (lemonade for Vivian), grousing about the heat, the children play in the treehouse, scrapping about whose turn it is to be king. The clothes Vivian has hung out stretch along the line like a row of minute sentries, ready to attack, if need be, defend the homestead. The porch floor is warm under their bare feet, and somewhere, very far off, a hawk calls.

"It was right there," Vivian is saying to Jane. She holds her glass of lemonade in one hand, points beyond the railroad ties with the other. Jane, sitting in a rusty lawn chair, nurses a beer.

"You sure it was a copperhead?"

"Looked it up, and besides, I should know by now."

"Ugh." Jane shivers and takes a sip. She is from New York,

so has had plenty of time to experience the frequency and likelihood of muggings, the crush of the crowds, the dank insides of
subways. Vivian sometimes questions the wisdom of living that
way, but now here is this snake, so what was the difference?
Choose your difficulty; pick a predicament, any predicament.

"It had elliptical pupils and this coppery head. Really kind of
beautiful. But now I have to look wherever I go—can't put one
foot down without checking out the ground first." She rests her
hand on her stomach, then gets up to demonstrate to Jane the
exaggerated snake walk. She minces her way from the porch to
the railroad ties, then back to Jane in slow motion. She balances
first on one leg, then on the other. Lemonade slides over the top
of her glass, cooling her hand as it slips past her fingers and down
her arm. It catches finally in the crook of her elbow, where she
licks some off, then she starts the walk back to the garden.

"It's like learning to walk all over again," she says over her
shoulder, balancing now in a sort of bastardized arabesque, arm
with drink held aloft like some torch carrier at the Olympics.
They are both laughing now, giddy from heat and mild fear, and
beyond them, the children laugh too, having momentarily settled
the squabble. And the smell of hot grass is everywhere, and in
that moment Vivian feels the perfect peace.

"One thing, one good thing." She is bending from her waist
now, still on one leg, the other stuck out in back.

"Watch it," says Jane.

"One good thing," she repeats, her hair hanging on either
side of her face, nose almost atop the railroad tie, "is that you
never ever see them—" but she doesn't finish because that is
when she sees the copperhead baking in a corner of the kitchen
garden about two yards off. It lifts its head to look at her, and
Vivian thinks she can see it thinking or rather willing her: get
the hell out of my garden. She springs back exactly as she did
the first time, but this time the copperhead stays put.

"What's the matter?" Jane's beer is halfway to her mouth.

"There it is again."

If Ray had been there, Vivian would have called him quietly

and quickly, would have kept an eye on the snake while he fetched the deadly shovel. Or his beloved machete, a present from Bullet, who found it on a trip to Guatemala—or was it Tijuana; she couldn't quite remember which. Ray would have swiftly and deftly decapitated the snake and they would have stood there in wonder and awe, though this would not be the first time—far from it—that they had encountered such danger together. But Ray is way beyond earshot, and Jane is an urban dweller, albeit a survivor, and all Vivian can say is "We need a shovel."

Jane is out of her chair now, poised for flight. The snake is coiled in an attractive pile of diamondy layers; it looks a little like the beginnings of the many pots Vivian tried to make in the one ceramics class she'd taken. The instructor—she had been half in love with him, as had everyone else in the class—would wind the coils round and round, producing in a few moments and twists pots she could never hope to make. He would make them, then toss them minutes later in the garbage can with the rest of the used clay. "Two points," he'd say, in a way that made her wonder just how serious an artist he was. She was young then, with no vision beyond imitating him precisely.

"We need a shovel."

Vivian runs for the shovel, has trouble with the stiff lock on the shed. She curses Jesus and herself and Ray for not having loosened it up long ago with WD-40. She sees herself struggling with the rusty lock while the snake waits complacently for her return. Or maybe the snake is at this very moment attacking everything in sight—she'd go back, armed with the shovel, and there would be Jane, stretched out, pale and writhing around in bloody pain, the lovely bodies of her children strewn hither and yon.

The lock gives, and she pushes the door open and stands in the dark of the shed. She looks over spilled bags of lime and grass seed and fertilizer, doesn't wait for her eyes to adjust as she bangs through rakes and hoes and dried clumps of grass from under the lawn mower, till she gets to the shovel. She grabs it, feels the splinter that immediately jabs her thumb. She runs back to Jane and the copperhead and her children and the sun, hoping there is no work to be done, that everything will be just as it should be. Jane simply points to the snake, lost in its own sweet dreams.

Vivian plants herself opposite, bulky railroad ties dividing them like a river. At the precise moment she raises the shovel, the copperhead lifts its head elegantly, sniffing—they can't sniff, she realizes later, they sense, feel the vibes—the air, for clues.

"Good God," says Vivian. Her arms, holding the shovel high, shake from fear and the force of her grip. Behind her she hears or, more accurately, feels the presence of Jane, who is behind her watching her watching the snake, who seems to know everything but does nothing. It is very still and very hot, and the children are quieter now, though they are probably unaware of this little porchside drama, or maybe they know and are watching from their treehouse perch, wisely staying put, letting the grownups handle this one. Vivian doesn't know, only knows the snake is right there, waiting for her to do something. The sun seems to burn through her thin shirt, seems to weld what little shirt there is to her back, her arms to her body, hands to the handle of the shovel. If Jane could have spoken, she would have said, Go ahead, just do it, chop the goddamn thing to bits so we can all breathe again. But Jane doesn't say anything, can't, and Vivian pauses a split second before pushing the shovel down hard toward the snake and earth. In that instant the copperhead moves its head again. And whether from that movement, or because her own eyes are shut as she strikes, or maybe it is just plain bad luck, Vivian misses by a good three inches, and the shovel shudders foolishly and vainly in the parched ground.

She doesn't see the copperhead go. Her heart is pounding so hard she imagines looking down and seeing the place where the skin covers it suddenly go transparent—like a plastic biology model—demonstrating up close, for anyone caring to observe, the strengths and limitations of a heart all out. Her unborn child gives her a sharp kick—chiding her for her ineffectiveness as warrior and defender of the hearth?—and suddenly she feels faint. She closes her eyes, then opens them wide; a flicker of the lid and she might miss something. Behind her she thinks she feels Jane's disappointment, as acute and sharp as her own, at the unfinished job.

"God damn it." Vivian raises her voice at the end the way she's heard her daughter do when she thinks no one is near. "God *damn* it."

"It's OK," Jane says, patting her on the back. "You scared it good," and after that, she nicely says nothing. Vivian can't look at her till she's retrieved the shovel, propped it next to the door, and banged into the kitchen to get them fresh drinks.

■ ≡ ■

In the next week she mentions the snake to anyone she sees or talks to, and everyone has a story. She mentions it to Ray when he calls a few days later from Vermont; he tells her the snake will probably not turn up again, but she knows better now than to believe that. The stories everyone has are like UFO sightings, just as unbelievable but with details slightly more lurid and exact. Certainly, everyone has one. *The snake was twelve foot long, eyes that stopped you dead. The snake chased this one woman down the road, nipping at her heels, tugging at her coat. The snake—colors indistinct—ate popcorn right from the man's hand, tame as you please. Snake fell down the chimney onto the hearth, dead of summer. A black snake swallowed this cute brown field mouse whole, then turned around and did the same thing to its terrified brother—true story, swear to God. The snake was inside the house. Under a dresser* (Ray's story; thank you, Ray, she thinks to herself)—*had to stomp it to oblivion once I got it out and trapped underneath the rug,* he'd said. *Sleeping inside the washing machine. Under the car hood. Snake bit onto the end of its own tail and made a hoop and tried to run down this dude. Down in South America you got 'em so big you think they're a damn log till you step on one and your old boot sinks down just a little too much.*

The friends talk snake in ecological terms, psychological ones, sexual—depending on the nature of their encounter and background. They are good stories, but the analyzing strikes Vivian as a bunch of hogwash, completely irrelevant. Just come home and get rid of this thing for me, will you? she'd said laughingly to her man Ray.

■ ≡ ■

The next Saturday she's not up for half an hour, and she's out in the garden drinking Red Zinger, enjoying the brief early-morning cool and the sound of the children playing. It has been going well with the children: they even, in their limited contact with him, seemed to like Ray. And now, with the comfortable sounds of their playing, it feels normal and real—they're one big happy family. She does not know how she can ever let them go back to Tucson. She quells the thought, won't think about that now.

And then suddenly there's the snake, must be the same one, certainly looks the same, tucked into the same corner of the railroad ties, waiting for the same sun Vivian will have to wear a hat against later. This time there's no Jane to prove anything to, and the children are inside and safe, but any moment they might walk out and disturb it, or the snake might decide to ease on into the cool of the house—Vivian, you've been listening to too many stories—might strike when no one's looking, and Vivian's thinking, This is it, my time has come, I've got another chance, and I must get the shovel. She thinks this crazily as she stares at the snake, who, eyes closed, seems unconscious of everything but the moment's peace.

Vivian walks like an Indian to the back door for the shovel, and she feels fortified, ready to go, adrenaline swirling through her sleepy, ripe system. She feels young—ten years younger!—brazen and muscular and tan, someone straight from the pages of *Shape* (her daughter's favorite magazine). She's filled with hope and vigorous intent; clearly she will be victorious. She grasps the shovel and is about to tiptoe back, when her daughter opens the door behind her and asks why she's sneaking around like that.

"Sssh, it's the copperhead."

Her daughter Delia's eyes widen, and darken, and she says, "Where?"

Vivian hushes her again and points to a corner of the garden. Delia tips her chin up as she looks over there, leans her small head forward to get a better look, and Vivian, watching her strain to see it, feels her heart filling with love for this girl, these children, and the child yet to come.

"Oh," her daughter breathes. She has seen it.

"You stay here." Vivian turns back to the garden. "And keep your brother with you. Where is he, anyhow?"

"Watching TV. Are you going to kill it?" Something in her voice tells Vivian that she, Delia, could certainly do it if she, Vivian, can't muster the nerve.

"I'm going to try."

Vivian is a foot from the snake when she hears Claude junior. "I can't see," he complains. She looks over at her son. He is leaning out from behind his sister's legs, seven years old and certain of everything. Delia is pointing to their mother, and Vivian points down, straight down, jabs the air with her finger. Right here, she mouths. Her son sees and is instantly quiet, instantly still, and in that unnatural, frozen moment, Vivian knows she must do something or they'll all be standing there forever like the faces on Mount Rushmore, stuck for the rest of their lives, waiting around for someone to cover them with sheets to keep the dust off, or tarps against the rain or rust or simply a slow fading away. From the corner of her eye Vivian sees her daughter put an arm around the boy—they are both still in pajamas—and as she grasps the shovel again, the long India-print shirt she put on when she got up that morning gets in the way, so she clamps it against her ribs with an elbow and inches forward. She has put on long socks and hiking boots, so she looks like a modern-day Mammy Yokum toting this lethal weapon, all gumption and chaw.

OK, she thinks, circling the ties. OK, OK. She contemplates the best position. The insects of the day are starting in on their noise; it burns in her ears, at the back of her neck. Far off, a train whines: same pitch as the insects, just farther off. The cool of the morning is gone, maybe never was.

Her daughter steps out for a look. "I can't see," she says.

"Get back in the house." Vivian thinks she sees the snake move its head, or maybe it doesn't, but then it twists around to look at her, it certainly does, God's truth. Looks directly at her but doesn't move, remains coiled, pot of clay, convinced the danger will pass if it just waits long enough.

Vivian raises the shovel. In that instant she realizes she has never killed anything so intentionally, and her stomach turns. The babe kicks. The children watch, entranced. She wills the snake to move, get lost, escape, spare her. The snake stays. She shifts her weight slightly. She is close enough now so that if it wanted to, the copperhead could strike and get to her, latch onto her leg like some toothy, elongated leech, bite the living shit out of her, send her to the hospital for a short, unpleasant stay. Wound the babe. She pauses. Her breath comes short—she smokes ten packs a day and has just run a thirty-mile marathon with weights on her feet in hundred-degree heat. Her arms shake. The shovel shakes. The world wavers and is insubstantial as water. Sounds are far off as the sea. She thinks she just might faint, maybe has already, except she is not fainthearted, is of sturdy stock, peasant stock, she always tells people matter-of-factly. Not true, but that is how she feels often—capable and resilient.

Go on, Mom, do it. *Do* it!

■ ≡ ■

Parts of snake lie on either side of the shovel's blade. The children stand closer, and Vivian is too distracted to tell them to get back, the snake could even now do damage. With just the tips of her fingers, and staying as far away as she can, she loosens the shovel from its slash in the earth. She waits only long enough to see that the snake is wounded, not yet dead, then she goes after it, slamming the blade down over and over, until the job is more than done. And yet still it seems to live, seems—impossibly—to move, the pieces tiny duplicates of each other. She thinks she must be hallucinating and crouches down, puts her head to her knees. She thinks she must be crazy, thinks she might be about to die.

Ray should be here, she thinks.

Afterward the children say, with admiration and mild fear, You should have seen your *face.* She is holding them, smiling, reassuring them that everything is fine, though her knees still shake and she feels slightly ill. She says to them, I had to do it, you understand that, don't you? I couldn't let that old snake get you guys.

Gradually she comes back, feels better and better, feels good, downright triumphant, absolutely victorious, crazy with power, better than she has felt in days, months, the last several years, much of her life. And she says to herself, half-jokingly, This is *pathetic,* but she thinks, transmits, throws the message out to Tucson and to Ray, miles and centuries off, Did you see *that?* And she relays the whole scene to Jane, over the phone, blow by blow, and in the next few weeks, she and the children fool around with what they call the snake walk, practice the precarious balance, eyes checking the ground, just in case.

But she leaves out of all accounts, even when she goes over it again in her own mind, how when she peered at the chunks of snake checkering the sun-baked earth, and poked at the blood and debris, she saw three perfectly marked, pencil-thin, six-inch babies about to be born, perfect and blameless and whole.

At the precise moment Vivian is plunging her shovel into the snake, Ray is standing with James on the ground floor of the spec house James is building in Vermont. They are looking up at a hole cut in the ceiling, which is supposed to accommodate the top of a circular staircase but is clearly way too small. Sunlight pours through the hole, spotlighting a larger, fuzzier circle of light a few feet off. The rest of the crew is banging away here and there, hammered orchestration of tools clanging like the busy insides of some steaming machine. It is very very hot. A fine layer of sawdust covers everything like pollen; it feels even hotter here in Vermont than it had in central Va., Ray is thinking, if such a thing was possible.

"No way they'll get a king-size up there," Ray says.

"It'll fit," says James, but they both know it can't possibly. "Besides, who says they got a king-size?"

"Anyone with enough dough to buy this house owns a king-size, believe me," says Ray, though there is no earthly reason why James, Priscilla's young boyfriend, should believe what Ray has to say about this, or about anything else, for that matter. Ray wouldn't have spoken up at all about the stairs, except that Priscilla had asked him late the night before, after he'd pulled up in his exhausted pickup, if he would check out the job. It was her money they were using to build the thing, she'd explained.

"I love James dearly," she'd said quietly to Ray just before they'd all gone to bed, "but he's a musician, not a carpenter. He does have a feel for wood," she'd added, "and an eye for"—here she had waved her long arms wildly, just as he remembered she always had—"proportion," she said finally. "But as for the actual building. . . ." Her voice trailed off, and she stepped back, which had relieved Ray enormously, because he was fighting an urge to keep her near him, hold her, smooth her hair, kiss her. Inappropriate, unseemly behavior, he told himself, considering her illness and how long it had been since he'd last seen her. And of course there were the children sleeping in the next room. And James in the kitchen. To say nothing of Vivian. In absentia.

James is tapping a post with his slender white fingers. "I don't know," he says. "Plans call for circular."

Ray sighs. He has been reading plans and framing houses long enough to know the circular stairs are a big mistake. People could float up and down them, kids could ride the curves—there was no denying their grace and pleasing lines—but sooner or later a set of usable stairs would have to be roughed in somewhere. All of which was reminding him annoyingly of the work he'd happily and intentionally left behind in Virginia.

"Architects should spend a few years on the inside," he says.

"We'll just cut the goddamn hole bigger," says James. "The stairs were Priscilla's idea." After which Ray simply keeps quiet. He walks out to the car while James gives the men instructions on what to do next. Ray lights another cigarette and, leaning against the hot side of the old Chevy wagon, toys with the idea of heading back to Virginia that very day. He has been gone over four weeks now, and there is little left to do. He had expected to find Priscilla alone and needy, whatever that meant.

Soon it is too hot to lean on the Chevy without running the risk of bursting into flame, so Ray eases down into the front seat, leaving the door open. He fools with the radio; Bono pours forth. Ray can just see him throwing his head around in that way he had. Even Bono would be stilled in this heat, he thinks. He leans back, closes his eyes to the sun. And he allows himself to think, just for a moment, about Priscilla, about how capable she'd become, about how infantile he still felt, at times. He remembers again, too fondly, the old De Soto and the musty upholstery and her Intimate and Percy Sledge and James Brown. B. B. King. Bono and B. B. singing the blues, B. B. singing easy circles around the younger man, eclipsing him, Bono digging it, not minding, understanding he was in the presence of something powerful. Is that how James felt around Priscilla, maybe? Possibly around him, Ray? Shit, young James was still chewing on Bazooka when he and Priscilla were slow-dancing to the likes of Percy Sledge and the King.

- ≣ -

"We don't know how to deal with the heat up here," Priscilla is saying. They are sitting in lawn chairs on the dock at the pond below Priscilla's house, drinking beer. "We're breaking all kinds of records."

Ray gulps down his beer, takes off his damp clothes, dives into the water. Though the top eight inches are warm, the water beneath is wonderfully cool. He begins swimming laps between the dam and the dock and is out of breath after six—too many Camels—but he keeps at it. There is no real need to be exerting himself this way, but he feels useless hanging around the dock with Priscilla and James. Their constant touching and general solidarity makes him uncomfortable and homesick for Vivian. He has had no chance to be alone with Priscilla; it is as if he himself is carrying the plague, as if, in their keen interest to keep the disease "in perspective" (as James had referred to it in his and Ray's brief talk earlier that day), they kept everything at arm's length, everyone at bay.

Ray would like to swim for hours, wear himself out to the point where he doesn't care what anyone does anywhere, but his body finally gives out, just won't cooperate, so he contents himself with floating, then finally, waterlogged, swims back to the dock. James holds out a beer as Ray hoists himself from the water, barking his shin against the dock's rough edge. He pretends it is nothing and, cursing inwardly, accepts the towel Priscilla offers. They sit on the dock not saying much, watching the children. In the late-afternoon sun, the children's small bodies are coffee-colored; they glisten like fish. Though there are just two of them, their shouting and splashing suggests a whole battalion. The sinking sun is pink, and without the white glare, everything appears brighter and richer than before.

Finally Priscilla wades in. She ducks under, then stands in the shallow water, swinging the boy back and forth. Her wet hair sticks to her back in intricate, snaky swirls. The evening light softens her; she is taller than Ray remembers, more angles.

Or maybe he is just getting used to Vivian's compact frame, expecting that now in every woman. For a moment he sees Vivian and her children in place of this woman and hers, and he feels a painful lump in his throat. Alarmed, he takes a swig of beer. It has been a long journey; perhaps he should not have come this far.

"How's the water?" James asks.

"Nice." Priscilla smiles at Ray. The little boy is trying to catch a water spider. "Wonderful." She leans back, eases out to a float. Ray tries not to stare at her dark nipples pointing to the sky.

"Surface tension," Rays says to the girl, who is asking why water spiders don't sink. "Water spider," he says, nodding in the direction of her mother.

Priscilla and the children laugh. "Water spider, water spider," the children chant. Red sky at night, sailor's delight. Soon the water will turn dark, onyx. The pop-top James snaps sounds like a gunshot.

"I've been looking forward to meeting you," James had said earlier. "Priscilla's talked a lot about . . . the old days." They were winding along hot back roads, the spec house behind them, pond beckoning. Ray grunted something noncommittal, mildly embarrassed. "Some of her friends can't hack it," James continued. He swerved to avoid a snake stretched dumbly across the hot tar in front of them, swung sharply back to his side, narrowly missing an oncoming four-wheeler. "But it's good for her to make those connections, close the gap, you know?" He paused, but Ray said nothing, being unsure quite how to respond. "She's beautiful and she's tough, but she has her weak moments, needless to say. Keeps her human." He laughed softly, as if at a private joke, and Ray thought suddenly then, and thinks again now, that James really was quite remarkable.

■ ≡ ■

"You'd think I'd be all skin and bones," Priscilla is saying. They are back on the dock, but it is night now. The moon is small and bright; earlier it had made James's gold earring seem to spark. Frogs and crickets sound their usual racket. James is cleaning up in the kitchen and putting the children to bed. We take turns, Priscilla says. She and Ray have been sitting quietly; Priscilla is shelling peas, bowl in her lap, which strikes Ray as an odd thing to be doing at this hour, but she says they planted too many and she wants to freeze these.

Somewhere an owl calls. After a time, clear high notes from James's flute trill through the thick night down to them. The music is sad and sweet. A kerosene lamp casts vague shadows along the dips and warps of the dock.

"He make any money with that thing?" Ray is longing for a Camel. He has held off in deference to Priscilla. He is burning up; his shirt is sticking to his back, his back to the lawn chair webbing, his hair to the back of his neck. He is thinking he could use a shot or two of whiskey right now, possibly tequila; he would like to be in some bar with plenty of strangers around to take up the slack, leave him alone. And maybe he would be listening to the frenzied guitar riffs of some junkie musician and wishing, at the very least, to be that person for the night.

"He's too good to put up with all the bullshit," Priscilla says. "You know, playing backup, studio gigs, the bar scene. Nobody cares."

"You and he seem pretty tight." Ever since his arrival, everything Ray says to her has seemed lame, or beside the point. What was his *problem*?

"We've got things worked out. He's good with the children." Priscilla rests her arms on the edge of the bowl a moment, looking at Ray. She is wearing a long sheath of a dress that on anyone else, in this close heat, would be torture. "I'm surprised, after all these years and women, you haven't had any."

"Kids?" Ray doesn't know why he hasn't mentioned the baby yet. "Costs too much," and they both smile at that.

"Everything costs too much," she says, going back to the peas. She tells him they've given up on the AMA and are working on a home cure for the cancer. James had stayed out of it until one

evening when she injected herself with a hefty dose of B-12 and
he found her unconscious and twitching on the green-painted
kitchen floor, eyes rolled up, back arched as if in the throes of
some splendid lovemaking. " 'Scared the shit out of me,' " she
says he said. " 'You need a manager.' " James appointed himself.

"We're holding our own," Priscilla says. They listen to James.
"How'd the house look?" she asks.

"For a musician, not half bad." Ray wants her to explain why
they're building a huge house with a circular staircase and mam-
moth rooms impossible to heat. Who would buy such a house
out in the middle of nowhere? How can she do such a thing,
start a project like this when she may not be around for the
finish? He wants to say, How can you be so smug, but instead
says, "Do you mind if I smoke?" His hand is halfway to his shirt
pocket, where he rests it, as if keeping his heart in place, till he
hears her answer.

"Go ahead. Most days I still wish I smoked. There's no logic
to it." He smokes while James regales them with his music. "Rick's
pitching in on the house too," Priscilla says suddenly. She is
looking right at Ray. "He's a banker now and is loaded. Piles of
money. Rick's always been generous; it makes him feel useful, I
think."

Ray remembers Rick—a bear of a man who never said much,
father of the two children. "He's a banker?" Ray remembers Rick
disposing of cases of beer and torpedo-size joints in record time.

"Rick's going to be worth more"—Priscilla makes dollar signs
in the air between them with her index fingers—"than all the
rest of us combined. Who would have thought?" She pauses.
"He's probably a kinder person than all the rest of us combined,
too."

"You're pretty kind," says Ray, and suddenly he feels the bad
eye throb and the good eye threaten tears. A few peas bounce
from the bowl onto the dock. Others roll toward Ray, looking,
he thinks stupidly, like errant crazy eyeballs, lost and blind. Some
roll between the cracks, are snapped at by feeding fish. Ray corrals
a few and drops them back into the bowl. His hand brushes

Priscilla's and she says, "Thanks," holds on to his fingers a moment, says, "You OK?"

"I'm fine," he says. "I just hope you're on the right track with this home-cure stuff. Sounds pretty fly-by-night to me. Might not be a bad idea to check in with the AMA every now and then; they do have a couple of years of research chalked up." He resists the urge to grasp her long white neck so that he might throttle her. He stubs out the cigarette and walks over to the water.

He hears her sigh as she pushes herself out of the chair, hears her set the bowl on the sun-bleached boards. She walks over to him, turns him around. "Look at me," she says. "Have I ever looked better?" Ray looks at her as long as he can stand, turns back to the water, says no, she never has, she looks beautiful.

"You know," she says, smoothing his hair, kissing the back of his neck, "if you were me, you'd be dead by now."

He is shocked at how callous it sounds, but he knows it's true.

"You need a haircut," she says. She puts her arm around his waist, her cheek to his back. "It's OK," she whispers, "everything's fine," but he says, No, it isn't fine at all, and she says again, Yes it is, until finally he is quiet and the notes from James's flute wrap and wind lightly round them.

They begin to dance. He feels all of her against him. He is ashamed at how much he wants her. He thinks of the time years before when he'd just flown home for good and they'd met so tenderly and awkwardly. But still she had saved him, if only for that one night, and now it's his turn and he feels woefully inadequate.

She seems to sense his distress, because she lets him kiss her, and now he realizes, with unfamiliar but daunting clarity, just how much he loves Vivian, loves her more than ever. He knows now he will make a wonderful husband and father. This fills him with exhilaration and relief. And he knows there is nothing on God's green earth he can do to save Priscilla, a fact that, of course, she has known all along.

And still they dance. They dip and sway. They barely move.

Through the sheer material of her dress Ray slowly and carefully moves his hands along her spine as if he is some delicate-fingered surgeon. He feels caught in a kind of enchantment, lulled and lured by the heavy heat and her closeness and their past and the music itself. He cannot imagine her dead, sees no reason to imagine her dead. That seems to have little bearing on what they are doing now, or might do. Soon it will be too late for simple sleep.

Perhaps if James stops, we will stop, he thinks vaguely.

He has come all this way to figure it out, and though it's not turning out quite as he'd planned—of course, he'd intentionally planned nothing, thinking that the ultimate freedom—it was going well. It was going just fine, suddenly.

How he loved Priscilla! What a sentimental, wasted old fool he was, and what wonderful people they were, the two of them, at this moment!

Priscilla stops dancing, steps back, slips the long dress off. Again Ray is struck by her paleness, the angularity. She watches him, steps closer. "Don't worry about James," she says as they resume the dance.

■ ≡ ■

In the middle of the night Ray wakes up. He is lying on the dock amidst wadded-up towels and bits of clothing. He touches parts of his body gingerly, checking for damage. For a time, the only thing he moves is his eyes, as if by moving anything else he just might come completely unhinged, might lose an arm or a leg over the side to some man-eating fish, his head might ease its weighty way off his shoulders and roll right off the dock, sink into oblivion and the soft silt at the bottom of the pond.

He is all there, he is intact, he is alone. Shifting his weight, repositioning his sore limbs on the towels, Ray feels a little old. Nothing a few laps wouldn't straighten out, he thinks, knowing there is no way in this world he will plunge into the water right now.

He remembers Priscilla saying, "Don't worry about James, this is inevitable," but James wasn't the problem, James had never really been the problem. It was Vivian, the vision of Vivian—he should write a song like that—the vision of Vivian was what Ray couldn't shake. All his life he had been unable to remain faithful to even the most wonderful of women. He said this to Priscilla, and said, This is the first time I have been tempted this way in a long time, and she says she understands, but this is different, isn't it, this is something separate from loving Vivian.

He says he knows that, he positively aches with that knowledge, but if he makes love to Priscilla, he will have to tell Vivian, and that will make him feel very very bad. And if he does it and says nothing, he will feel equally bad.

So he said to Priscilla, in between kisses—her hair, her skin, smelled, impossibly, like lilacs; it made him crazy—We can't do this, and she said, We can keep on doing *this,* can't we? meaning kissing and kissing only, and he thought, Well, why not?

So they lay on the dock and kissed, but when she began to slide her hands under his clothes, and when he began kissing her neck arms breasts—when he felt himself begin to lose it—he stopped. He flopped away from her, took deep breaths.

She said, You think too much, and he said, The truth of it is, I don't think enough.

But they went back to it a little longer, and once she murmured, It certainly does feel natural after all this time, and he said, It certainly does, and she said again, Well? pulled back to look at him, hair falling to one side, shoulder sharp in the light, and he just shook his head.

Suit yourself, she said, but this could be your last chance. Which he thought was unfair. Hard enough to be denying himself the pleasure of a night with her, without the added reminder of the general precariousness of her health.

She said, I decided when I found out I was sick to go after what I wanted—for obvious reasons—and that has always included you. You are high up on the list. She pointed a finger at him: I want *you,* she said, like the poster, finger pointed dead at him.

And he said, You've got me, you've got me, you have *always* had me.

And she said, Yes, but I want you now, and he said, finally, just no.

And that was when he realized there'd be no end to it, no solution; even when she was dead there would be no end to it: a body could sit around wasting his life away, wondering how it might have been, what he had missed.

And all *that* meant was that he simply had to say no now and live with it. Simple enough, but he wasn't used to living life this way, and it seemed to be requiring, at this moment, a ridiculous dredging up of all the willpower he could muster.

I will think about you, he said to her, for days, weeks probably, but after that I'll be OK, I'll be fine, and so will you—at which point she let out a little snort of disdain—and who knows? he said, maybe things will be different someday. Maybe I'll come back.

And she said, Things are always different.

The last thing he remembered saying as they lay there watching stars shine and fade—James's flute was silent now—the last thing he said when they both knew she would not get what she wanted just then, and neither, necessarily, would he, was, It feels good to be lying here next to you, holding you, and she said, Don't it though. Which had sounded to Ray like something a one-eyed cowpoke would say sitting in a saloon, pretty gal on his knee, glass in hand, after a gritty day in the saddle. And he murmured, kissing her shapely white ear, Of all my friends, you are the dearest, and she said, Is that so?

■ ≡ ■

The sun, already hot, is punching through the leaves of the trees surrounding the pond. In a far corner, a kingfisher stands,

erect and wary, watchful of the man on the dock and the occasional careless bass. Here and there fish rise; a frog harumphs.
Ray stretches and moves to where a patch of sunlight warms the
dock. The sun feels strong and soothing, though he knows it won't
be long before they are all running for shelter, wild for shade,
insane with the heat. He thinks he hears the clank of a pan—
James up and about, throwing together a little morning chow for
the troops. He thinks he hears a child laugh, someone singing.
He thinks of Priscilla and all they did and gets up suddenly,
invigorated and a little confused, and dives neatly into the pond.

He gasps sharply as he hits water. It is much cooler than he
had imagined, and for a moment he thinks he might sink after
all, that his heart might not recover—for all his thoughtful
logic—from the shock. But in the next moment he is moving
toward the dam, swinging his arms in and out of the New
England water, a little erratically, until he hits his stride. He is
feeling like a strongman, a muscle man, the greatest man on
earth. He touches the dam, makes a modified flip, swims back
to the dock. His arms slap out her name—*Vi*-vi-an, *Vi*-vi-an,
Vi-vi-an—but it is Priscilla's slimness he feels as he roars back
to the dock.

And then, in a flash, as he is about to touch the dock, he sees
her dead, sees Priscilla floating serenely just beyond him—ro-
mantic mythological painting—hair spread out, fine filaments
floating about her, beatific smile. Peaceful but most definitely not
alive. And again he almost dies himself, almost sinks from life,
feels himself choking, but somehow he makes it to the dock, hauls
himself out. And when he looks back, there is nothing there that
wasn't there before, and he flops down on his stomach, exhausted
by the physical exertion and the fractured night.

And he knows now it is time to go home. If he could, he
would instantly transport himself there, beam himself back, let
Priscilla be. There is nothing more for them to say or do. She
has James, music, children—all their comfort. And he has, as
much as anyone can have anyone, Vivian.

His breathing, still slightly knotty, steadies, and now he can see Vivian, bright and alive, child moving inside her, behind his closed eyes. He sees her welcoming him with outstretched arms. He will have to drive his pickup carefully and reasonably back to Virginia, keep within the law. He wants to make it back in one piece. He feels ridiculously impatient, but he will use the hundreds of miles between them to shake off any lingering traces of his full and ofttimes lamentable past. And he sees himself, as he stares behind his eyes, finally finally reaching the end of the line, holding her, walking with Vivian in fields near the house, asking her to receive him this one last time in all his faith and faulty glory.

■ ≡ ■

A sign is nailed to the fence post at the front gate: YOU HAVE REACHED THE END OF THE LINE. Ray wonders if Bullet, too, has heard the catchy song, but he has little time to think, because before he is even out of the truck, Bullet is standing in the front yard with arms outstretched, glass of Old Crow in each hand.

"Welcome, old friend!" he bellows to the sky. "Welcome to the last frontier! Everybody's out looking, God bless 'em, but it's right here under their very nose!" He tips his head back when he yells, wags it to and fro as if he has no sense whatsoever of balance or space or plain old normal behavior. He looks like a blind man, Ray thinks, but he can't help laughing. Bullet's dogs, curs really, sniff at Ray and the truck.

Ray walks down the path, stops in front of Bullet, says, "Hey, old friend, how's it going?" and they lock in a crushing embrace. Old Crow sloshes out of the glasses onto the back of Ray's shirt, but in all this heat, it feels good—instant cool. In fact, Ray just now would rather soak in the stuff than drink it. And suddenly he's thinking how he could have stood, for just a little longer, the dull-eyed monotony of the road. Once he started in with Bullet, there was no turning back. His only hope was Peg, who, according to Bullet's last report, was back and happily ensconced with the kids. He wouldn't have stopped—he was anxious to get back to Vivian—but the truck was acting up a little, probably needed a tune-up, and it was easy enough to get back to Charlottesville (with a brief detour to Suitland for Darryl) in half a day from this part of Maryland. Besides, at least with Bullet the craziness was familiar.

They walk down the worn path and into the house, leaving the dogs at the door. The old farmhouse is made of chestnut logs, faded yellow clapboard outside, tin roof. The furniture is worn and mismatched—Goodwill relics, all once fine, same as Ray's stuff. They stop in the kitchen, where an old wood cookstove, stacked with dirty plates and pans, takes up most of one wall. Potatoes and turnips sit in the sink, dried red Maryland clay still caked on. The men pause a moment, looking blankly at the vegetables, then Bullet dumps more bourbon into Ray's glass, and while he's fixing his own, Ray says, "How's Peg?" He is very hungry, has eaten only sardines and crackers since morning. All day he has been looking forward to Peg's wondrous cooking.

"Peg's gone." Bullet keeps pouring.

Not again, Ray thinks, but he says, hoping "gone" means she's in town, "But she'll be back." It's a statement rather than a question.

"You tell me. Took the kids and the car and the family silver and just left one morning after breakfast. Next thing I know, she's calling from goddamn Tuscaloosa, wanting money."

"Tuscaloosa?"

"Her folks live down there." Bullet is leaning over, squinting out a small window at the back field. The sun has set, and the kitchen seems to darken instantly. Ray imagines the settlers who built the place poking guns out the few small window openings at dusk, fending off wild Indians, hungry wolves, and invading armies, strong brave wives handing men ammo, occasionally taking shots themselves, reassuring whimpering children.

"I lose my wife and kids, and the goddamn buffalo, all in one week," Bullet says dreamily.

"Buffalo?"

Ray feels giddy and slightly ill, though it's too soon liquorwise. Probably the heat. If he'd been paying attention, he would have noticed how pointlessly large and still the house seemed as they wandered through. Evidence of the missing family is everywhere: Peg's hairpins, dusty on the dresser, rock stars staring mutely from the walls of the tiny bedroom under the eaves, small mud-caked shoes lined up inside the back door. It was no place for just one man. Or a man and his oldest friend. Or a man with ten friends, for that matter. Ray should have been prepared for anything as far as Peg was concerned, he is thinking. But about these buffalo. . . .

"Bought me a herd a week ago, six females and a bull. Some old coot the other side of the mountain raised them. You don't have to live in goddamn Wyoming to have buffalo. Christ, who'd want to live there, anyhow? Look at their winters." Bullet shivers and looks over his shoulder at Ray.

"Huh," says Ray.

"Thing about the buffalo is, they keep taking off, escaping and marauding and doing whatever they damn well please, trompling everybody's corn and potato crops. And they keep ending up at this old man's place. Course the old coot just loves that, especially considering how much he charged me for them." Bullet fills his glass, then motions to the back door. "They live *here,*" he says, pointing to the dirt outside the back porch. Ray looks where Bullet points, sees nothing.

Bullet bangs out the screen door, jumps the side porch railing; he leads Ray to the edge of the back field. The field slopes down to a stream and, beyond the stream, eases back up to where woods begin. It is hillier and more rocky than Ray's land, but flatter than the land he's just left. The field is empty; the grass is high and dry. It looks unused, neglected and forlorn, and in the late light is fading fast.

Bullet waves his hand toward the field, magicianlike. "This is where they live," he says. "This is where they graze. And that"—he points to the middle of the field—"is where the gazebo's gonna go."

"Gazebo?"

"All my life I've wanted to sit in a goddamn gazebo watching my goddamn herd of buffalo."

First Ray's heard of the lifelong dream. "You got enough land to keep them?" he asks. If he remembers right, Bullet has about twenty-five acres, mostly wooded. When he thinks of buffalo, which isn't often, Ray envisions them roaming the plains, covering the prairies in great brown streams.

"You think I didn't check that out?" Bullet looks pained. "They just need to stick around is all. They got minds of their own." He tips his glass, swallows what's left, puts the glass on top of the nearest fence post. "You'd think all this wire'd keep 'em in." Bullet pushes his palms against the wire as if testing its strength, but not, Ray notes, hard enough to cut himself—a good sign. "They need to learn to love the hand that feeds them." He holds his hand up, and Ray can barely discern the small indentations dotting his palm.

It is darker now. The whippoorwills are starting up. Somewhere in the woods a screech owl calls. Ray is feeling fuzzy and weary; he has a hard time imagining any gazebo anywhere. Bullet puts an arm around him and takes him back to the house. "They're the legacy, see. A herd of buffalo for my kids to mess with. That and my lousy teeth." They both smile at that, though there are no buffalo for miles, and not a kid in sight.

■ ≡ ■

Ray isn't really surprised Peg is gone, but he is sorry. He has always liked her. She put up with Bullet, which should have earned her a Purple Heart and a peaceful life. She must love him, Ray had always figured, or she would have left him for good years ago. The only time Ray ever saw her angry at Bullet— though he imagined plenty must have transpired between them in private—was when he mistreated his dogs. Bullet had always had dogs, like every other friend of Ray's, and he would take his dogs with him, early on, to bars and parties and road trips, like everyone else. But the difference was that Bullet's dogs—until Peg took over—were always on their own, fed (usually) but spiritually orphaned. They all had names like Tank or Bear or Dog or Sam, though there were occasional lapses like Jimmy, Cajun. They were all big and had that hungry look to them. Ray didn't quite trust any of them, just as he didn't quite—across the board—trust their master. From a dog's point of view, it must have looked pretty discouraging. Imagine finding yourself in Bullet's care.

Peg kept Bullet in line with the dogs, with all animals, as best she could. Ray remembers one particular night when a bunch of friends were sitting around the woodstove—so it must have been winter, Ray thinks—shooting the shit, and someone told the story about a drunken Bullet biting off the head of a newborn kitten, crunching and chewing and gulping it down with relish. There had been several witnesses, equally drunk, though no one could quite remember who. Similarly, the retelling was a little drunken. Peg was sitting there, and when she heard that, she stood up right in front of her husband and demanded the truth. "This was before your time, darlin'," Bullet said, "when I was young and crazy." "But did you do it?" she wanted to know. And for some reason, either he didn't think she meant it, or he couldn't bring himself to tell the truth one way or the other, or maybe he just could not remember, but he wouldn't answer her, kept cracking jokes and talking about how great it tasted. But he gauged her wrong, and she gave him a murderous look and left the room and wouldn't speak to anyone the rest of the weekend. Ray knew there was always the remotest possibility that Bullet had actually done this horrifying thing, but still, it was easy for such stories to circulate: people loved having someone on whom they could foist all the atrocities and fantasies they themselves hadn't the nerve or stomach, the depravity, perversity, or imagination, to commit. Bullet probably never touched the kitten, but he certainly kept other people's lives in check.

So Peg put up with Bullet, but as Vivian had warned Ray,

sometimes love wasn't enough. Many nights Ray and Peg had sat in the kitchen at the scarred oak table long after Bullet had crashed—or when he was off somewhere—talking of nothing in particular, or maybe discussing the kids, or the garden. Or what Ray was up to, which was usually struggling with some house he was building that was way over budget and far from being finished. In a way quite different from Charlene with her barbecue, Peg came close to being the perfect woman in the flamingo blouse. (Vivian would give him such shit if she knew about this dream woman. So go marry your mother, she'd say.)

Sometimes Ray thought—pre-Vivian—that if it weren't for Bullet, he could love Peg, could ease right into his friend's place, be her man.

He tried to talk to her that icy weekend. He caught her in the kitchen and told her what a good job he thought she did with his old friend Bullet, he was such an asshole sometimes, how did she stand it? He bashed on, in what he intended to be a light mode, designed primarily to make her laugh. That was what he liked about her, he said: she had so much more sense than almost anyone he knew, certainly than all their friends and acquaintances. Then he told her that Bullet was a lucky man, and in case no one ever got around to letting her know, all his other friends thought so too.

Peg had stopped whatever it was she was doing—she was always working at something. He remembered she was at the sink, wet hands, and she turned and looked at him with such hatred that he thought she must have misunderstood, and he was about to repeat what he'd said, but he was instantly confused and was unable to do so before she said, "You bastards," and for an awful moment he thought she might cry, and now he was afraid of her and wondered how he could ever have thought of living with her. "You bastards."

Next morning she was easy as ever, though still unusually silent, but he had never understood what had gone wrong that night, and he was sorry he did not, but he wasn't about to ask her to explain. He had meant it as a compliment; he had thought she would be pleased; he had thought she would agree. He was just being honest.

He stands in the field with Bullet, head swimming from whiskey and the miles he's driven, and he thinks about Peg and wishes she were there to hear about Vivian and the baby and how he perceived their future.

■ ≡ ■

After a huge dinner of fried turnips and sausage and potatoes and onions (produced with surprising flair and speed by Bullet), the men sit in the kitchen listening to the radio. Following leads from the sheriff's office and frequent radio reports, Bullet has been able to track the herd. Track them but not catch them.

"Goddamn DJ's having a ball," says Bullet.

"And for the latest buffalo report. A lone bull was seen early this morning by a passing motorist wandering along old Route 616. Headed east, a few stragglers in tow. Man said he had to swerve to miss them so as not to total his week-old Toyota. Said the Toyota responded well."

"Thank you, Paul Harvey," says Bullet.

"Also a Mrs. Shifflet of Thelma just called in to say she thinks she sees buffalo at this very moment on the ridge back of her place. Could be your regular cattle, she says, could be bison. Not that she's ever seen bison, mind you. Says they're moving slow and look too big for beef."

"Jesus H. Christ," says Bullet.

The DJ says he'll keep them posted.

Ray laughs. He thinks he might be on the edge of delirium; he should have driven straight through to Virginia.

"The females follow the bull anywhere, just like a bunch of goddamn sheep," Bullet says while they wait for some young singer they never heard of to finish wailing out his brief lifetime of grievances. "The bull goes off the cliff, they all go."

"Sounds like something a bunch of women would do," Ray says stupidly, just to say it. He should get up, leave the kitchen, stumble up to bed.

"An ad for Michelin radials (in anticipation of winter, folks), an interview with the school superintendent about putting air-conditioning in the high school auditorium—kids can't play their instruments, slip right out of their hands, it's so hot. Speaking of which: more of the same, hot and humid, find yourself a pond, people, or a cold tub, plug in those fans, rev up that AC, don't go jogging anytime soon, we are under siege, *yes indeed."*

The DJ plays a few more songs, and then he loads the airwaves with buffalo anecdotes, buffalo jokes, buffalo lore, buffalo trivia, and Ray says, "Must be pretty dull around the old studio," but Bullet's face is tightening up like a huge strained muscle turning in on itself, and now Ray is the one cracking the bottle, doing the pouring, keeping their glasses filled. Maybe he can knock Bullet out with the whiskey before anything comes of all this.

"And now for all you buffalo fans and East Coast cowpokes, all you easy riders, all you Jack Nicholsons and Peter Fondas, all you Rawhides out there, this one's for you. We know you're out there, you know we love you."

Gene Autry rolls his song out, smooth as butter, "Oh, give me a home," and suddenly Bullet is up, chair knocked back, clattering to the floor. And he says to Ray, "First thing in the morning, we bring those fuckers home," and he bangs out of the kitchen and up to his empty room.

Ray lets Gene finish, even listens to a remake of "Shuffle Off to Buffalo" by some hot new group out of Chicago, and then, though his eyes burn and his body begs for bed, he sits on the back porch with Bullet's rangy dogs, playing the old guitar to an empty field and the moon and the thin white-edged clouds that scatter across the night sky like some ghostly herd.

■ ≡ ■

In the middle of his dream, Ray thinks he hears a telephone ring, and he stirs, meaning to answer, but then he hears someone stumping down the stairs to take care of it—Bullet?—and so he lets it go, drifts back to where he was. But the dream is lost, replaced by light, fitful dozing through which he hears vague shouts, muffled cursing, Peg's name, not enough noise to wake him fully but just enough to make him wish, when he sees Bullet leaning over him the next morning, shaking him, that he had the day—or at least the next few hours—to give over to deep sleep.

■ ≡ ■

They are bringing the buffalo home.

They started out in the eastern part of the county, but now are headed clear across to the other side. They have listened for half an hour to an elderly lady describe how she watched helplessly as the buffalo ruined her English box, trampled her azaleas. They even chewed up clothes freshly hung on the line.

"There ought to be a law," the lady had said, trembling with rage. "There ought to be a law."

There was a law, but no real proof. Bullet listened, then gave the lady a hundred dollars to help with the replanting. All the time she was talking, his eyes darted over the hills behind her place, searching for his lost children. Ray had stood silently by, feeling bad for all of them.

They stop at a country store to buy some beer and barbecue (nowhere near as good as Papa Stumpy's, Ray notes), and check in with the sheriff for an update. They make another brief stop where they hear the buffalo have made a recent appearance, but again they miss them. Each time, though, the path is more recently trod, the evidence bolder. And in each place, based on stories and the physical evidence, the buffalo seem to stay longer. They flatten corners of pastures where they bed down for hours; they settle for picked-over timothy just to be near, it seems, a bunch of lazy milk cows. They seem reluctant to move on, weary from wandering. It is as if they, as much as anyone, wish for the journey to end, yearn for a place to stop and rest their bones.

Now it is late afternoon, and the men are hot and hungry and tired; they have missed the buffalo by halves of days, by hours, minutes. They are drinking Black Label, which, though it's cool going down, eventually seems to heat their bodies just short of the boiling point.

"You sure these buffalo actually exist?" Ray says. They are on their way to the estate of a famous English rock star, who had called the sheriff's office to report a sighting. Ray is think-ing it is time to push on, get back to Vivian and his life; the buffalo seem impossible to capture and keep, as elusive as perfect health.

"We're hot on it this time, Ray," says Bullet, gunning it. He is wearing an old straw hat, which he occasionally takes off to wipe the sweat from his temples. It looks like a hat you might buy on a quick trip to the Bahamas—built-in green visor—but Bullet told Ray he could get one just like it at the country store where they bought the 'cue. When he blots the moisture from his brow, the red rim left by the hat looks like the result of some medieval torture machine made specifically to squeeze the cranium, oust the brains, clear the decks once and for all.

"Can't be too much longer," he says. They pull off the highway onto a long, straight, cedar-lined drive. "Looks like the shaggy fellas showed a little taste this time," Bullet says. He points to the ornate wrought-iron gate and gateposts. He is driving way too fast. The road seems to go on for miles, but because it is smooth, there is little possibility for accident. In the back of the Jeep, rope and the jumble of farm tools, scraps of wood and odd bits of chain, rattle and clatter. A day of driving all over the county with that backseat din and Bullet's manic chatter, plus the annoyance and genuine pain of being regularly knocked in the head by the butt of Bullet's old 30.06 resting in the gunrack behind them—to say nothing of the extraordinarily life-sapping heat—has saddled Ray with a colossal headache and the profound wish to be anywhere but there.

They are nearing the end of the drive, which now winds into a circle before a huge stone mansion. As he wheels around the corner, Bullet turns from the waist to face Ray, who wishes he'd stick to the simple business of watching the road. "All my life," Bullet says slowly, "*all my life* I've wanted to sit in a gazebo and watch a herd of buffalo—*my* buffalo—grazing. When I was a kid, I saw this movie where some woman murdered her husband and buried him right under the gazebo in the backyard. I didn't even know what a gazebo was, but right off I loved the sound of the word, you know?"

As a matter of fact, Ray did know what Bullet meant.

"This gazebo was stuck off behind the house, beautiful and remote—a little like a carousel—and this woman and the officers investigating the murder drink a lot of lemonade and gin and tonics out there in the gazebo, and they talk about the suspects, and the weather, but no one *ever* suspects *her*. Or the gazebo."

He glances at the mansion, stops the Jeep with a jerk. Ray is thinking Bullet has never waxed so poetical, and he is briefly and unexpectedly moved.

"As for the buffalo, what's to explain? Grandest creatures on earth, barring dinosaurs. But I landed on earth a couple million years too late for that one." He pauses. "Hence the power of the search," he adds. "I just want to bring them home. That's not asking too much, is it?"

"Hell no," Ray says right off. It's just simply well-nigh impossible. "We'll bring 'em home for you."

But Bullet is looking at Ray as if he's being difficult. "I mean, what else on God's green earth is there?" he asks, and bangs his shoulder against the Jeep door, which has a tendency to stick. Third try the door gives, and Bullet is halfway to the house before Ray's even found his door handle.

The windows of the house are wide open, and they can hear music. It stops and starts, seems to repeat itself. Ray hears drums—congas?—a horn, the twang and snarl of electric guitars. Someone sings something, stops, tries it again. Someone laughs, and the music stops. For once, no clutch of dogs runs to jump at them.

There are cars, though, a pack of them in one curve of the driveway and a gray stretch limo the size of a small yacht sprawled in another curve. Also several parrots or cockatoos and macaws, hanging in huge intricately woven cages all over the wide, white-columned veranda. At the back of the house is a bus painted purple, script scrawled across it in green: *Inky Black et al.* Huge trees dot the lawn, some so big four men couldn't circle them with arms joined. Pastures and fences stretch from the house way back to soft, worn mountains rising gently in the distance, the same ones that miles away touch Bullet's land. In the fields between, clumps of Queen Anne's lace and chicory make the drying land look like a fresh spring sky—hours and acres of clear blue and white. An assortment of outbuildings and sheds flank the main house. At any moment, Ray thinks, the field hands will appear, hot and tired—and resigned—hauling great loads of tobacco or cotton, moving slowly, moaning their mournful song. And he thinks, *This* is the place for a gazebo, this is the place for the herd.

The music inside the house is not mournful.

"What we got here?" says Bullet—as if he's on a reconnaissance mission is what springs to Ray's mind instantly. "Just what have we got here?" He steps onto the porch. "Bunch of punks is what we got."

"We got the great Inky Black," Rays says. "You've heard of him. Been around for years."

"Can't say I've had the pleasure," says Bullet, just as Inky Black himself, in cutoffs and a T-shirt that says MAKE MY DAY, strolls out onto the wide porch to meet them.

The birds squawk and flap. Inky Black shushes them, pokes at them gently through the bars of their cages. "I'd love to let you out," he says to a gigantic macaw, "but this is Maryland, not the bloody equator. You wouldn't make it past route 616."

Bullet is studying the macaw.

"You the buffalo man?" Inky Black asks Ray.

"I am," Bullet says, extending his hand.

■ ≡ ■

When he first saw them, Inky Black says, he thought he was hallucinating. He's seen stranger things in his time, mind, much much stranger things, but when he opened the front door and saw these buffalo spread out all over his lawn like living sculpture (his words)—moving boulders—he remembered where he was, in America, land of opportunity, frontier land, and he knew anything was possible.

"Beautiful creatures," he breathes to the men, and Ray can feel Bullet bristle at having someone other than himself, rightful owner of said herd, elevated by the sight of the bison. It is as if he, Bullet, has been cruelly cheated, as if, perhaps, Inky Black has stolen the animals, hidden them off behind one of those picturesque outbuildings for his own personal use and pleasure. Might trot them out one night during the tour, middle of the second set, exploit them, make fools of them—all those gaping faces. *Ladies and gentlemen! I give you . . . the* amazing . . . buffalo!

"Beautiful amazing creatures." Inky Black is leaning against one of the white columns. "So. I'm watching them, you know? and the lead bull—"

"Only one bull," says Bullet.

"OK," says Inky Black slowly, carefully, waiting to see if this man with the cheap straw hat has more to say. "The *only* bull, the big daddy, steps up onto the porch, right about where you're standing"—he points to Bullet—"and the floorboards are cracking and breaking, and the whole fucking house seems to be swaying, and I'm standing at the door *watching* all this and I'm enchanted, dead enchanted—I am *transfixed*." He pauses, chucks the macaw under the chin. "And we just stand there, this buffalo and I, looking at each other. Finally I tell Jacky to get the sugar cubes from the kitchen, which he does, and then"—Inky Black stretches out his hand to demonstrate, holds his guitar-worn fingers out to Bullet, tattoos all up the arm—"*then*"—he takes a few small steps in their direction—"just like this, I offer this buffalo the sugar, and he looks at me awhile, just checking me out."

Inky smooths his hair with his other hand, remembering. The birds are absolutely silent. "And he *takes* the sugar, eats it incredibly daintily" (Thought he was going to show us that too, Bullet says later), "and then I give him another, and another, till the whole goddamn box is gone. It was beautiful, man. Made me want to go out immediately and become a U.S. citizen, for some reason." He pauses again, lets the arm drop. "And then, when the box is empty, he moves off, but—and you will not fucking *believe* this—before he goes off the porch, he walks up to the door and puts this enormous shaggy head of his into the hall there, and he just stands. Checks out the chandelier and all the stuff on the walls." Ray sees through the door portraits and coats of arms and Moroccan Arab strips hanging there, wonders how it looked to that bull. Simply a maze of shapes, dark and light? Or did he imagine this might be a place he'd want to take up residence? Breakfast in bed, tea and scones in the afternoon. "And then," says Inky Black, resuming, "he retreats, turns, and ambles off, just eases away, and the rest of them watch him a moment, then they follow, move out en masse—there seems to be this telepathy thing going on—and I watch them go off into the woods, and on up into the mountains, and I am just *moved*." Inky Black shakes his head, looks down at his busted porch. "Poetry," he says. "Thought I was beyond all that."

A microscopic breeze ripples his hair as they gaze back at the mountains. Inside the house, the music starts up. Sounds like tomtoms, war chants. Someone wails plaintively. Inky Black laughs briefly to himself, through his nose, snorts really, says, "Only in America," and Ray makes a mental note to be sure to buy the next album. In fact, he thinks fleetingly of asking if he can do a guest shot sometime during the upcoming tour. Bullet's dream might be to have a gazebo surrounded by grazing buffalo, but Ray's was—had been ever since he had pretended his old tennis racket was a Gibson and had aped Elvis—to be a rock-and-roll star.

Bullet has tromped down the steps and is headed for the Jeep. "They've gone back to the old man's place," he says over his shoulder. "He lives just the other side of the mountain. We can make it there before dark."

"He's real anxious to recover the herd, in case you hadn't noticed," Ray says, thinking something needs to be said. He would at least have thanked Inky Black for not shooting the buffalo, say, or kidnapping them, but Bullet is in the Jeep now, revving it.

"I don't blame him," says Inky Black. "Truly majestic creatures. . . ." He walks to the edge of the porch, calls out good luck to Bullet, who nods in answer as he pulls the Jeep up for Ray so fast that Ray wonders if he'll be forced to leap at it, stuntman style, as it rolls by. But Bullet pauses just long enough for him to get the door open and hop in without losing or breaking a limb, and they roar off down the driveway, Ray praying nothing is coming the other way. At this point, and with a glance at Bullet's stricken face, he couldn't guarantee that they would actually stop for anything or anyone—not at a railroad crossing for a passing train, not for an innocent pedestrian on a crosswalk, not for a stray hound, crazy with running for the scent and heedless of everything but that.

■ ≡ ■

They reach the old man's place half an hour later. When Ray suggests that they stop on the way for some beer, Bullet doesn't slow down, acts as if he's not heard. They don't talk much. Heat seems to be pouring out from the Jeep's heater onto the men's legs—Ray even puts his hand down there, swears he can feel it.

Once, over the clatter, Bullet yells, "Peg called last night."

Ray has had to rest his hand on the stock of the 30.06 to keep it from knocking him senseless. Every now and then his head grazes the flimsy canvas top of the Jeep as they bang down hard on the pitted country roads.

"Where is she?"

"Still in goddamn Tuscaloosa, steam bath of the world. She says she needs my goddamn social security number, needs it for some forms she's filling in, to get some money or for some damn reason. And I tell her, Look, if you haven't committed that number to memory by now, then it's too goddamn bad, but then she starts crying, poor girl, twangs at my heartstrings"—he drawls this on out, as if he's Hank Williams, Jr.—"she breaks down long-distance, and so I take pity on her and I give it to her."

"She coming back anytime soon?"

"Didn't say."

"Peg's a good woman," says Ray.

"No need to tell me *that,*" says Bullet in disgust. Then he looks at Ray, who wishes yet again that he'd keep his eyes and attention on the job at hand, and he says, "She always did like you."

And now his expression makes Ray feel instantly and irrationally uncomfortable, and so Ray says, "Oh, come on," but Bullet's face is set again on the road, so he adds, "Peg's a wonderful woman."

"Yep, she's a wonderful woman, all right. Deserts her husband, carries off his children, breaks up my happy home. Shit, the buffalo were for her as much as anyone." They slow down, but just barely, to maneuver the turn onto the old man's deeply rutted road. Bullet turns so sharply Ray is practically thrown from the Jeep.

And now talk is impossible. Ray glances at Bullet, sees him buck and bounce. His body aches from being folded into the Jeep for so long, his head and insides feel as if they are stuffed with ninepenny nails. He looks at Bullet and sees them back in Nam, back in a Jeep in the jungle, can't help himself, they are searching the flickering foliage on either side of what passes for a road, straining to see into its green and dark shadows, searching for gooks. Ray strains now, on this old man's road, to detect things in the shadows that can't possibly be there. He remembers looking so hard for the enemy back then that after a while he couldn't trust himself to see—or dodge—anything, not one goddamn thing. It's OK, he says to himself, jerking his head back to look straight ahead. You're safe, this is Maryland, this is the U.S. of A. You are in love with Vivian, you will be a father soon, it's your dear friend here who is crazy. And now he sees split-rail fences dart past, jumping and jangled, and he sees the brown trunks of trees, bland sides of grazing cattle, a pinkish flat sky beginning to give itself over to night.

All we are doing is bringing the buffalo home.

Beside him, Bullet, grimly silent, is leaning slightly forward. His shirt is drenched, sweat glistens on his face. He looks, Ray thinks, like the figurehead at the prow of some weathered schooner, blind eyes gazing tirelessly and steadily and brightly forward, out to sea, heedless and helpless of everything but their destination.

They reach the end of the road, they practically land, as if formerly airborne, and suddenly it is very still. Weathered gray outbuildings, junked cars, bits of machinery, pieces of unidentifiable scrap metal, and lumber clutter the small clearing where they've stopped the Jeep, but there is an order to this landscape. It is clear that the old man need only walk a few feet to find whatever it is he requires to repair a particular piece of broken equipment, furniture, some defective part of his life. He seems to have little use, based on this functional ornamentation, for the world beyond, which Ray appreciates, that being for years— incongruously coupled with the rock-and-roll dream—one of his lifelong goals. These days, though, Ray wonders about that perfect insularity—helpful if the A-bomb dropped but a tad deficient when it came to general living and the human heart. Perhaps he is swinging too far from where he's been, still off track. Undoubtedly the old man would outfox and outlive them all; he had things figured out here at the end of his lousy driveway. Ray sees a barn sitting near an old log cabin; pigeons roost along gaps in its sides. He imagines its cool insides, the dusty hay smell.

Bullet is halfway out the door when Ray puts a hand on his arm. "Have you thought that the buffalo might not ever come home?" he asks. "Have you thought of getting your money back and just leaving them here? Could make life a lot easier. Cheaper too."

Bullet looks at Ray as if he has just suggested shooting his own mother. "Not a chance," he says. He looks down at where Ray holds on to his arm, looks at Ray's hand as if it were diseased, says, "I thought you were with me on this."

Ray doesn't recall ever being asked where he stood. "I'm just saying this might not be the end of it, you know? This could go on and on, ad infinitum." He loosens his grasp. "You're not as young as you were," he says, trying to lighten up.

"It ain't going on and on, hoss," says Bullet. "This is the end of it right here, right in this very spot." He jabs a finger at the ground. "This is it," he says.

They hear a door slam, and Ray sees an old man in overalls watching them from the front stoop. Ray sighs, opens the door.

"The guardian of my children." Bullet jerks a thumb at the old man. "Jesus Christ. Last time he almost wouldn't let me take them back."

The old man looks angry, is already yelling something at them Ray can't quite decipher. Bullet starts down the dirt path to the house; Ray begins to follow, but Bullet stops, says, "I'll take care of this."

"No," says Ray. "Come on." He pushes past Bullet, who grasps his arm.

"Look, McCreary, your heart ain't in it, which is OK, but I don't need someone else to fight with about this. That one old man is enough. Go check out the barn. It is a thing of beauty, all mortise and tenon, not a nail in it." Bullet's voice is almost friendly now, companionable. "Go cool out," he says.

"I just think you gotta think about the alternatives," says Ray.

"It's too late now," says Bullet. "I'll call if I need you." He begins walking again toward the cabin. "I'm coming, old man," he yells. "Deaf as a doornail." This to Ray, over his shoulder. Ray watches the two men walk down to the cabin, then disappear behind it. Through the trees, clumped into a small corral, Ray sees the herd. They look resigned; they hardly move. He hears the bull bellow as he walks to the solace of the barn, a magnificent sound—that Inky Black would relish.

Inside, it is cool, as he had imagined. Bullet was right; the joinery is clean and uncomplicated, more than adequate. Built to last. He sits for a while, watching what little evening light is left mark the dusty floor in fine stenciled designs, then he climbs a ladder to the loft, where he lies down on the hay and drifts into a light sleep.

And he dreams: about some crazy musician dressed up as an Indian who sneaks up on a buffalo and kills him before Ray can scream out a warning, and after the show they are sitting in Naugahyde armchairs in the musician's motel room, drinking spring water from Dixie cups, and Ray is sweating as if he's being interrogated, which he isn't. And Vivian is saying something about how the concert reminded her of Beethoven's Ninth but without the snow, and the Indian-musician is saying to Ray, curiously and kindly, Evidently it was all quite real to you, and Ray, peering cautiously over the edge of his cup, says, Evidently. And outside, he and Vivian push through a small group of Iroquois from upstate New York, who try to whack them with placards protesting, in lurid colors and prose, the band's representation of Indians as cruel, bloodthirsty savages.

Ray doesn't know how long he sleeps, but he is awakened by shouts, bangs, screams, and he jumps up, terrified—because of the dream?—and cracks his head on a beam, curses. And it is as if the dream, whatever it was, was vivid, hard-edged, and this life he wakes up to is blurred and painful, and utterly alien. He hears more explosions—thunder? fireworks?—and then he hears the bellowing again, anguished cries, and he gets up, stumbles to the barn wall, puts his eye to one of its many chinks, and he sees, cannot believe he sees, Bullet, his closest friend, braced against the corral fence, firing over and over into his beloved herd, the old man frantic, screaming, jumping on him, clawing at him, a monkey on his back.

Bullet easily tosses him off. The herd is thundering from one side of the pen to the other, crashing into whatever is in front of it, crashing into bullets, falling in on itself, folding up. Killing itself, Ray thinks wildly, and now he is halfway down the ladder, falls the rest of the way, runs to the men and animals, screaming himself, running faster than he has ever, his strides immense— he seems to cover miles in seconds, but the distance lessens agonizingly slowly. His hair, wet from the heat, pulls back from his face, stretches it tight as he runs, flattens his features, and he falls, darts back up, runs to the carnage, but there is less and less activity, less life, the brown waves are tiring, smoothing, and by the time he gets there, it is done, it is too late, they are all gone, they are all Bullet's now, and why is he always always always late?

III

PIG ROAST

In the cool October night, a hog is being hoisted out of the back of Ray McCreary's pickup and eased onto a waiting plywood pallet as if about to undergo open-heart surgery: cleaned, hairless, resigned; one hundred eighty pounds dressed. Beyond the pallet where the fire glows hot and red, a steel spit shines. The moon is three-quarters full, and they can see the smooth pale skin, as pink as a baby's but not near so cute, the body a little long, too lean. Behind them, the schoolhouse looms silver and spooky at the edge of night. Someone tries to wedge an apple into the hog's mouth, but the jaw is tight. Lockjaw, someone says, laughing. Tight-lipped, ain't he? Not *about* to squeal. Someone else tries; no luck. The jaw won't budge. The people ring the hog uncertainly, momentarily disconcerted by the stubborn jaw and the open eyes that stare, stupefied, as if caught in the middle of some unspeakable act. They might as well be paying last respects to a dead distant relative before haggling over who gets what of the estate, because in the next moment, with knives and gusto, they will be cutting into that hog's hide, poking garlic slivers into each crack for flavor and fun. They have been peeling garlic for hours around the fire, and their fingers sting from the reeking juice. No problem with vampires, someone says.

This little piggy went to market, says Ray, as he sharpens his Swiss Army knife. He keeps time with the rhyme, whooshing hum of steel on stone the perfect percussion. He goes on with the rhyme, his voice rising at the end of each line like a child's, or as if he were speaking a foreign language, where the inflections were different, gentler. French, maybe? a language with which he is totally unfamiliar. He doesn't know why he should be chanting such nonsense in front of a dead hog in the middle of the night, but one thing is certain—strange thoughts bordering on panic have been occurring to him frequently these days, probably, he reasons, because of impending fatherhood and the newness of marriage, just twenty-four hours old. The occasional panic that strikes him when he stops to think about what all this entails drives him to the liquor supply, or the dope stash, or his medicine cabinet in search of painkillers of any sort. But always, too, these days, he stops short, stays his hand, wanting to keep his system free of obstructions. Above all, he wants to think clearly from here on out, wants everything in good working order, no snags.

Of course, there were exceptions, and fair enough. His wedding day, for instance, and this pig roast, celebrating everything decent and worthwhile: the signing of a new building contract, his return from the north, his marriage to Vivian, fatherhood. Fatherhood! Who would have thought! How on earth would he come up with the one hundred K, or whatever it was, it took to raise a child to age eighteen in America today? How would he raise this child, steer him/her through life's joys and calamities? Look at his own fractured and feverish time on earth! What would he do when the child whom he would raise to be creative and resourceful wanted to join the FBI, for instance? Or be a corporate executive, or become Miss America, for Christ's sake? What to do, what to do? It boggled the mind. No wonder he ached to escape, he thinks, watching the pig and taking a slug from the pint of Jack Daniel's stuck in his hip pocket. There were no answers to all this. You just did your level best. The key was to do something, anything, rather than be done to. For him, anyhow, that was the key.

An acorn hits the plywood like a chunk of hail, then another grazes his forehead. Tipping his chin to look at the trees and moon, he wonders who the angry little god was up there who kept hurling nuts down onto the heads of hapless humans. As if a knock or two on the skull could possibly make a difference. "The sky is falling, Chicken Little," he says, and nearby someone laughs. Suddenly the pig smells too fresh, and Ray feels dizzy and silly, and nicks his thumb on the edge of the knife. Sucking the cut, he crouches next to the fire, poking at the coals with his good hand.

Where was Vivian? How beautiful she'd looked yesterday as they faced the sheriff and the freshly blackened woodstove in the living room of the old schoolhouse. She was wearing a sort of Indian jumpsuit thing with harem-like pants, and gardenias in her hair. Her face was flushed. At one point, she said she felt fine but faint. The sheriff waited solicitously and politely while Ray whispered words of encouragement. Her children were not there but would be back at Christmas. His mother had made a colossal effort to get there, had left her beloved Indians on the reservation in Montana to be there. Christine and Jerry had made it, had been having heart-to-heart talks with Darryl ever since they'd arrived. Darryl was glad to see them. Jane from NYC was there. A few old friends. But the group was small and the affair thankfully short. Rivers of champagne after, everyone dizzy and lighthearted, lightheaded. Though it was fairly cool, Ray felt the perspiration wind its damp way down the valley of his spine as the sheriff read the vows and he and Vivian repeated them. Ray had bought a white dress shirt for the occasion—he himself had ironed out the creases the night before—and he felt, oddly, for once in his life, grown up.

"When he talked about Adam and Eve," Vivian said later, "and when we said the vows, I felt the baby squirm." They were whispering because all around them were people sleeping and snoring and dreaming, and doing their own share of whispering. Bodies were everywhere. Vivian always referred to the baby as "she," and somehow Ray, too, knew she would be a girl, wanted a girl. He would teach her everything she needed to know about men, namely to ignore them, for the most part, or, more pointedly, not to expect too much. Or rather to expect much but to acknowledge their intrinsic humanness. And as to the question of humanness, she should realize that a man couldn't do it all for her, just as she couldn't do it all for a man, and the point was to maintain your own independence but compromise just enough to allow for the shortcomings of your partner, and so on and so forth, and it was all so individual, wasn't it, in the long run, there were no hard-and-fast rules, except to pay attention.

That night, as he drifted off to sleep, Ray marveled at how peopled his life had become.

Vivian, eight and a half months pregnant, has been resting. She heard the pickup and had thought she would help with the pig, but when she walks up to the field and sees tomorrow's dinner shining dully like some landed pike, she thinks better of it and goes back down to the house to put her feet up. Half an hour later she returns, pausing at the edge of the field to be sure it is safe. She sees the women hanging back, knives in hand, while the men struggle to secure the pig to the spit. A few children, without weapons, half hide behind the women, eyes wide as the pig's.

Tying the pig to the spit is hard work, much more complicated than anyone had imagined. No one seems willing to hug the animal to his or her chest to get it right. Finally they work it into place, wiring its haunches tight to keep them from splaying obscenely. Though just seeing the pig laid out like that, trussed up, is a bit obscene in and of itself, Vivian thinks. With legs stretched out forward and aft, it looks like a thoroughbred sprinting to the finish of some endless race, nostrils flaring, eye on the prize. She will stick to coleslaw, she thinks; she will turn her talents to cabbage and huge pots of beans. Leave the meat to the men. She eases down into an old green metal chair just outside the circle at the fire.

Some of Ray's hair catches in his jacket collar, and some falls forward as he stirs the fire. If she could see his face, Vivian knew his cheekbones would look sharper than usual in this slanted light, almost Indian. She hoped the baby would get his cheekbones and his love of fire, her feel for painting. She would like to be painting Ray at this very moment, but for the first time in her life, the smells of turpentine and oil have been making her sick. She sticks to sketching, but lately has been feeling far too restless for the concentration that took. She would get back to it. She had wangled a year off from teaching. She would make it a point to remember what she would later paint—the orange cast of this fire, the pink pig, silver moon.

Once she had asked Ray if he had learned about fire as a Boy Scout, and he said no, he was self-taught. Had he ever gotten into trouble with it, she asked. He looked like the kind of kid that just might burn the house down by mistake. Well, yes, as a matter of fact; he and another boy had burned up an entire field once. Corpus Christi was hot and dry that summer, and the field was gone before they knew it. Was he scared? contrite? He didn't remember being scared, but he had felt bad about it and, several years later, told his father. And what had his father, that fine man, said? You could have killed somebody, and be more careful in the future.

It annoyed her how easily Ray ignored the obvious when it was unpleasant or mildly complicated. It annoyed her, but she also envied his ability to detach himself so easily when in the thick of troubling situations, if only temporarily. Eventually, of course, he paid: it was simply a question, she supposed, of when. She watches him crouching by the fire with the others, looking fleetingly Neanderthal, and she loves him deeply. She wonders how they will fare, knows there is no way she can know this. After all, she had worked hard to free herself of the nicest of husbands (or so everyone said, and she agreed, though he had been unable to talk to her—what do you want, blood? one friend had said), and for a time she was convinced that she did want too much. She had been the model mother, and her husband had worked hard, come home, played with his children no more or less than any other father. But when she left, ah, when she left, he became the model father, would not even let her see her own children. You're not fit. I'm leaving you, not the children. We are a family, and you're ruining this family. And she had to admit that she was, but either way, stay or go, the family was not what it should be. And now she had her children back, and that struggle was closing, and another child was on the way, and here she has just married a man whom she loves deeply and who excites her and who seems more and more able to talk, though he had been unwilling to say much about the massacre of a herd of buffalo by his friend Bullet.

■ ≡ ■

They were fixing dinner the day after he got back when she asked about the buffalo. He had left Bullet the morning after the shooting, stopping long enough in Suitland to get Darryl and in Washington to buy fresh crabs. He had not slept well his first night home, and when she asked, he told her the whole business.

Two huge pots of water simmered on the stove, bubbling invitingly. It was getting cool, early September, and Ray was so grateful to be home that he was unusually talky. Vivian was melting butter for the crabs. He was leaning on the stove, watching the pots boil. The crabs, as if knowing what was in store, scrabbled around hopelessly in the bushel basket at his feet.

"Why'd you let him do it?"

"I didn't let him do it. I had no idea what he was up to."

"But you'd spent the whole day with him." Vivian tipped the pan with the butter in it this way and that. "You should have seen it coming."

"By the time I got down there, there wasn't much I could do." Ray went to the fridge to get a beer. Vivian looked at him, then looked back at the butter.

"He was crazy from missing his kids," said Ray, "crazy that Peg had left again. I'm not excusing him, just trying to acquaint you with his state of mind."

"It's horrible," she said, turning off the flame under the butter. "Sick." The crabs stepped up their scrabbling.

"I never said the boy was smart. He's always been crazy."

"Then why do you hang around with him?"

"I don't *hang around* with him. I hardly ever see him. I needed a place to crash. And I've known him for years. We're soul mates. Some people you're stuck with, for better for worse." She was squeezing lemons vigorously into the butter. He didn't want to tell her that after the strain of being with Priscilla, he wanted to be able to relax wordlessly and probably foolishly with his old pal.

He touched her arm, but she wouldn't look at him.

"I wasn't the one doing the shooting, remember?" But the look she gave him indicated he might as well have been. "I just happened to be there. I got stuck in his weird little game for a while."

"No one needs to get stuck," is all she said.

"Thank you, Herr Doktor."

Ray already had thought about all this, in fact had thought of little else on the drive back from Maryland, had talked wisely to Darryl for those few hours and felt that he was bringing to bear almost everything he knew when he talked to the boy. There but for the grace of God, et cetera.

All he wanted, finally, was to get back to Vivian, to the warmth of her ripe body, her strong arms, and here she was giving him the third degree.

He knew he was arguing now simply for the sake of it, and

he wished he could stop, wished she would stop. It was the vision of her that had kept him on the straight and narrow while he was gone; he would measure his life against those of his friends and feel blessed. But now here they were, and no slack from her, and he was getting mad. He squinted at her through the steam—the pots were wildly boiling—and he tilted his head back lazily. "I'm not into playing God," he said. "Besides, it's better than shooting his wife and kids—or me, for that matter—because that was the alternative, that's where he was headed."

"You don't know that."

"I know that." He pauses. "Come to think of it," he says, "he wouldn't have shot me. He needed someone to drink with after."

He had meant it to be funny, but she just stood there looking at him, and she was furious, he could see that; she was holding the knife in her hand, and it wouldn't have surprised him if she took a lunge—he almost wished she would, so they could wrestle, fall down, get this over with. For a moment he forgot she was pregnant; she was wearing one of his flannel shirts, extra large, and the red plaid somehow muted her largeness, made her appear as small and slim as when they first met.

"Sometimes," she said, in slow, measured tones that he wasn't sure he'd heard before, "sometimes you drive me absolutely crazy. You can't just let things go, you can't expect things to take care of themselves. While you were gone"—and now she's flailing the knife around—"I had to kill a goddamn fucking *copperhead,* because if I didn't, it might have bitten one of the children, or one of the dogs—*your* dogs—and if I had just let it go, I wouldn't have been able to live in peace, wondering when it might turn up again, where it was hiding out. I have never killed anything so consciously before. It was awful. I hated doing it." She put the knife down, stepped closer to him. "How could you just stand by and not do anything?"

By now Ray was thinking that she was worked up over something that had little to do with buffalo—clearly, she was ready to strangle him, no matter what he said. Later, he would let her know what he had learned on the trip, how he had turned a few corners, and he realized he'd better do it fast, that there was no percentage any longer in not saying what you thought to the person you loved best; but how can he say anything when she is letting out a choked sort of shriek and is grabbing the bushel basket of crabs and throwing them at him, tossing the contents of the basket at him as if she's throwing dirty laundry water out the tenement window. The crabs had bounced innocuously off his chest and arms, though one managed to snatch the edge of his shirt sleeve and hang on for dear life.

Ray was so startled he didn't move at first, then he picked a few up from the floor and tossed them back at her, the one attached to his sleeve swinging like some lame pendulum. And she threw them back. Wayward crabs scrabbled sideways across the kitchen floor, finding refuge beneath the stove and the oak table, hiding in corners, claws raised, ready for anything. Others seemed to play dead, rolling around the floor like guillotined heads, awkward and senseless. When one pinched Vivian's ankle, she screamed and tripped, almost falling into Ray, so they joined forces, were on the same side, defending themselves. In the end, it was with a certain sadness that they tossed the crabs into the boiling pots.

By the time the crabs were scarlet and edible, Vivian and Ray were half undressed, leaning, semi-lying on the kitchen table. The red flannel shirt was unbuttoned, and Ray couldn't keep his hands off her full breasts, the rounded belly. Before they could go further, she stopped him and said, unaccountably, "I hope no one comes in," which was unlikely, as it was late and they were alone in the schoolhouse—Darryl was at a movie in town—and then she said, "Do you really find me attractive this way? Tell me the truth."

Ray was peeling off his jeans and didn't feel like stopping to answer, or consider anything just then, but she asked again. "Do I still turn you on?"

"Lord, babe," he said, laughing though mildly exasperated, "you always turn me on."

"You have to look at me, Ray. You can't tell without looking at me."

He got the jeans off, drew a deep breath, backed away from her, and looked at her. He slowly finished unbuttoning his shirt, then held his hands up, studied her through the small square he made with his fingers, in the way he imagined photographers and painters would do. And he thought how sometimes she looked, in her pregnant state, round and waddly, almost cute. Other times she looked like an innocent child, the picture of wistfulness. Other times she looked old and heavy and puffy. Alcoholic. Eternally tired. Still other times she looked like the Madonna herself, pure love and distantly holy. At this moment, though, at this very moment, she looked, he decided, like a whore, a sultry beauty with endless, tantalizing sexual tricks. She was gorgeous. Her mouth was the most luscious he had ever seen, her body the most inviting. He touched her leg.

"Well?" she said.

"Yes," he said. "Yes, you do." Though he had practically forgotten the question and could tell by her eyes that she had too.

He let her remove his shirt. He knew better than to list everything he'd thought; some things, some notions, some truths—in spite of his recent revelations on the road and with the crabs—should never see the light of day.

■ ≡ ■

Ray's mother, Eve, joins him by the fire. Linking her arm in his, she gently pulls him up, and they walk to the edge of the field where the woods begin. The people around the fire seem as remote as the stars. Every now and then, all at once, their chatter reaches Ray's ears, as if they are talking in unison, and their conversations and sentences are bound together, delivering themselves to him in one fell swoop. Like the talk of some lazing giant.

of anger and pity, and had slapped her gray braids abruptly over her shoulders and walked away from him.

Ray lets go of the tree, feels the impression the bark leaves on his cheek. Eve pats his arm, says, "You are going to make a wonderful father." He thanks her and kisses her hair where the thin line of scalp is white and fragile as a shell.

They return to the pit and stand with the group, watching the spit slowly turn. Someone passes a bottle and Vivian moves closer, wanting some. Someone tries one last time to get the apple into the hog's mouth, but ends up throwing the fruit into the fire in mock disgust. The falling apple sends up a shower of sparks, makes everyone step back a little, as if only now realizing the power of the flames.

It is Christine who tried to wedge the apple in place, which surprises Ray; he knows for a fact she is squeamish at the sight of blood and used to wear rubber gloves to pump gas. But under the three-quarter moon, and in the face of the naked, helpless hog, things are different. The guests are like figures in a Brueghel print, peasant bodies moving in and out of the firelight. Mead, laughter, glinting knives and teeth and whites of eyes. Riddles. Clues in the folds of the men's tunics, the women's skirts, children's dreams. Their smiles, the way they eat and dance and sing.

■ ≡ ■

At the four A.M. basting, Ray and Jerry roast a chicken over the coals. Everyone else is in bed. An hour later, they pull legs off the small charred body, wiping their slick mouths on the backs of their hands, their hands on the legs of their jeans. They wash the chicken down with the Jack Daniel's Jerry brought. They chuck the stripped bones into the fire, where they burn like twigs of seasoned oak. The pig turns slowly, eyes brown as pennies now, skin cracked and hard as a desert.

Ray lies on a sleeping bag, watching Jerry baste. There are

things they could talk about: Jerry was in the navy, in the Mekong delta the same time Ray was. They usually end up grousing good-naturedly about what it's like for Jerry to be married to Ray's sister—interesting, to say the least—and how when you're over forty, nothing is ever the same. They also talk about Darryl, who has said he might be ready to return with his parents to Suitland after the pig roast.

The hog's rump slips uneasily where the meat is cooked and tender. It is as if, though roasted, it still has a will of its own, as if it might shake loose from the spit and jump across the fire to Ray, give his leg a little nip, then chase him around the field, before squealing in triumph over the ignorance of man and trotting off into the night. Pondering this, Ray decides he could use a lot more Jack Daniel's, or a lot less. Either way, the dark insides of his bag invite him to sleep, and he buries his head in its depths just as Jerry says that life will never be the same after the baby's born. All this talk about how life is never the same after such and such.... When was life ever the same, he thinks as he drifts off.

And he dreams of coming upon a huge conch resting on the ocean floor, so huge he can slip inside, which he does, but once there, dazzled and confused by what seem to be the bright lights of a huge empty city, he cannot find his way out, and the king of the place, a sort of androgynous mermaid type, tells him to relax, that life is good inside the shell, that after a time he will no longer feel the urge to escape.

■ ≡ ■

He wakes up hot and agitated. He has worked his way so far down in the sleeping bag, for a moment he thinks he is still trapped in the shell, and he struggles unnecessarily with the bag's opening. Then he hears gravel crunch in the driveway. Dogs barking. A predawn gold glints in the east. No red sky, no need to worry. The dogs keep up the racket, and Ray pushes his head out of the bag. Across the fire, Jerry is a lump of cushiony warmth, and between them, the pig is looking more and more like something that Ray can actually imagine eating.

The dogs keep barking as Ray sits up to listen. He thinks he hears a motor revving and instantly flashes on cops, MPs, the border patrol—Indians?—as he always does whether or not he has reason to. In the next instant, he hears nothing, just the cool, silent aftermath of the night, and he chides himself for his lack of faith in life's serendipity. Awake now, he slips on his boots, wraps the blanket his mother has given him tight against the damp dawn. He pokes at the fire, tosses in a few chunks of wood before walking down to the house. Behind him, Jerry's snores are perfectly timed; they linger in the air, soothing and low.

Patchy white frost brightens the stubby field grass like sunlight at noon. Ray shivers and pulls the blanket closer. He is thinking he should go inside to check on Vivian, maybe bother her a little— she had seemed so quiet earlier. He is walking around to the back of the schoolhouse on his way to the woodpile when he almost collides with someone coming the other way. Ray would have been more alarmed if the man hadn't appeared to be zipping his fly, harmless enough. And besides, Ray had stopped being cautious way back by the fire and Jerry's reassuring snores. But when the man throws up his hands as if in surrender, or as if about to shove Ray backward—palms flat and pale—Ray steps back, instantly wary. And when the man says, by way of greeting, or explanation, hands still up, "Long time no see," and Ray sees it's Bullet, he feels no better.

■ ≡ ■

"I wouldn't ask you to do it, McCreary, but I'm desperate."

They are sitting in Bullet's brand-new Winnebago, drinking rum-laced coffee brewed on the camp stove. They are leaning on a small fold-up Formica table screwed into the side of the Winnebago. The café-style curtains and matching green-checked seats remind Ray of a motel room he hopes he never has the grim pleasure to sleep in. Ever. It occurs to Ray that he has had little sleep, and exhausting dreams, and quite a bit of whiskey, and that maybe this isn't happening at all, that Bullet isn't sitting there asking him to stash a couple of hundred pounds of homegrown— Maryland's finest—in the basement of the schoolhouse. Or under the stage, even better, Bullet suggests. Ray is glad everyone is asleep and away from them, not privy to his own skewed weariness and his friend's glittering madness. A barrage of acorns hits the thin roof of the RV, and Ray remembers where he is, and why, and wishes, of course, that he were back in the bag.

"Jesus," says Bullet, looking up. "We under attack or something?"

"Acorns," says Ray. "Big as billiard balls. Could mean a mild winter, could mean a shitty one."

"I don't know about you," Bullet is saying, "but I am planning on having me one hell of a fine winter this year. Bountiful. Beautiful and bountiful."

In the weak, battery-powered light, his face is gray and vaguely shadowed, fleshy, no angles. And though it warms Ray, the spiked coffee is way too strong—too much rum, too much coffee, sour tinny water. He puts down the mug and wraps himself tighter in the blanket. The rooster is carrying on now as if it is his final day of reckoning, as if he knows that if he isn't careful he might end up in the pot, or sizzling over an open fire along with certain other barnyard friends. It seems important that he remain on pitch, that his timing be perfect.

"Someone oughta shoot that bird," says Bullet, and he laughs, but Ray wonders uncomfortably if the 30.06 made it down to Virginia, and if so, where it was, if it was nestled somewhere out of sight in some warm corner of the vehicle, just within reach of Bullet's itchy finger.

"Where's the Jeep?" Ray asks. He tries not to think about the dope, though he smells it, sharp as fresh-mown hay. He tries not to think about Peg, the buffalo. He feels a monumental headache coming on. He should be getting back to the fire, basting the pig.

"Traded it in on the RV. They made me an offer I couldn't refuse." This makes Bullet chuckle, Ray groan.

"Hey," says Bullet, "don't knock it. They threw in a CB and a skylight." He points up at the window that frames the early-morning Virginia sky, like some precise Magritte painting. Ray stares at the sky longer than is necessary, still stunned by Bullet's arrival. How had Bullet known to turn up on the very day that for Ray signified all the good fortune and happiness still to come? How was it Bullet always managed to sniff him out in his weakest moments? He was still sorry, in a way, not to have shot Bullet after the massacre of the herd, or at least jumped him. It had seemed the only justice possible, though hopelessly irrelevant by the time the dust had, quite literally, settled. And Ray was re-alizing more and more how infinitely impossible it was to even the score on this and on all things: you simply took note and bashed on (if you chose to continue), trying to achieve and main-tain the precarious balance by never committing the same mistake twice. The men pause, gulp at their coffee.

"All I need is to store the stuff in your place while I drive down to Tuscaloosa to get Peg. I can't be driving all over the countryside loaded up like this." He stares at the match he's lit for no particular purpose. He stares first at the flame, then at Ray. "And when I get back," he says, "with or without Peg, I'm gonna sell the stuff and head west. This time I'm really going."

"Sell it to who?"

"You got friends around, right?"

"Wonderful," says Ray. "You don't even smoke the goddamn stuff; I'm clean. . . . Watch it. You one-timers are the guys that get popped every time."

"Us one-timers are the ones that make a shitload of money." Bullet tosses back the rest of his coffee, grimacing as if he's tasted something red hot. "And fast." He leans his arms on the edge of the table, puts his face close to Ray's. His crooked teeth wink in the unreliable light. "Like yesterday isn't soon enough, you know?" Then he says, "It's funny, but I really seem to have a knack for it. Fucking plants got up to fifteen feet, some of them."

"So stick to tomatoes or potatoes or cabbages."

"Can't make much money on cabbages, son," says Bullet.

Another round of acorns pounds over their heads. "Jesus Christ," says Bullet, shaking his head, glancing at the roof. "They're gonna ding up my clean machine here." And Ray is thinking it is as if they are prisoners stuck aboard some small sailboat again, the captain and crew clumping around on deck above them, torturing them into living or dying by making them crazy with the clamor.

Ray says, "You look like you could use a decent night's sleep." And he thinks, I'll deal with this later. It's time to baste the pig.

"I could of used a decent night's sleep for a couple of months now, McCreary, but I got no time. Got too much to do." He runs a hand through his short hair while Ray lights another Camel. "You still smoking those things?" Then, "You want a cut of the dough when I score?" He is looking at Ray with red eyes. "You want in?"

"No, thanks." Ray speculates again on the whereabouts of the 30.06. Then, discouraged, he says, "Look, Bullet. You can't keep the stuff here. I'm roasting a pig up there in the field, Vivian is about to have the baby, my mother is here, there will be people all over the place tomorrow—or rather today." He stops to sniff. "And the stuff is pungent, you know? You can smell it a mile off. It ain't exactly quiet, that smell. We don't need any surprises right now."

Bullet's head is tipped back, his eyes are almost closed. He looks the way he did that day in the sea, asleep, almost dead, except Ray can see his Adam's apple move just slightly when he swallows. "You know how it is," Ray says. "You can park the RV here for a while while you get some sleep, and feel free to stick around for some pig, but none of the stuff goes inside."

"Hey, man," says Bullet. "I was counting on you. Just do me this one favor."

Ray picks up his mug, not wanting the coffee, looks down into the lethal-looking mixture of coffee and rum. He sees his nose large and ludicrous in the murky dregs, hates the ambivalence he feels. He cannot look at Bullet but hears him begin talking in the same low voice he used on the old man, as if he is imparting top-secret information, or crooning some love song, or divulging the key to some mystery or private thought to Ray alone.

"Peg keeps calling from Tuscaloosa, wanting money, wanting *me,* poor girl. B.J. needs braces, George is going to this special tutor so he can make it through the eighth grade, Peg is seeing a head doctor." He taps his own head with a thick finger, opening his eyes wide in what Ray figures is Bullet's idea of a look of madness. Bullet leans over the Coleman to mix more coffee. "It's the little stuff eats you alive," he says. "I'm gonna bring her on home. Leave the kids with their grandparents, take off on a trip." He moves his finger from his head to the mug and stirs the steaming liquid. "I closed up the farmhouse for the winter. Got this moving house here, got my savings all squared away." He gestures toward what must be the marijuana, a large dark mass of something covered in black plastic. "All I need is my loving wife by my side."

Ray feels himself momentarily weaken. After all, weren't he and Bullet after the same fine goals just now? Eternal peace and ever-loving happiness?

"I'm all for you and Peg working things out," Ray says, "but you really can't take the stuff inside. It's too risky. I don't even like having it here in the RV, to tell you the truth, but that's OK for the time being."

"You going straight on me, McCreary?"

"Got too much at stake here."

Neither man speaks for a moment. A smatter of acorns showers the roof of the Winnebago. The rooster has calmed down; now the goats are starting up. It feels to Ray as if he should be falling into bed, giving himself up to sleep and, once again, to his dreams. It feels as if Bullet should be miles away, not here in front of him, demanding this favor. Shouldn't he be flattened by what he had done in his life, by the slaughter of the buffalo, for instance? He seems to endure, like—Ray couldn't think what—like *plastic.* Nonbiodegradable. When we're all burned to nothing, or even if we just plain die of old age, there Bullet will be, alive and well, looking neither older nor younger than he had ever looked, just like plastic. Or cockroaches, was it? Some species of flying ant? Somewhere Ray had read about what would remain when life as we know it is kaput. But plastic and cockroaches had no soul, and certainly Bullet had soul. Lord knows, the boy had soul.

"You still alive, Ray?" Bullet asks. When Ray opens his eyes slowly and looks at him, Bullet says, "I really want that woman back."

■ ≡ ■

At the six A.M. basting, in the thin light of what looks like a promising day, Jerry and Ray take turns dripping the special pig baste over their slow-cooking charge. It is Charlene's recipe, collected especially by Ray on a special trip to Papa Stumpy's. Since she'd last seen him, Charlene had married Johnny. Now Johnny worked with them at the diner, making fresh pasta. He was Irish and was always after Papa S. to go into the potato line: "You got your fried, you got your baked, you got your scalloped, you got your boiled, you got your mashed, you got your au gratin. Something for everybody."

Johnny had wound out the litany, and Papa Stumpy had groaned, "Spare me."

They had all laughed.

Charlene's hair was knotted into a simpler French twist, and, as she explained to Ray, Johnny took up so much of her time she was thirty-five pounds lighter. She felt, she said, less pressed to work on her hair. Nerves was what did it with the weight loss, she said, nerves and worrying over Johnny, did he really love her, would he make it to the church on time—if at all—the day of their wedding, would he do right by her, and so on. Now, three months later, she chided herself for her lack of faith.

"He is the perfect husband and father to my Joey," she told Ray. They both gazed at Joey, who was at work with two rubber spatulas, pounding away on a cabinet door. Papa Stumpy and Johnny were in the back, making fettuccine.

"You see," Ray said, his mouth full of barbecue, still the best he'd ever tasted. "You *are* lucky."

"Luck's got nothing to do with it. You get what you work for. Tit for tat." Her hands were on her hips, and suddenly she looked as large as she had the first time he'd seen her. The flamingo woman, if ever there was one.

Johnny poked his head around the corner from the back. "I'm taking her away from all this," he said to Ray. "I'm going to win Publishers Clearing House and we're going to take a cruise around the world, buy a second home."

"Buy a first home," Charlene said, but she was smiling.

"Get some new vehicles—Mercedes, BMW."

"Dream on," Charlene intoned.

"See the Orient," Johnny continued. "Might even take you along." He chucked Joey under the chin. Joey tried to bite his hand.

"Over my dead body," Papa S. yelled from the back. "Who would make my barbecue?"

"I would," yelled Ray, wishing with all his heart that he were Italian, or at least as Irish as Johnny, lover of potatoes.

Everyone went back to work.

"Men." Charlene shook her head. "You wanta know something?"

Yes, indeed I do, Ray was thinking.

She leaned over the counter close to Ray. "I'm getting my tubes tied Wednesday. No more babies for me. Not after I got my waistline down to twenty-four."

Ray almost choked on what little barbecue remained. "You're kidding," he said.

"No more babies." Charlene was emphatic. "Don't get me wrong. I love Joey, even though his father, who shall remain nameless, was a worthless SOB. I love you, Joey," she said to her son. "But one is enough. That's it."

"What does Johnny have to say about all this?"

"Not much, mostly because he doesn't know yet. He'd probably have a heart attack if he knew. A blow to his ego."

"Don't you think you'd better tell him?"

"I'll tell him soon enough. It'll be all right. He agrees with me, see, that one kid is enough, and he takes precautions, but sometimes he gets a little careless, and what I don't need right now is another kid."

She looked as radiant as he'd ever seen her, Ray was thinking as he listened and chewed, probably because of how strongly she felt and because of the emphasis with which she mouthed each word. She stopped talking to rub a towel vigorously over the counter next to Ray. Still, he missed the intricacies of her former hairdo and knew any reference—however complimentary—to her former size and assets would be met with disdain and maybe even anger.

But he had to say, "But that's where I think you're wrong. People like you and Johnny should have a hundred kids. Kids are the hope of the goddamn future."

"And so where are your kids?" she said.

When he didn't answer, she said, leaning forward again, "Look. My mother had nine of us, so I know whereof I speak. When you and I were young—or when I was young, anyhow; I don't know about you—that's the way it was. But the world these days. What a mess. And as for the future. . . ." She shook her head and scooped up Joey, who proceeded to play with her huge, pizza-size earrings. "If the future depends on Joey, we're in big trouble—right, Joe? You gonna be President of the United States one day? You gonna teach 'em how to cook pasta? You gonna learn how to sign your name with ten different pens and which fork to use first? You gonna put Mama up in the West

Wing when she comes to visit?" She kissed her son and put him down.

"Who's gonna be President of the United States?" Johnny yelled from the back.

Charlene put a finger to her lips. "Sssh," she said. She winked at Ray. "You are, honey," she called back. She smiled at Ray, who smiled back. He paid for his barbecue, wrested from her the secret of the sauce. "It's a question of ginger," she breathed. As he was putting his wallet back in his pocket, he told her again how good she looked. "I could never go back," she said, "never."

■ ≡ ■

The hog seems to have shrunk overnight, so that it looks now to Ray almost too pretty to eat. Its ears remind him of mini-conchs, the delicate rippled edge. Beyond Ray, and way down the drive, Jerry thinks he sees someone carrying what look like bundles of Christmas parcels from what looks like a Winnebago down to what must be the basement door under the main bedroom. He thinks of saying something to Ray but doesn't bother. Ray is rhapsodizing over the sauce and his general feeling of goodwill, and besides, Jerry has no reason to believe anything unusual is going on. In fact, someone carting packages to the basement makes just about as much sense as his sleeping next to an open fire all night when he doesn't have to, basting this wasted-looking hog. He takes another slug of Jack Daniel's, offers what little is left to his brother-in-law, and they hazily toast the fading night.

■ ≡ ■

"Ooooh, gross," squeals one girl to her friend as they watch the pig turn on the spit. "Ooooh, look at his eyes." They are standing about ten feet from the pit, hands covering their faces, fingers cracked just enough to take a peek. They are not looking at the pig just as they will not fall in love with at least one of their teachers by the time they're nineteen. It is high noon, and next to them a few old people sit in folding chairs, chatting quietly, oblivious—this being their hundredth pig roast—to the pig's eyes, its hard saddle of a skin, the haunches. Their hands are folded in their laps or around plastic cups of beer. They wait as patiently for their food as they do for each day to begin and end.

Everywhere else, people are wandering around or sitting or drinking or talking. They are there to help celebrate Ray's recent good fortune, both general and particular. Ray has invited everyone he knows in Charlottesville and its surrounding counties, and miraculously everyone has come. Though there are factions within the group who would not dream of situating themselves close to certain other factions, there is plenty of room for all, and Ray anticipates no trouble.

"Trouble?" Vivian had said, eyebrows raised. "This is a party."

"I guess discomfort is what I meant," says Ray. And this was before he had any inkling that Bullet might be a participant in the festivities. Bullet would fit in fine with some of the men Ray worked with—men of few words and, Ray had to admit, at times men of little action. Actually, Bullet and these men—teenaged, country, skinny and silent, spidery mustaches—would have little to say to each other. He could see them watching Vivian sideways from thin eyes, like foxes, whenever she came on the job: the boss's woman, nice little piece. When they broke for dinner, they huddled together as if eternally chilled, eating sardines, crackers, and Cokes. Blood kin, they did not talk among themselves and said little to Ray. But they had the houses they were building, and for most of them, that was enough. And now they had this pig to eat, and that was more than enough.

Ray mills around with his guests, locates his mother talking animatedly to Jerry. Watches his wife carry a pot of beans up to the tent they've rented from Dolly's Funeral Home. He smiles as he watches her, likes it that she is unaware he's there. The edges of the funeral tent flap merrily in the crisp fall breeze. The band they hired pulls up in several vans and pickups. Ray is feeling like the king of the heap; he is feeling fine. Acorns fall relentlessly.

At two-thirty, Jerry, Bullet, Ray, and Darryl lift the pig away from the fire, onto the plywood. The pig is back to looking helpless and soon as it's cut into looks like nothing at all, or something else altogether, certainly not like anything that once scrambled or ambled this earth on small cloven hooves, grunting and rooting for nuts. The men set its head on one corner of the plywood; it stares beseechingly skyward. They use wire snips to cut the body from the metal bar. They pull bits of wire from the ham hocks as if they're splinters. The girls squeal, they cover their eyes, and Darryl can't resist, he raises the severed haunches over his head, up and down, up and down, as if he's pumping iron. He grunts and huffs; the girls squeal. He beats his chest, lets out a Tarzan yelp. Ray shakes his head, thinks Darryl's still got a lot to learn. He watches his friend Bullet hack away at the pig, wonders what lies in store for him for the remainder of his time on earth. Wonders, in fact, just how much time God has allotted for Bullet to remain on this earth. Wonders again what God has in store for him, Ray. Wonders briefly about God himself. He watches Jerry, face slightly ashen, trying to hold the pig in place for Bullet's knifework. He thinks how glad he is that this man is married to his pretty sister. Thinks how happy he is to be married to Vivian. The baby turns a cartwheel in Vivian's womb. The girls squeal. The old people wait.

Bullet and Darryl take over with the pig. They work the meat like artists, playing to the crowd that has gathered around them, taunting them, luring them. The crowd stands back a bit at first, wary of Bullet's wild gesticulations with the knife, concerned about the pig juice staining the front of his safari shirt, his cries of "Pig meat!" But he tempts them to come closer, and Darryl, in his black leather jacket, apes him: yep yep yep, step right up for the sweet meat, folks.

The guests open their mouths for a morsel. Eve passes around a platter piled high with steaming meat. The young girls edge closer now that the pig is in pieces. They still moan a little over the eyes, but the novelty is gone, and they begin flirting with Darryl instead. Ray joins Vivian under the tent, where, munching on an apple, he watches the proceedings from a safe distance. He smells the smoky fragrance of her hair, whispers things he knows she likes to hear. And then, to cap it all off, in a gesture he knows borders on a shameless baring of the sentimental soul, he climbs up to the belfry of the old schoolhouse and lets the bells loose. They have not rung since Bullet got them going earlier in the year, and though it takes Ray more effort than he had thought it would to move them, he does it, and they ring out jubilantly and soulfully over the heads of his family and friends. He pulls on the ropes till his muscles ache. He watches his friends gaze up at him, some with mouths open to dark O's, some with knowing smiles. Even the men from work who say little look pleased. For a moment, he thinks he might pass out from the effort of the pulling; his vision seems to blur. He can see clearly the center of the picture: the pig laid out, Bullet's knife, Vivian. But the edges are rough. He attributes the fuzziness to his general euphoria and great excitement at entering this new phase of his life. He lets the ropes go, the bells wind down, and gradually the people below return to their business. A few minutes later, Eve is standing at the top of the belfry steps. "Sit," she says.

Ray sits. She sits facing him on the belfry floor. "The bells sounded lovely," she says. Ray notices she is holding a narrow, leather-fringed pouch that looks as if it could contain a clarinet, or possibly a bone-handled carving set. It is decorated with complicated beadwork, geometric designs of red, black, and yellow. His mother is running her fingers over the beads as if they're braille. They sit silently facing each other. Ray's legs begin to go numb; he gently shifts positions. "I have something I want to share with you," Eve says.

Ray thinks at first she is going to tell him something about his father. He watches her finger the soft leather fringe. Was his father a clarinet player, a closet musician? If he had lived, would father and son have played wonderful hideous duets together, he on the Hummingbird, his father wheezing away on the clarinet? Would they have subjected Eve to the full force of their musical genius and verve, or would it have been more private, the two of them playing late into the night, telling their stories, getting so drunk they would ask each other questions, give answers, look into each other's eyes knowingly and blindly while they played, until finally Eve, and probably Christine and whatever boyfriend was kicking around, would have to yell down (or up) the stairs for them to shut the hell up or come to bed? Would it have been like the Marine Corps that way, man to man, story for story?

Eve puts the pouch down on the floor between them. She lifts the flap and pulls out a long-stemmed pipe. Bright feathers are tied to the base of the stone bowl; animals' heads are etched into the wooden stem. Ray wonders what she will pull out next—a little stash of some magical substance to take them sky-high, clear up to the Happy Hunting Ground? He cannot imagine getting high with his mother, can't, these days, imagine getting high with anyone.

His mother is running her brown fingers over the pipe as if conjuring up a genie. She is not smiling. Ray folds his hands in his lap and waits. But Eve doesn't move, or speak, simply looks at him with so much love that he is embarrassed. "What about the pipe, Ma?" he says, but she is seeing her late husband sitting there, she is talking to him in her head about their children, their smart pretty daughter and their smart wayward son, what they can do, what they should have done to steer them right.

"Ma," says Ray, touching her hand.

"The peace pipe," she says slowly, "is a symbol of harmony and goodwill. I haven't always understood you, and there were times after your father died when I probably wasn't a good mother to you, and I have to bear the burden of that guilt. All the same, I can't help but feel that even if I had been there, much of the time it wouldn't have made any difference. You would have gone on and done what you had to do, like all young men."

"Not young anymore, Ma," Ray says.

"I know that, dear. Believe me, I am fully aware of that fact." She shakes her head, holds out the pipe. "This is for you. Consider it my white flag. I want you to have it to remember me by."

"I don't need a pipe to remember you by," Ray says, taking it from her. He turns it over in his hands. "It's beautiful," he says. "This is embarrassing."

"Sometimes," says Eve, taking his hand in hers, "it's good to be embarrassed." He helps her to her feet, then walks to the belfry window. Below him, in the field, his friends look small and colorful and energetic, but now he has trouble picking out one particular person down there. He turns to his mother. "Let's go," he says, but she stays looking out the window, thinking he cannot imagine what.

"Thank you, Ma," he says. "I'll give it to my daughter when the time is right." He takes the pouch from her, slips the pipe in. Putting an arm around his mother's small shoulders, he leads her to the steps. "And don't worry about me. You were a good mother, Christine was a good sister, Dad was a good father. Really. Now let's go eat some pig." She smiles finally, hugs him, and they walk down the steps, one behind the other.

The band has just about finished setting up; they stand around adjusting knobs on amps, tuning their instruments. Ray goes over to watch; Vivian is there, talking quietly to the man who looks like the leader. He is a friend of hers, she has told Ray; he paints houses to pay the bills, plays music for his soul. In fact, on Sundays he plays bass with a local gospel group, and the congregations— all black—are always polite enough not to shout out, Who is that *white* dude up there? Ray had felt an unfamiliar pang of jealousy rush through him when she'd told him about this musician. How had she met him, he wanted to know. He painted my apartment.

The band strikes up a lively rendition of "Turkey in the Straw," which gets jazzier and more and more unrecognizable with each stanza. The few people who try to dance end up sashaying around to their own personal beat, partners being unnecessary and well-nigh impossible under the circumstances. The band plays on an old rug provided by Ray, which covers the cool, spiky field of grass like a piece of AstroTurf. A wildly complicated and dangerous-looking set of extension cords and wires hook them up, on their patch of turf, to the schoolhouse, several hundred yards away. They are like a satellite, yet another satellite rolling easily around within the magnetic field of the schoolhouse. Rolling easily rather than madly careening, is the way Ray likes to think of it.

He puts in a request for something danceable. The band obliges with "Respect," the female singer belting it out as if she's never known a moment's peace. The fringe on her cowhide jacket quivers with impatience and desire. *"All I want you to* do *for me...."* Ray mouths it along with her, puts his head back to howl it out: *"Re-re-re-re-re-re-re-re-*spect" ("just a little bit," the bass player sings high, "just a little bit").

By now everyone is at it, bodies contorted into the most suggestive and innovative postures, Eve carrying on with Bullet: he is impossibly zonked, outlines curvaceous female torsos in the air between them; she seems to float just out of his reach, observes his antics with reserve and mild amusement. Christine and Jerry move in a tightly choreographed and oft-executed dance routine; they could be participants in a nationally televised contest. Darryl and one of the young girls dance as only the young can—sweet smooth bodies aware that much lies in store for them but uncertain as to the particulars, so what is there to gain by holding back now? Time enough for that. At least that's what Ray thinks when he bumps by mistake into the girl, whose face is hidden by the smooth sheet of hair she swishes from side to side as she tries to keep up with Darryl.

"Rock out, unc," shouts Darryl, and Ray complies; he is not much good, but he has always loved to dance. From the corner of his eye, he sees Vivian's friend Jane standing at the edge of the rug watching them, trying to ignore one of the plumbers, who is leaning her way. He makes a mental note to be sure to ask her to dance soon.

The next number is slow and sultry. The rug clears, and Ray leads Vivian to its empty center. He bows and they dance a sort of modified minuet, at least at first, elegant and discreet—no reflection of Ray's condition: mildly drunk and getting worse, feeling giddy and loving it. He controls himself on the AstroTurf and is careful with his partner. Vivian's dancing is graceful, as always, in sharp contrast to his own energetic efforts.

People from the crowd ease onto the rug. The old folks watch from their time-worn periphery. And now the plumber gets Jane out there with him, and they do a cross—in double time—between a mad tango and the jitterbug. People get out of their way; it is their purpose to cover, during the number, every square inch of the dance floor. The band loves it; everyone loves everyone. The pig is good, the company charming, the skies perfect.

Ray holds his wife of a day and a half with great tenderness; he tries hard to be understated as he steers her around the rug, resists an urge to tip her back right down onto the ground, lie there next to her, do whatever they feel like doing. He remembers the time he sat in the front row of a small club in D.C., the Cellar Door, probably, pleased to have gotten such a good seat, wanting to concentrate on the band, but failing because of his concern that at any moment one of the two female vocalists, hugely pregnant, might, in her open-throated passion, topple off the stage, right into his small, unwilling lap. He had worried about this the whole show; just the thought of touching a pregnant woman had made him uncontrollably nervous, maybe because he had recently been threatened with a paternity suit by a young woman he didn't much like and whom he hardly knew. But also he had visions during the entire two and a half hours of having to assist in an emergency delivery right there on the café tables, littered with half-drunk beers and cigarette butts, and the thought of all that responsibility had made him weak for days.

It was like being first on the scene of a twisted, smoky traffic accident: you didn't really want to believe such things happened, but knowing they did, what you wanted even more was for them to occur just after you'd passed the slick spot, after you'd rounded the bend, so you could, with a clear conscience, continue tearing down the highway and through the night, going where you were going, singing along with Patsy Cline, say, or Lucinda Williams, or old Percy, at the top of your lungs, making good time, heedless of the dangers lurking behind you, the tragedies of the world.

Since his return from the north, and D.C., Ray's concern for Vivian and their child has surfaced so often she sometimes says it might have been better on his nerves and hers if he had stayed away till after the birth. They both knew, of course, she didn't mean it. Short of heart failure or the apocalypse, Ray had better be there.

He guides Vivian to the edge of the rug, where they stand watching the others a few moments. Jane is doing fine with the plumber, who is surprisingly good. The band strikes up an Irish jig without missing a beat, and most of the dancers carry on as if it were perfectly natural to be hopping around to some Irish tune on this rug at the edge of a field out in the middle of nowhere. Eve and Bullet are still at it, though Bullet needs no partner; he could easily go it alone out there. They watch him stomp around on the rug like someone trying to extinguish a boot-licking brush fire. After a while, Eve steps back, gives him space.

Vivian leans against Ray. "Brian," she says, tipping her head toward the band, "plays beautiful Irish tunes that would un-doubtedly be lost on this crowd right now. Maybe we'll get him to play some later." Which doesn't necessarily make Ray eager to hear the beautiful tunes, just makes him resolve to work a little harder at his own guitar.

He leads Vivian away from the band and the beans and the people. They walk to a rise at the end of the field. They sit, then lie back on the wheat-colored grass, watching clouds slip past. Ray points out mares' tails and mackerel backs. They close their eyes, letting the sun shine as bright as it likes. And Ray lets himself float up there, where he observes the activity below as a pigeon might, or a sparrow hawk. He imagines suitable prey— succulent mice, an abnormally small child. When he reaches for Vivian and she isn't there, he thinks he might have dozed off.

But the sun is still warm, and when he sits up to collect himself, things look about the same, and he knows he has much of the day, and all of the night, still left to go. He stays where he is a moment, sees that Bullet and Darryl have taken on Jerry and the plumber at the horseshoes pit. The shoes cling and clang sharply as the men toss. In between pitches, they joke a little, mutter to themselves, but when it is their turn, they bring to bear everything they've got—which, in the plumber's case, is several local championships—and they are as intent on winning as they are, in the next moment, on chugging beer. Ray stands, stretches, and walks their way. He is happy to see Darryl joining in with such hearty camaraderie. Maybe pitching horseshoes had its drawbacks (though Ray is at a loss to come up with even the remotest objection to the game), but it seemed far superior to anything else Darryl was likely to pursue in the recreational or job line. In the few months he'd spent with Ray and Vivian in Virginia, Darryl had expressed an interest in exploring everything from becoming a mercenary to spending the next decade in school (not counting the half year of high school he still lacked) in order to become a country vet. Or maybe he would be a scuba diver: less school, more pay. A better return, though? morally speaking? in the ethical sense? Ray had spent a lot of time talking down-home ethics with his nephew; he'd done his best to give a strong plug to life's deceptively simple but deeply rewarding dips and swells. Usually, when he finished what he hoped sounded more like wisdom than like some middle-aged man rattling on stupidly about the world's beauty and dangers, Darryl invariably took up the mercenary rap again. At which point Ray remembered who he was, he himself, and who he had become, and rather than feeling sorry that he had bored his nephew with his—of course—sound advice, he vowed to be more careful in choosing the time and place to do the talking. Timing, in this case no less than in any other, was of the essence.

"Hee hee hee," Bullet laughs. He is slapping Darryl on the back when Ray walks up. "This boy can pitch shoes blindfolded," he says. "He can pitch 'em inside outwards, upside down. You got the knack," he says to Darryl, who is looking pleased with himself. Down at the other post, Jerry and the plumber appear to be kibitzing strategy. "You ready?" they yell, separating, facing the other two.

"We're ready," Bullet yells back, and the plumber throws, gets a ringer, which draws groans and mild taunts from Bullet and Darryl.

"Too bad you can't make money pitching shoes," says Ray.

"There are ways," Bullet says absentmindedly, though Ray is in no way addressing Bullet. "Plenty of ways."

"Sure," Darryl says. "Join the circus, right?" And they both laugh, Ray does too, and he can feel this nagging little sermon coming on about the difference between working on a dream and wasting time, but he restrains himself. He strolls off toward the band, wanting to shake this irritating but interesting sense of responsibility.

■ ≡ ■

By midnight there is nothing left of the pig but its head and some bones and an assortment of oddly shaped, unappealing-looking joints and hunks of meat. These Ray awards to the dogs for their unwavering good behavior. It is quiet and still and cold. Ray has shifted from feeling fogged and slow to a kind of clear-headed but distant wakefulness, the same sharp bright edge that used to characterize the end of exhausting LSD trips. Or the sudden jolting that occurred at high noon the day after a night without sleep. This night, as then, he sort of enjoys the jolt; he knows it's momentary, that soon he will be in another dimension altogether, barely conscious, ready for sleep.

The guests, miraculously, seem to have departed or gone to bed. Or at least they are not with Ray and Vivian, who are lying by the dying fire on top of some blankets, and beneath others, watching the stars, scattered and wan in the October sky. Here and there paper plates and crumpled napkins flutter in the moonlight like wounded birds. The Dolly's Funeral Home tent is an enormous black square in the blue-black night. Where the rug was, the grass is flat and bent as if permanently steamrolled. Now and then an acorn falls, hitting the tent with a soft plop and rolling ineffectually down and off. Others fall straight down to the field. None falls on the lovers.

Somewhere near the Winnebago, Bullet dodges nuts while showing Darryl how to throw a knife in the dark at a tree ten feet off without damaging the knife, yourself, or someone you love. And somewhere else, someone is playing clear lovely Irish tunes on his guitar, and even Ray is enchanted by the notion that a man who earlier played low-down, good-for-nothin' soul had it in him to produce this delicate lilting sound. Like James and his flute, he thinks, wondering what it is he himself lacks in that department. Knowing the answer would be basic talent: you got the feeling, man, and the thoughts are crystal-clear; it's the execution that's fuzzy. But that's OK, that's OK, they can't build houses, can't bevel a sweet cornice, and they don't have Vivian, most assuredly they do not have the wonderful Vivian, and you do, but then again, you don't really, so though your execution on the old guitar may be a bit blurred, make absolutely certain your execution—your life with Vivian—is crystal-clear, perfectly orchestrated, without blemish, beyond reproach.

Whippoorwills call. The rooster sleeps. Night falls.

■ ≡ ■

Ray is at the part of the dream where he becomes Cézanne and hates the world (Vivian's influence, her knowledge of art, her favorite Cézanne print in their bedroom making its presence known), loves only what he paints and isn't one hundred percent sure about *that,* when the phone rings. He does not want to hear a phone—he and Vivian had stumbled down to the schoolhouse finally when the music stopped ("he says the music was written originally for lyres," she had said sleepily)—because it cannot possibly have rung back there in the mist on the Gulf of Marseilles, and that is where he wants to be, both in and out of his dream. The message in Marseilles would have been written on some café serviette, discreetly delivered, *merci, monsieur,* or might have been quietly spoken, murmured, words issuing forth from an exquisite rosebud mouth, a mouth familiar, somehow, with lyres.

"Speak," he mumbles into the phone. Vivian stirs beside him. She smiles at her dream, and he wonders why. Beams of light shining through the pocked and wavy windows mottle her body interestingly—strong lights and darks. Does she dream of Brian? Of the babe? Of her loving husband?

A woman laughs through the phone.

"Who is this?" Ray hears someone fumble at the other end, drop the receiver, giggle. "Do I know you?" he asks.

More fumbling, clanking. "Ray, it's James."

"James." It takes a moment. "James," Ray says again. "Do you know what time it is?"

"Sorry. Priscilla got to the phone before I could stop her, and she has no idea in hell what time it is. Do you, babe?" Ray hears.

"What do you mean?" Ray asks, but in his heart he does not want the answer to that one. So he says, "You missed a good party. The pig's nothing but skin and bones." Vivian's digital clock blinks red through the dark: 3:59. Jesus Christ. He closes his eyes, leans the receiver against his ear. He seems to hear the entire schoolhouse breathing, or rather holding its breath. He wonders if anyone else was awakened by the ring.

"Believe it or not," James is saying, "we had planned to come down there for the wedding, or for the pig roast, anyhow, but then Priscilla decided to tie one on all by herself, so we never even got out the door."

Ray can feel James's fatigue crawl right through the telephone line and into his own lifeless ear. He moves the receiver away from his head as if trying to avoid exposure. But it is way too late for that, and he knows it. "I didn't think she drank anymore," he says lamely, right in the moment that he hears James say, "She's feeling pretty good now, aren't you, babe?"

Both men pause. "What's wrong?" Ray asks finally. "Did something happen?" And instantly he regrets the question.

"What kind of a fucking question is that?" James snaps. Then he says, "Nothing more than the usual."

They seem to be struggling with the phone. Or at least that is how it sounds to Ray, who is feeling helpless and absolutely ineffectual. He wishes he had the strength and wherewithal to hang up. Instead he waits to see who will come on next, and while he waits, he watches Vivian breathing softly in and out, in and out, and he thinks, dressed or not, Vivian is always appealing, always real. Whereas this telephone conversation is about as unreal as you can get, and is, he has the strong sense, only headed for deeper and darker pits.

Priscilla is there now, saying, "I just want to have a good time, and James won't let me. He's such a goddamn nursemaid sometimes." He can hear her messing with the receiver, clunking it against the wall, or the counter. He pulls his head away again, then carefully replaces it against the receiver. She sounds like someone he's never known, someone who, if he met her by chance in a bar, he would make very sure to have just one beer with before carefully and deliberately walking out the door and out of her mess of a life.

James has the phone again. "This is too much," he says. "We're hanging up. Sorry to have woken you."

"Hey," says Ray. "Wait a minute." For a moment he thinks it's too late; he hears only a loud silence.

"There's nothing you can do," James says. "She'll be OK in the morning."

"Let me talk to her." He hears the phone move. Next to him, Vivian murmurs something and brushes his leg with hers. "Priscilla?" he says. "Priscilla? Can you hear me?"

"Speak," she says. Then she says, "What the *hell* do you want?"

"What's going on? Are you OK?"

"I'm fine. I'm celebrating your marriage. I'm celebrating my life with James, whom I love dearly. I love you, James," he hears her say away from the phone. Now she's back with Ray. "Do you remember when I met you at the airport that time when you came back from Nam?"

"Of course." He hears a glass clank against the phone, hears her swallow. He remembers her slender neck, the way she kissed him, the way she would sometimes lean across whatever was between them, no matter where they were, to touch his hand, make a point.

"That was a fine night, wasn't it?" she says. "That was the best."

And he says, "Yes, it was," but what he remembers is the awkwardness, their ambivalence. Didn't she remember she was the one who seemed, in the long run, not to want it? She had the Harley boyfriend, the latest groovy records. He probably would have done anything for her, immersed himself in boiling oil to stay with her. That is how he thinks of it now, anyhow.

She is saying something about Vivian, he is almost certain. "And I hope you live a long and happy life, and have a passel of children."

"Where are your children?" he asks, for no particular reason.

"In bed, of course," she says. "James takes good care of them."

"So do you."

"Oh, yes," she says, "I do a tremendously good job of everything. I am an *extremely*"—she draws the middle of the word out ludicrously—"an ex-*treme*-ly smart and capable woman. Strong too. And I am beautiful and I am talented and I am persuasive, but I was unable to persuade you to sleep with me, and I count that," she says, "as the colossal failure of my life."

"Let me speak to James," Ray says. "Go lie down."

"Fuck you," she says. "Here is the great James."

"She's been hurting lately," James says. "I never really know till it's too late. If she'd only—if you'd only let me know," Ray hears.

"Don't talk about me as if I'm not here," he hears.

"From the cancer? She's hurting from the cancer?" Ray hears only mumbles. "Hey. James."

"I'm here. That and other things."

"Like?"

"The usual stuff. Whether she should wallop the kids, maybe send them back to Rick. What to do with the house. Whether or not she loves me, or who on earth she does love. The usual."

"I'm sorry," Ray says. "I am truly sorry. She seemed so fine last summer."

"She has her ups and downs," James says, "pretty much like the rest of us."

"Not hardly," says Ray. "Please tell her from me she's a fine woman and I love her." He hears the phone move again, hears Priscilla say, "I love you," doesn't know who she means. "I love you," he hears again. Next to him Vivian sighs and smiles. He hears Priscilla kissing James hundreds of miles to the north. He feels himself being pressed between them as they embrace, the receiver nestled between them, as intimate and unconscious as a third skin. He feels Priscilla's fingers in his hair, her breath on his neck. He smells lilacs. He feels Vivian's body against his, smooth and kind. He feels her hair brushing his cheek. He wants to touch his wife, but he doesn't want to wake her. He feels himself, the receiver, fall away from Priscilla and James, bang against the kitchen counter, roll off. He feels himself dangling down the wall, forgotten, abandoned, absolutely unnecessary, swinging like a dead man as they kiss and murmur and make up in that green Vermont kitchen.

Ray feels angry. He feels enormously sad. He feels a certain sense of relief, and inevitability. He wishes he could just go back to sleep and ease on into the dream. His bad eye, which hasn't acted up for months, chooses this moment to throb as if he's just been shot. He wants, selfishly, to wake Vivian.

"Hey." He is yelling at them now. When Vivian stirs, he says more quietly, "Hey. You two having a good time up there in Vermont?" Then he says, "I'll call you soon," though it will be much longer than he ever imagined before he sees them again. He hangs up and wonders how much of it he should try to figure out, and how much he should simply let go. He sits up in bed, lights a Camel. Vivian turns to him. "What's the matter?" she asks.

"Didn't you hear?"

"All I heard was you lighting the match," she says, pushing her hair out of her eyes. And then she says, "I think this baby is going to be born soon."

■ ≡ ■

An hour later, Vivian feels the first twinges of labor, and an hour after that, she is in labor proper, so called, Eve informs a distraught Ray, because it's such hard work.

"I was in labor with you for three days," she tells him, "but Vivian seems to be moving along nicely. Good strong contractions." Eve makes a fist, punches the air for emphasis.

Ray calls the midwife they have been seeing regularly the last several months, but she is somewhere two counties away, attending to the long and difficult birth of twins. "She'll be there eventually," says the midwife's husband. "Best thing you can do is stay calm, time the contractions, and have a drink or something. She'll be there."

"I certainly hope so," says Ray. He wishes he had taken the time to look over the books the midwife had recommended. He hadn't read them because he was busy working on the building contract, but also he wasn't sure of this midwife. Stupid reason not to read what she suggested, he's thinking now.

The midwife had advised Vivian to walk a lot and rub her stomach with olive oil to minimize stretch marks. This service Ray had performed for Vivian, to their mutual enjoyment, and for that pleasure he secretly thanked the woman. But there was something about the way her single brown braid twitched impatiently down her back to her waist, something about the granny glasses and long skirts with mirrors at the hem and the Earth Shoes, that put him off. Perhaps she seemed too casual, or perhaps she seemed too officious. In any event, Ray found her a little scary. He had the distinct and uncomfortable feeling that during her visits she and Vivian discussed behind closed doors the emotional shortcomings of men, how childlike they were, especially in times of crisis. How, in the heat of battle, so to speak, they were either struck dumb or behaved like madmen, nitwits, nothing rational.

This battle talk was pure speculation; for one thing, Ray had not actually overheard one word, and for another, he had said little to Vivian of his days in the war. Just having Bullet around was enough to sour the whole idea of postwar craziness, as far as Vivian was concerned. Once she'd said, "At least Bullet doesn't seem to wallow in it, like some people I've known." Ray had felt like asking her, Who? but all he'd said was, "I guess wallowing in it, as you put it, is as bad as ignoring it altogether." And she'd said, "It's just the way life is. Choose your complication. The only thing to do is bash on."

And bash on is what Ray would like to be doing right now with this baby on the way, but the midwife is unavailable, and he wishes he'd taken the goddamn time to read the goddamn books, but then again, this is not, after all, Vivian's first child, though it has been seven years since the last one, and she herself has said that each time the experience is completely and utterly new, just as fresh and strange as falling in love.

Ray rouses Christine, who leaves Jerry to his particular dreams of the pig. She goes to check on Vivian, while Eve busies herself in the kitchen. A feeling of helplessness clutches at Ray like an advanced case of angina. Suddenly he feels faint and slides down the wall to the floor, rests his head on his knees. And now Jane is there, putting a cool hand to his forehead, asking him if he is all right. Earlier, she had annoyed him by asking him, as they danced (he supposed it was a question), "You'll take good care of my friend Vivian, won't you?" He had always sensed mild disapproval from Jane. "Of course," he'd said, tipping her back so far that her hair practically touched the ground behind her. He held her there so long she finally had to beg to be returned

to an upright position. For a moment, he'd felt cruelly and child-
ishly like letting her drop, but that notion had been instantaneous
and so fleeting that Ray could hardly believe he'd thought it. Next
moment they were dancing away happily, and now, in his weak-
ened state, he can see that her remark had not so much to do
with Ray as with her deep affection for Vivian.

"Are you all right?" she's saying.

"A little dizzy, but better," he says. "Thanks," and he takes
her hand from his forehead and holds it a minute. "This is worse
than the jungle," he says, and she nods in sympathy. From the
floor, they watch Eve at the stove.

She has appointed herself temporary midwife and is boiling
water, mixing strange-smelling herbal drinks, with fresh ingre-
dients straight from the reservation. Watching her work, Ray
thinks of the beautiful Indian girl in *Little Big Man,* how she
struggled through childbirth in proud silence, piece of rawhide—
was it?—clamped between strong white teeth. Was the enemy
near, was that why she hadn't cried out? Or had she done it to
keep the pain and mystery to herself? And was that selfish, or
noble, or just plain stupid?

Ray stands up, thanks Jane, goes to see Vivian. Lying next to
her in their room, rubbing her back and smoothing her hair and
murmuring wise and foolish words to her, he tries to recall the
peace he'd felt earlier with her up by the fire—any peace he had
felt anywhere, at any time—but he comes up short. This is just
an affliction of the moment, this is no sign of your life, he tells
himself as he watches his wife drift off into restless sleep. He gets
up carefully from the bed and trudges back to the kitchen for a
cup of coffee and a smoke. His mother laces the coffee with
whiskey, which tastes good this time, not like what he had with
Bullet centuries earlier in the dark of the Winnebago. What a
lunatic.

Back with Vivian, Ray watches the headlights of early-
morning travelers flicker through the woods like fireflies, growing
dimmer and dimmer until, at last, they are one with the delicate
dawn.

■ ≡ ■

Someone is saying, What the hell do *you* want? In his dream someone is crying, Ray! Ray! we need you, come here! Someone is screaming, and it is Ray himself, no, it is a woman—Vivian—and she is saying, I need you. He puts out a hand, touches her arm. She clutches it with old man's fingers, feeble clawings, then scratches deep. He is awake now, absolutely, and hears his mother saying, What the hell do *you* want? On his arm, threads of blood surface. He hears a man—Bullet?—saying he needs Ray. Another voice says something, a man's voice, unfamiliar and not particularly friendly.

Vivian is whispering, "Who's here?" and he leans close.

"It's me," he says. "Everything's fine."

She shakes her head, eyes closed. "I mean out *there*," she says, nodding toward the hall. Ray gets up, walks to the door that separates them from the rest of the world.

Ray had been dozing just a few minutes, but in that short time, the morning has firmly established itself. The schoolhouse upstairs is bright though cool, and Ray, at the threshold of the bedroom door, takes a deep breath in anticipation of what will be, no doubt, a memorable day. Still, he is unprepared for the sight of Bullet at the landing at the top of the stairs, and an enormous state trooper with the bulk and bearing of a Titan close behind. Eve has placed herself between the intruders and the bedroom; one look at her and Ray knows she is prepared to fight to the finish, peck out eyes, lacerate skulls, whatever it takes to keep the enemy away. The midwife, newly arrived, goes back and forth between the kitchen and the bedroom with pots of boiling water; she pays no attention whatsoever to the commotion in the hall. The one look she shoots to Ray seems to acknowledge that this is what she expected to find in such a place all along, no need for him to pretend otherwise. He can't wait to set her straight, but he will have to do that later.

"I don't know what this is all about," he says. "I don't even want to *think* what this is all about, but the one thing I do know is that we have to go back downstairs." And he pushes past Bullet, comes to the state trooper, says, "My wife is in labor in there," stares him down until the trooper steps obligingly to the side, and they all three clomp down to the first floor. Ray leads them into the front room, replete with the debris and general chaos of the past several days. Clothes and shoes—especially shoes, and boots, endless footgear—are strewn everywhere. The hammocks, with blankets and spreads trailing out like lazy arms and legs, seem freshly abandoned, as if their occupants had just sprung for the windows a moment before. Ray scans the room quickly, almost as quickly as Trooper Cronk does, looking for incriminating items of any sort. It's automatic and instinctive—the cursory once-over. Ray doesn't remember leaving the peace pipe there on the couch, but it's there, all right, looking invitingly discreet. And in that moment, everything seems to stop. Ray feels the burden, knows he must do something, say something, make things right. Suddenly his life to date seems grossly mismanaged, as if he's been ill all this time, bedridden, sheltered by pain and IVs and pretty nurses—so much so that he is unable to do anything other than stand and stare with the others, waiting for something to break. No one moves or speaks until a cry from Vivian, tumbling down the stairs and into the cool emptiness of the front room, jars them back to life, and the world keeps turning.

"Sorry about this, pal," Bullet says, "but I ran into a little trouble. You got any cash on you?" He flaps a piece of paper in front of Ray, who stares at the paper, then back to Bullet.

"What happened?"

Bullet looks at Trooper Cronk, who appears to be ignoring all of them. He is standing in the living room like Sergeant Preston of the Yukon—ranger hat, badge, shiny high black boots. No sled, no snow, no encouraging smiles, but he does have a dog caged in the back of his vehicle out in the driveway, and it's throwing Geronimo and Frenchie into a frenzy. Ray can see them circling the car; he hears the caged dog's snarls and feels faint.

Trooper Cronk is clean-shaven and red-faced and wears a

half-inch wedding band; this fills Ray with relief. Trooper Cronk, then, is a family man, a husband, lover of children and steak and beer. He's probably a father three times over, fourth on the way. He will understand, then, how Ray cannot take the time just now to have a little chat.

"What happened?" Ray asks again. Another moan from Vivian. "For Christ's sake," says Ray.

"You got a smoke?" Bullet's voice sounds a little jumpy.

Ray doesn't move. Bullet glances around, sees some cigarettes on one of the tables, takes one out, lights it. He smokes as if he has always smoked. His hand is steady; he blows out smoke in an exaggerated stream of fatigue and savvy. "We took the truck out—"

"What?"

"We took the truck out—"

"Who did? What truck?"

"Darryl wanted to show me the work he'd done on the truck"—Bullet is shouting now—"so we took her on out, and let me tell you, that kid is one hell of a mechanic."

Ray goes to the window, glances at the spot where he parked the truck after they'd unloaded the pig. Nothing there but chickens pecking at nothing. He turns back to the room. He waits. He has this dreadful feeling in the depths of his stomach again, and the room wavers as if he, all of them, are stuck underwater, not stuck so much as suspended—dangling bodies, voices not their own—caught in a disturbing, ear-splitting void. The old white noise shrieking.

"Where the fuck is Darryl?" Ray asks. He feels ready to beat to brainlessness just about anyone who comes too close right now.

Bullet looks at Trooper Cronk and speaks loudly, words carefully spaced. "When I saw Darryl was in no condition to drive," he says, "I took over, but I had a little trouble negotiating that hairpin curve up the road a ways. You know the one. There should be a sign."

"Sign's there." Trooper Cronk's voice is higher than Ray had expected. "Sign's been there a good two years." He is looking around the room as if assessing its contents for the auction block. Outside, the dogs, who had been quiet awhile, are barking frantically.

"Where is Darryl now?" When Ray says this, as if he cannot bear to hear the answer, he turns to look behind him. The boy might suddenly have shrunk and be hiding inside one of the boots Ray had kicked off earlier, for instance. Might have snuck inside there for fun, trying to trick them, ridiculous adults. Might be wedged between the wall and the back of one of Vivian's paintings. Could be anyplace, but must, absolutely must, be alive and well.

"He got a little banged up," Bullet says, "but hey, he's OK, he's OK. Just got a little bruised is all. The kid's tough. Wants to be a goddamn mercenary, for Chrissake."

"He wants to be a goddamn fucking veterinarian. Where is he?"

"Martha Jefferson." This from Trooper Cronk, who seems to have just noticed where he is. "He's got a mild concussion, but they want to watch him awhile. And this boy"—he means Bullet—"owes the state of Virginia a little something."

"Ray?" It's Vivian, and he tries not to break into a run to get to her. If he runs, if he does just that, he might keep right on going, might grab his wife and jump with her out the window, or crash straight through the wall if it comes to that, leave a jagged cartoon hole in the plaster. Might fly right up the chimney to get them out of there. Find some ferns to lie on beside a river, and get on with things.

He leaps up the stairs two at a time, leaves Bullet and Trooper Cronk to find and discuss what they will.

"What's wrong with you?" she asks when she sees him.

"Nothing. How are you doing?"

Her rumpled hair is spread all over the pillow, like hopelessly tangled electrical wire. Ray's hand shakes as he tries to restore it to some kind of order. She smells of roast pig and smoke and lemons—probably the herbal drink. He wonders how he ever could have considered life without her, how he could have thought it heroic to go it alone.

"What's going on?" she asks.

"Bullet got a speeding ticket. No big deal, though of course he's broke. How are *you* doing?"

"Bullet," she says, turning away. "Your friend Bullet." Doesn't he ever stop talking? she'd asked earlier. Now she says, "I'm OK," but he knows it isn't true, and can't be, shouldn't be, until the house is theirs again.

The midwife, on the other side of the bed, says, "I'll take care of her. You just get rid of them." Mirrors wink at the edge of her hem like gnashing teeth. She gestures angrily with her head to the door when he doesn't move. Go *on,* she mouths. Eve, who has just come in with another mug of something lemony, says, "It'll be all right, dear. You go, but take care." He kisses Vivian, whispers he'll be right back, and goes down to the men.

Down in the front room, Bullet is laughing at something Trooper Cronk has said. It is that laughter, as much as anything, that Ray remembers for a long time after. That, and the way his sister looks at him when he tells her where her son is, and why.

"Trooper Cronk used to go to school here," Bullet says.

"That was a long time ago, before your time," the trooper says to Ray, though the men appear to be about the same age. "Miz Goodman's desk was there"—he points toward the front of the room—"and my desk"—and now he's walking right over to the couch and the leather pouch—"my desk was right about" he points down at the couch—"here."

All three men stare at the peace pipe and its leather pouch, as if it contains the answers to everyone's questions and problems. The air is heavy with what no one says. Upstairs, overhead, the women scuff and move across the floor. Ray says, as deliberately and calmly as possible, *"If it is not an inconvenience, I would like to settle this outside. My wife is about to have a baby."*

They move slowly, reluctantly, it seems to Ray, toward the front door. He feels as if he's herding them, stray cattle, steathily and skillfully in his stocking feet. The hall is streaked with clumps of red clay the trooper and Bullet tracked in. Behind the guest room door, Jerry and Christine talk in low voices. Ray has not yet told them about Darryl.

And underneath all of them, tucked away in the basement, is enough of Bullet's homegrown to put them all away for a good long time; or, at the very least, cause everyone a great deal of trouble.

They stop just inside the door. "I have to pay right now," Bullet says.

"Why's that?" says Ray. Good God, when would it ever end?

"His license has expired, plus he's from Maryland." Trooper Cronk says "Maryland" as if it tastes bad. "No personal recognizance."

"Goddamn it, Bullet. How much?"

"Forty-two bucks."

Again Ray leaps up the stairs. He takes some cash from the top of his dresser, stuffs it in a pocket. He does not want to look at Vivian, who, even if her eyes were open, would probably not know him. Eve and the midwife mop her brow, whisper soothing words. He is, in that instant, insanely jealous of these two intruding females. They should be downstairs, dealing with all the mundane bullshit, his crazy friend. He is the father of this child. He is sorry as soon as he thinks it, knows the only thing to do is finish up the business with the men, and do it in such a way as to never let it happen again.

On his way out, Vivian stops him with a hand on his leg.

"Get them out of here," she says.

■ ≡ ■

Down in the front hall, Ray counts out the money to Trooper Cronk.

"Forty, forty-one, forty-two." Singsong, as if he's just learned what it is to count past thirty. When he's finished, he reaches for the door, but Trooper Cronk begins writing out a receipt, thereby effectively blocking the move.

Block that kick! Block that kick!

The crowd roars in Ray's head. He drops his arm and takes a step back. One of the goats has clambered onto the front porch and is peering at them through the glass at one side of the door. Ray feels as dazed as the goat looks. He folds his arms in front of him while he waits for Cronk to finish.

"How many people you got living here, anyhow?" asks Trooper Cronk, still writing. Ray listens to the paper crackle under his pen. Bullet is looking out the window, past the goats, looking at his Winnebago, thinking Ray has no earthly idea of what.

"Not that it has anything to do with all this," Ray says, "but just my wife and I." His voice quavers, though he enunciates carefully as if instructing Trooper Cronk in elocution, or as if the man is hearing-impaired. Or as if he, Ray, in his deliberation, is speech-impaired, beyond repair, can't talk so good.

Trooper Cronk seems to find nothing of interest or amusement in Ray's answer, but he is thinking, as he fills in the blanks, If this dude wants to mess, I'll mess, so he says, "That a licensed midwife you got in there?"

"Friend of the family," says Ray, and for the first time Trooper Cronk shows the slightest irritation at having to do his job. He looks directly at Ray, and his eyes, clear and hard blue, just about as blue as Ray's, seem to twitch and flicker with recognition.

When he sees the eyes, each hair on Ray's noble head and on the back of his neck stiffens and stands at attention as it takes on a life of its own. He feels himself swirling, microscopic and lost—upside down—in the eyes watching him. He tells himself to keep calm, stay cool, take your time, because he does not want to spend the birth day of his firstborn—or any other day, for that matter, ever again—with filthy urinals and angry drunks and hard wooden bunks. He smiles weakly at Trooper Cronk, who goes back to his scribbling, but now Ray can hardly breathe, the air is so close, the space so tight there at the end of the hall. He smells the men and he thinks he has not smelled such fear, not felt the need to tread so lightly or with such care, since mincing his way through mine-rigged rice fields many years earlier, fearful of putting the boot back down that just made it another step, in the same breath wanting to stomp down square and hard on a live one, thereby blowing himself and everyone else to kingdom come, sparing them the inconvenience of trying to stay alive this way.

In the room at the top of the stairs, Vivian is huffing and puffing as if on the verge of cardiac arrest, and these men in front of him won't let him open the door and let the air in, and Ray feels himself wanting to push for the light and, like the baby, squeeze past the bones.

But right now he cannot move, for fear of rupturing some delicate peace, so he stands quietly, just waiting, vowing he never ever will put himself in such a position of helplessness again. But when Vivian cries the next time, he moves past Cronk and opens the door. The fresh morning air pushes in. His dogs take a break from circling the trooper's car to glance at him for further instructions. The young goat scampers off. Why is the rooster so quiet, he wonders.

"You got to go," he tells the men.

On his way out, Trooper Cronk gives the receipt to Bullet. "You're getting off light," he says, then he stands with his back to the schoolhouse, takes a deep breath, tips his chin up to take in the day. He scans the semicircle of the driveway, sees the Winnebago, cars and trucks parked in no particular design. He takes in the funeral tent, the trash lifting and floating just above the ground in the light morning air, the odd metal contraption— poles and wires—rigged at the edge of the field. "Looks like somebody had themselves a party," says the trooper.

His hand is on the door of the cruiser. The dog in the back is quiet, looks mild as a lamb. Farther up the driveway, the Winnebago sits huge and dumb. Geronimo sniffs at the cruiser one last time, then, while the men watch, maps out his territory, first on the left front radial, then on one of the Winnebago's back tires.

"Urinating in public," Bullet howls. "We pay a fine for that too?" and he lets loose with a laugh so loud the other two men are instant allies in their stunned silence. So that Trooper Cronk, instead of staying to sniff out what he instinctively knows is pay dirt—felony material; he feels it like a douser twitching at the eternal source—simply looks at Bullet's ravaged, ancient face, shakes his head, says they could all do with a good night's sleep, squeezes his bulk into the impossible space behind the wheel of the Plymouth, floors it, and roars out the driveway to the big soft arms of his lonely wife. As soon as he's gone, Ray runs for the house. Bullet stands by the Winnebago while the chickens peck crazily at the flung gravel as if it's cracked corn, and the goats stare blankly from afar at the whole mad scene.

■ ≡ ■

Inside the front door, Ray is face-to-face with Christine and Jerry; he tells them what has happened to their son, gives them instructions on how to get to the hospital. "I couldn't feel worse if he were my own son," he says as he holds the door open for them. And that is when he hears the bright startled wail of his daughter spilling down the stairs. The three of them pause, cannot move—stuck in stone—and no one can bear to cheer or offer congratulations. Christine and Jerry simply and silently leave.

When they are gone, Ray leans against the front door. The knob clicks back into place loudly. Outside, Christine and Jerry pull away. The rooster Ronnie, released from some kind of un-known bondage, crows nonstop. Ray's daughter cries out a wel-come to the world; women's voices muffle and soothe her.

Ray knows it is a daughter, and he knows she is lovely— broad-shouldered, straight-nosed, brilliant. He feels infinitely sad that the world should strike her as so distressing so soon, and angry beyond reason that he was not on hand to welcome and comfort her. He covers his eyes with his hands and hears the prayerful murmurs of the women. He rubs his face all over, short blunt whiskers catching on his hands rough as rasps, and his feet are cold and he thinks of Darryl's face—young and smooth and unwhiskered—and he prays it is just as it was.

His throat hurts so much, he thinks he must be dying. It hurts so much he needs to cry. He sees himself huddled against the front door of this old schoolhouse like some derelict or cringing delinquent student, and he would like to free up his throat to howl, but he cannot, as much from shame as anything. Most of all, he wants to see and touch his daughter, but there seems to be no hurry now, those first few moments having been lost. Only a vital need to set things right to ensure he won't lose anything else. Ever. But when he hears Vivian say, Someone get Ray, tell him to come see his daughter, he saves them a bit of trouble by making it to the top of the stairs before they are even out of the room.

They are there waiting for him—his family—propped up against pillows, looking rosy with health, flushed from the exertion. Ray stops at the door.

"I'm sorry," he says. "I am so sorry."

"We missed you," Vivian says, "but what matters now is that we made it." And Ray can see, from the exhausted brightness of her face, that she has not needed him there, has managed perfectly well without him. She has taken care of the business at hand, namely to get that child born, and she has done it expertly and courageously. The love and exhilaration apparent in her voice and face he will remember always, as much for the way it absolutely excludes him as for how it envelops him.

The baby is nuzzling at Vivian's breast. She has a finely shaped head, Ray decides. "I like her nose," he says; "she has a definite nose. And eyebrows." He is still standing at the door, feels again glued to the spot, cemented in, stuck there for life. Vivian maneuvers a nipple, dark and more erect than Ray has ever seen it, to the baby's mouth. She finally attaches herself, sucks for a minute, lets go. And he is thinking, So this is it, this is the moment after which things are never the same. Thank God for that. Thank you, God, thank you thank you thank you thank you thank you.

"Would you like to hold her? At least touch her?" Vivian lifts a hand out to Ray. He moves into the room, tries not to look at the bloodied stains on the bed, bright reds, deep browns mottling the sheets like some horrific topographical map of his life. The forms of Eve and Jane and the midwife waver at the edges of the room, shadowy, barely there. He ignores them, wills himself to forget them and their mute accusations. He runs the back of his fingers over his daughter's cheek. Truly he has never felt anything so soft.

"What did we decide to name her?" he asks.

"We hadn't quite figured that out. Mona, maybe? Francesca?"

"Francesca?" Ray says. He lets his fingers just barely graze the top of her head. "Did we discuss Francesca as a possibility?" He isn't paying the slightest bit of attention to these names. He only knows this daughter's softness and the firm determination of her nose, her tiny shell of an ear. "We'll come up with something," he says. He is content, for now, simply to look at her.

A V of Canada geese honking outside the window momentarily distracts him. A joyous sound, it reminds him of the bells; they seem to be announcing the birth of this perfect child, and he moves from the bed to the window to watch them fly past. He waits until the last straggler has vanished beyond the highest fir trees and then glances down to the driveway, his eye caught by some movement there. What he sees is a man moving large bundles up the driveway from the schoolhouse to the monstrous Winnebago. It takes him a moment, but not really very long, considering everything that has happened in the past few hours, to piece together what Bullet is doing. And he can feel something finally beginning to snap at the base of his skull, in that delicate precise spot where his neck joins his shoulders. He feels that precise, pinprick spot go fiery hot, spiky hot, as if someone has pushed an orange-tipped poker straight from the fire into the base of his neck there, and the fire, or rather its heat, smacks itself right up to the brain, to the very top of the brain, where there is little room to contain the heat and virtually no escape short of blowing some sort of cranial gasket. To avoid doing himself and the occupants of that blessed birthing room irreversible damage (though actually he doesn't much care about himself, it's the mother and child he fears for), Ray stumps across the floor and out the door, slams his way down the stairs, bangs out the front door, and, without a word to Bullet, without a look in his direction, hauls out an old cement-mixing wheelbarrow from under the front porch, very heavy and cumbersome and layered many times over with chunks of dried cement, and shoves it, is practically pulled by it, down the incline to the basement door. He thumps the barrow over errant bricks and bits of wood and things he can't see and has no wish to know. At the basement door, Bullet catches up with him.

"What the hell are you doing?" Bullet yells. He stands in the doorway between Ray and the dark, loamy-smelling basement, avoiding the nudges of the wheelbarrow as Ray pushes past. "You helping me load this shit?"

Ray doesn't answer. He works quickly for a man who's been up most of the night and is recently a father. But the bundles feel light, and he feels equally insubstantial, as if he could toss them forever and never know it, toss them up to decorate the sky, where they would turn into stars or planets or new inhabitants of the moon.

He piles them high, pushes the wheelbarrow to the door.

Bullet blocks his way. Ray sighs and sets the handles of the barrow down. "I don't recall," he says slowly, "saying you could stash the stuff here."

"I'm moving it back to the Winnebago," Bullet says.

Ray lifts the handles and pushes toward the door, so that Bullet must move or become part of the masonry wall. Bullet moves, and Ray pushes the wheelbarrow up to the edge of the field, where he dumps the load. Behind him, Bullet dogs him. "What the fuck?" he says. "Hey, man, this is my life we're talking about here. I just need a few more days."

Ray says nothing, rolls the wheelbarrow back down the drive for another load. He still wears no shoes, and though his socks are thick, he would welcome having gravel poking into his soles just now, bloodying him. He fills the barrow again, bumps it back over the threshold and up to the field. It is arduous, pushing all that up the drive, but Ray could do it all day, all year, in fact for the rest of his life. Wishes the entire basement were stuffed full so he could work through this terrible sense of worthlessness and waste and pure rage. The burning in his skull has remained constant, has neither abated nor increased, is simply still dully there. He works methodically, like an automaton; the next time he goes down to the basement, for what should be the last load, Bullet does not follow, but Ray knows now what he must do.

This time Bullet is waiting for him in the field. "Just give me one more day, McCreary, and I'll be outa here."

"Nope. Stuff's gotta go now. You can load the Winnebago up here and be on your way. Give Peg and the kids my love."

"Fuck Peg and the kids," says Bullet. In answer to which, Ray pulls back his right arm and, without quite realizing what he's doing, slams his fist into the side of Bullet's face, knocking his down. Bullet sits, duncelike, feet outstretched, hand at his cheek, looking at Ray.

"So," he says, and he seems almost to be chuckling, "I finally get a rise out of you, McCreary." He narrows his eyes. Blood threads its way from his nose to his upper lip. He licks at it but seems unmoved by the pain. "You done lost your cool, now that you got that pretty wife and sweet child up there." He removes his hand from his face, looks at it as if it is part of someone else's composition. "Shit, man," he whispers, "didn't think you had it in you. Mr. Cool way back when, Mr. Cool out on the water. Even when you pulled me out that time, you said any fool would have done the same thing."

Now he's looking at Ray, pulls his knees up, pushes himself off the ground. "But things are different now. You got a wife and kid, a family, got a nice place to live, money coming in. You think you got it all."

"What else is there?" It is all Ray can do to speak. The fire at the back of his head is raging. It is out of control, choking him, blinding him, making him dumb. It is charging him up full throttle. He feels perfectly capable of taking Bullet apart limb by brawny limb, of making pulp of this man he's known so long.

Bullet is on his feet now. He is saying to Ray, without looking at him, "You think you got it all under control, but look around you, man. It ain't necessarily so." He hums the tune, closes his eyes to do it, eyebrows high.

Ray looks around him. He sees midmorning light sharpening the edges of oak leaves. He hears acorns falling like shot. He smells the clean frost of October. He tastes the tart apples he has been eating by the bushel lately. He knows he is doing the right thing, and he is grateful for the opportunity and the clarity, though he admits to feeling slightly feverish and crazed—nothing new there. And he says to Bullet, who is walking to the Winnebago, "You got to get this shit out of here. Now. Right now."

But Bullet doesn't answer, simply disappears into the sliding door of the RV. So Ray shouts, "You hear me, Bullet?" But still he gets no answer. He walks toward the Winnebago, then abruptly changes course; he is trotting down the driveway to his shop, where he rummages around rusting tools in dusty corners till he finds the gas can. He shakes it—a promising lap of something liquid—then sprints back to the tumbling piles of pot at the edge of the field, tears at some of their black plastic wrap to expose the fresh green under. And now not even Apollo himself can stop Ray. He is dripping gasoline all over the pile, into its dull insides. He pats his hip pocket for matches, finds none. Pats his breast pocket—pay dirt: Camels and matches. Pulls them out to strike one, conflagrate the whole fucking mess, be done with it, be done with all of it forever amen.

Matches stubborn, won't cooperate, and then he hears the sharp crack of a rifle, knows without looking it's the 30.06, doesn't even want to turn around to confirm the fact, knew it was just a matter of time, got to get on with the business at hand. He rips out several matches from the book, tries it that way. No go.

Another shot. And another. Is his hair lifting gently in the wake of a bullet speeding past his left ear? Impossible. But right now, in this clear stunning moment, who's to say? Is that the old man now moaning, Oh my God, oh my God, what have you done? And is Ray saying (or did he just think it), He's only trying to scare the buffalo, wanting them to get on home. But there is that dreadful sick feeling he hasn't had in years, and he is soaking wet, he is sweating, and there is entirely too much noise, way too much, pandemonium of wailing bellowing shrieking. The noise is killing him. And the old man is screaming, He is a murderer, they are all murderers, and Ray wants to say, You've got it all wrong, we are honorable men. But even he can see that the herd will never graze again, except in someone's fleecy dreams, or on worms six feet under. And now, in front of the schoolhouse, on the birth day of his daughter, in the din of ricocheted shots, on the happiest day of his life, he sees again the panicked herd veering to right and left in the corral, curved horns tipping like bonnets, leaning en masse, almost horizontal as they pound across that tight space, the bull leading them nowhere. And he sees again, is horrified by, sickened by, the huge brown mounds stained red-black, hears their grunts of disbelief, sighs of despair, submission, shaggy shivering still-lively hides spread out all over, just shy of death. And he sees himself running up behind the hunter to wrestle the rifle away, but it is way too late, and so he goes finally into the woods above the barn and walks and walks and walks, punching at the trunks of trees, bruising and bloodying his hands unnecessarily—what good is it now?—and unable to feel a thing.

And from that time on, it seemed that every time he turned around, there they were—buffalo: on stamps, Indian-head nickels; in songs; in the offhanded expression; in dreams.

But Ray is not dreaming now, he is nowhere close to dreaming, he is all there, he is clear-eyed and alert, as awake as he's ever been.

He lights a match calmly, slowly drops it onto the grass. The pile ignites instantly, no tentative flickers, bright orange. It burns hot and fierce as the dry fields of Corpus.

This is very satisfactory, Ray thinks, this is entirely satisfactory, and he turns to Bullet, who is walking toward him with the 30.06 pointed skyward. He lets fly another shot. Acorns rain down. Not a sound from the animals. No one shouting from the schoolhouse. Perhaps no one hears but these men.

Behind Ray, dope crackles and pops. It invites the men to warm themselves, open their shirts, give it all up. But then Bullet points the 30.06 directly at Ray's heart, and fires. Ray tilts to the side, but the bullet grazes his arm, singeing his shirt, and the piercing hot spot in the back of his neck transports itself right down to the spot on his arm. Bullet moves the 30.06 back up, and this time Ray lunges for him. The rifle falls, rattles out of reach, and the men roll over and over, clutching at each other like lovestruck, mating fools, killer bears, romping children. They grunt and kick and punch and yell, and they separate and slowly straighten and do a repeat performance. They circle and circle; they pant. They stare. They hate each other; they adore each other. They just might kill each other; when they look at each other, they see only the enemy.

The jab that brings Ray to his knees, tears to his eyes, comes suddenly and unexpectedly. Bullet jerks his black cowboy boot back and Ray sinks to the ground, holding his crotch, weak with pain and surprise. His eyes practically roll back in his head when he's hit, and he's not sure he can hold on, stay with it, remain one with the universe.

He leans forward. He touches his forehead to the ground before him, as if in homage to the fire and its exceptional heat. And tears keep coming, whether from pain or exhaustion or distress or the thick smoke, he's not certain. Could be anything. Or all of the above. In any event, he doesn't much care anymore. He is absolutely and thoroughly and unequivocally spent. And yet he can feel, shimmering through the far side of this pain, the promise of peace at having come so far so fast (bearing in mind most of his life to date), and so maybe the tears are for that.

Next to him, someone is moaning and saying over and over, "I'm sorry, I'm sorry," and Ray remembers Bullet, who has col-

lapsed next to him and is swaying and howling like a man be-
reaved. Ray turns his head, forehead still resting on the ground;
he looks at him. At first Bullet is kneeling, doing the wailing,
then he flops onto his back, resting an arm over his eyes. He
turns quiet. The arm resting on his chest rises and sinks rapidly,
then slows to the point where Ray wonders if he's gone comatose.
He doesn't want to fool with it. He turns his head, his nose, back
to the earth, where, for now, they seem to belong. It is a comfortable position; he feels he could stay that way forever. The
earth smells strong and good. He could become a part of the
landscape, this organic-looking mound of purity. Vivian could
paint him, the baby could climb on him as if he were a jungle
gym. At this moment, nothing seems so perfect as that.

He hears Bullet take a deep breath. "I am just so tired," Bullet
says.

Ray finally lifts his head. He is coming back to life. His neck
is getting stiff; he can tell it will be even worse with time. But
the general pain is subsiding. He slowly leans back, rests on his
heels. He breathes in the sweet smoke. Geronimo and Frenchie
come sniffing around. He holds Geronimo close beside him, ruffles his coat; Ray rubs his face in the thick fur of the dog's neck.
"If I hadn't married Vivian, I'd have married you," he says to
the big white dog, who seems, absolutely, to understand. Ray
stares at the flames; they are still plentiful but appear to be losing
power. He inhales deeply. Next to him, Bullet does too. He is
still supine, apparently lobotomized by the disbelief that what is
happening here is indeed happening. Eventually he mumbles
something Ray can't quite catch.

"What?" says Ray. He knows now the danger is past.

"I said, what a waste it is to be burning this gold mine of a
stash." Bullet sighs. "There goes my future."

"Nah," says Ray. "There goes your reprehensible past."

"My reprehensible, delusion-filled past," Bullet chants, and he
takes a huge, lung-punishing breath and begins, quietly at first,
then uncontrollably, to laugh. And Ray can't help it, he does too,

and they sort of lean into each other in front of the fire until they have finished.

Finally they straighten and stand. The fire bathes them in a tropical heat. They open their arms to that heat. They push their hair back from deep, lined foreheads. They rub their bruised bodies, nurse their penitent souls, smoke Camels in silence.

The pain inside Ray's head is just about gone, as is the pain in his leg, the pain in his groin, all pain everywhere. He feels so loose as to be near boneless (which is not to say spineless, he tells himself stupidly, but merely boneless, no hard edges, no more trouble). He pats Bullet on the back, leaves him staring blankly at the fire, and walks slowly down to the schoolhouse. He thinks he sees someone in the upstairs window, watching him, but the sun shining on the glass simply mirrors trees and sky behind him.

He will go see his wife and daughter now. How nice it will be to have a daughter to swim laps with someday. He can tell she has the makings of a swimmer: long legs, strong arms, wide shoulders—his body. And that nose! She has the physique already; he will teach her what she needs to know of endurance. He will tell her it doesn't have to be so hard.

From an upstairs window, Vivian and the baby watch Ray. Vivian whispers into the baby's ear, "That's your father down there. He loves to play with fire." And whether from the sound of her mother's voice, or the sight of Ray, or the October light, or from some secret only she knows, the baby seems to smile, though it is unlikely she sees much beyond this glossy windowpane and her own wondrous reflection floating there.